FAT CAMP

James Sabata

Visit James Sabata's website:
http://www.JamesSabata.com

Follow on Social Media:
www.facebook.com/JamesSabataAuthor
www.twitter.com/JamesSabata
https://www.imdb.com/name/nm8516263/

Copyright 2018 James Sabata

Cover Art and Illustration by Lana Liz
(https://www.instagram.com/brekninger)

First Edition

MENU

This book is dedicated to anyone who has lived with an eating disorder or found any other reason not to smile while looking in the mirror.

I hope you find a way to see the beauty that others see in you. It's taken me years and I still only see it occasionally, but it's definitely there...

PROLOGUE

The weight of her intestines pushed against her hand as blood streamed down her arm. A hopeless yelp surrendered in the back of her throat; her teeth clenched so tightly no sound could escape. His laugh echoed behind her. She turned, trying to crawl away, but with one hand locked on her stomach, she was left with three limbs. Her balance gave way and she fell to the dirt.

His boots hit the forest floor in a slow rhythmic manner as he stalked behind her. Looking over her shoulder, Jessica's hand moved from her stomach, extending open, reaching for grass as though she could somehow pull herself to safety. He savored the bloodletting as her body crumpled to the ground. She spasmed with each labored breath.

"I give up." A whisper; barely audible.

One gloved hand shot out, gripping the hair near her scalp. He pulled up quickly, forcing Jessica to her knees. Not letting go, he moved in front of her and knelt. Eye to eye, a smile spread across his face. Jessica wished to apologize; to explain. But no words came out as the sound of the machete ripping through neck tendons echoed through the silent forest. He stood, staring at the moon for a full thirty seconds before releasing his grip on Jessica's dyed roots. The disembodied head bounced slightly, before resting next to her body.

CHAPTER 1

Or at least that's the way I heard it. When it happened, I was all the way on the other side of the camp. Nowhere near the lake. I was out cold, asleep in my own bed in the cabin farthest from the dining hall.

I was still in that same bed several hours later; long after my roommate, Georgie Perkins, and most of the other campers began the day. I wasn't sleeping. I just did not give a shit. I'd given up. I was going home. Six weeks at Fit Camp and I'd lost twenty pounds. That might seem like a lot to you, but that was five percent of my body weight. You know, what you probably gain and lose every day just drinking water. I'd tried. I ate the insanely small portions they called a meal. I sweated my ass off every day. They said they wanted to save my life but everything they did just made me feel like I was having a heart attack. This was no way to live.

I'd finally earned my family visit and invited my sister, Nicole to be the one to visit me. I could have up to three guests, but I didn't want to see my mom. The one thing I'd really gotten out of Fit Camp was the therapy aspect and the therapy taught me my mom was one of my biggest triggers. If she wasn't offering to buy me a bra (sixteenth birthday party, in front of everyone), or telling me my shirt was too tight (pretty much any time I stretched for any reason) and to "sit up more" for pictures (grandma's retirement party), she was inevitably just ignoring me. Well, except at dinner, when she'd remind me that "Just because I cooked enough for six people doesn't mean you have to eat enough for five."

My sister may not have been my best friend in the world, but she was dating my best friend in the world. I'd convinced her to visit me, using him as an excuse so that she couldn't turn me down. I'll never understand what they see in one another, but if I could use it to my advantage, I was going to do so. With any luck, Nicole would arrive, check in with me, spend her gross, sweaty naked time with Seth, and then I'd spring it on her.

"I'm coming home." I'd say. It wouldn't be a question. I wasn't leaving options. She wouldn't be used to this and would have to react in a positive manner. My therapist taught me that. No open questions. Be forceful. It was the opposite of who I had always been, but it was the only way I saw this working. I'd tell Obi, Timothy, and a couple others goodbye. Then I'd sit on the back of my sister's convertible with both middle fingers in the air as we drove to Pizza Hut in time to catch the buffet.

I rolled onto my side, ready to go back to sleep. I knew what the others were doing, and I had no desire to join in. I was done. Outta here. But as I rolled, my gaze met the most beautiful brown eyes I'd ever seen. Emily Clausen, my sister's best friend. I'd hung the picture up to motivate myself through Fat Camp. To always remember what I was aiming for. A cheerleader doesn't go for a guy who's 400 pounds. That's common sense. But she was extremely nice to me and always talked to me or asked me to be the one to help her with her Algebra homework or to be her lab partner in biology. Clearly, Emily saw something in me that I didn't see. Something worthwhile.

Staring into those soft brown eyes, I apologized to her. Out loud. "I'm sorry it wasn't enough. I'm sorry I couldn't do it, even for you. One day I will. I learned enough here. I know how to lose the weight. Just wait for me, okay?" And I laid there, watching that picture like she was going to move somehow. And I closed my eyes, imagining what it would be like to kiss her.

"MCCRACKEN! I suggest you pull your oversized ass out of bed right this second and get moving. I don't care if you're procrastinating or masturbating. You are done as of right now!"

Gordon "Sarge" Stanheight had some lungs. I didn't hear the door swing open, but I sure as hell heard him scream, "I thought you were related to a two-toed sloth, but my guess is it must be a three-toed sloth. Is that right, McCracken?"

"I guess so?"

"You guess so? You're too lazy to know your own relatives? Why are you still in bed, you gigantic void of motivation? When's the last time you showered? Time to move, you human petri dish."

My blanket ripped off me in a single jerk, but my sheet remained cocooned around me, even as I jumped to meet his gaze. I thanked God himself we were all too big to have bunk beds. My body rocked back and forth as he sneered. "Weebles wobble but they don't fall down, McCracken."

"Yes, sir." I replied, more out of routine than anything else.

His eyes ripped through me with a disdain reserved for mosquitoes. "Are you in the Fitness Protection Program?"

"No, Sir."

His volume increased. "Did you hear the bugle?"

"Yes, sir!" I lied.

"Did you hear me call formation?"

"Yes, sir!" I lied again.

"And rather than grace us with your enlarged shadow you thought you'd just lay in bed staring at that picture of that brunette? Did you get your hand stuck in your thigh sweat while you searched for your wittle weenie, McCracken?"

"Sir, no sir."

"Well, I'm sure glad you found it just fine, McCracken. The way you refuse to burn calories, you're the only one that will ever be reaching for that Lil Smokie." Stanheight's fingers gripped the sheet still hanging around me. I stood before him in just my stained boxers.

"Well, McCracken. This is one time I'm glad you're not standing at attention. Not that I'd be able to tell either way. Get your gear on and hit the course. If you're not at that starting line in fifteen minutes, you're running every drill twice today. I've burned more calories yelling at you than you've burned all week." Stanheight closed in, only an inch from my face. A mix of coffee and tree bark hit my nose. "That's about to change. This is Fit Camp, McCracken. You're gonna start hauling ass, no matter how many loads it takes."

"Sir, permission to speak freely, sir."

"This isn't the military, son." He said, without a single hint of irony. "What do you need?"

"With all due respect, I've decided to throw in the towel and... and go home."

Stanheight stopped. The air changed in the room as he stared into my eyes. "You sure about that?"

"Yes."

He inhaled deeply, looking around the room at the knapsacks and suitcases jammed under my roommate's bed. He looked back at me. "How do you plan to get home?"

I stared down at the floor. "I'll have my sister take me. When she's here tomorrow."

"I can't say I'm not disappointed in you, McCracken. And if you're gonna be man enough to waste your mother's money like this, the least you can do is find the self-worth to look me in the eye while you chicken out." He turned toward the door, stopped, and looked back at me. "Oh, McCracken."

"Yes, Sarge?"

"Tomorrow isn't here yet. Your ass is still mine. You got fourteen minutes to be at that starting line." One eyebrow cocked up on his forehead. "Otherwise, I'll fit the next six weeks' of training into your last day. Got it?"

The door slammed with the same authority carried in every action of Sarge's life.

<u>CHAPTER 2</u>

Two weeks earlier, I'd sat in my therapist's office for my twice weekly individual counseling session. Most kids in camp only had a once a week gig, but I'd been given two as soon as Dr. Munson found out my father's death was still such a huge trigger for me. Her office was in the Counselors' Quarters; a large building toward the far end of the camp containing the administrative offices and the sleeping quarters for the counselors. The building was literally a resort hotel, used for weddings and such the rest of the year. It was beautiful. I assumed Dr. Munson lived up there with her husband, Greg, who was one of the counselors, but for all I knew, maybe she drove in every day. I had no idea if they had children or not.

Dr. Munson was the kind of woman young boys can only dream of. She could've been a model. Her eyes entranced me. They were different colors, but insanely beautiful. Usually, about ¾ dark green with the ¼ maybe a light brown, but I swear to you when she was in a good mood, the green parts had a tint of blue to them. When she was annoyed with something or upset with her husband, they moved to a darker brown color. I spent most of our sessions unable to look away from her eyes and her awkward smile.

But when I did look away from her eyes, the rest of Dr. Munson's body was just as amazing. She had lighter, but not pale, skin and a few freckles she attempted to hide with makeup. Her fingers often danced through her flowing blonde hair as we spoke. Her cotton dresses whispered secrets to me that I tried my best to ignore, but it was impossible. She was the one woman on campus that any man would have killed to sleep with, but it was her personality that turned me on.

She received her MA degree in 3/4 the time it normally took, and she'd published several papers along the way. Talking to her was easier than talking to anyone else in my life, even Seth, who had been my best friend since second grade. I loved how she stopped to think about what I said before she responded. And her advice was always spot on. Dr. Munson had a way of laying out the obvious answer I'd been avoiding and making me look at it and accept that it was the correct thing to do.

She could have talked me out of leaving Fit Camp in a heartbeat. But that day in her office, two weeks beforehand, I hadn't yet considered leaving.

I kicked back in the leather chair, one foot out further than the other. I wasn't exactly slouching, but for once, I wasn't thinking about how my chins looked or sitting up straight, fixing my shirt as if that somehow hid the truth. I was so lost in thought I hadn't paid attention to how I looked for once. Which is amazing, because I was literally explaining the things most people don't understand about being four hundred pounds.

"They can't comprehend how much it hurts to even try to move some days, let alone doing so at the same pace as people 3/8 your size. They seem to think we enjoy being fat. I'm lazy, yes. I love food, yes. I don't *enjoy* being fat. I just hate working out. I can watch what I eat for a full week, work out repeatedly and weigh in with a two-pound loss to show for it all. Then I can go out for pizza, not even eat enough to feel completely full, and magically gain three pounds." Dr. Munson smiled lightly, but in an encouraging, understanding way. Not the way people normally reacted.

Her fingers endlessly rolled her hair like a father twirling his young daughter as she dances. "And then you have to start over. Which sucks." She said.

"Yeah, but it's even worse than that. Because every single time I have to start over, I'm reminded that I failed. Again. Whether internally or externally. My mom will follow up with 'Oh, you're on a diet again?' or 'If you'd stop drinking soda…' or, worse, 'Oh come on, Phillip. One piece of candy won't kill you.' But like any addict, that one hit gets me right back into a full-blown dependence. The continuous cycle of the ups and downs of the scale mixed with the reality that I'll never be 150 pounds is almost unbearable."

She turned to stroke the Calla Lily in her vase. Calla Lilies were her favorite flower. That's the kind of thing everyone knows about his or her therapist, right? As she turned back, her expression looked legitimately curious. "Have you tried explaining this to your mother?"

"Usually, no. Most of the time, I just try to ignore the things she does. I don't think she means to be rude. I think it's just how she's wired. But I told my sister, Nicole. And Nicole told me to talk to mom. So, I finally did. I sat down, and I explained all of this." I stopped as suddenly as I'd started. I had backed myself into a corner and didn't wish to continue.

So, I sat quietly for a minute as Dr. Munson made a couple notes on her scratch paper. She was obviously waiting for me to continue, but when I didn't, she gave in. "And what was your mother's response?"

"Fit Camp."

"And you don't want to be here."

"No. Well, maybe. I mean, I see how it's helpful. I'm down fifteen pounds already in the four weeks I've been here. So, it must work. But it's hard when…" I cut off again; afraid of the words I'd almost said.

Dr. Munson leaned in, the collar of her dress hanging slightly. "Phillip, it's okay. This is a safe place. I'm here to help you. Say whatever you need to say. Even if you don't mean it. Get it out of you."

I took a deep breath, trying to buy time. I stared at the collection of Thomas Campbell poetry on her desk. When I looked up at her again, I found myself looking into her eyes. I saw the flecks of blue in her irises and I felt safe. So, I just said the horrible thing I'd been thinking. "It's Seth."

"Seth? Seth Jenkins?"

"Yeah. He's been my best friend forever, so I thought he would understand. I told him all about how my mom wanted to punish me by sending me here. I thought he'd get how upset I was. I mean, he's not as big as me, but he's severely overweight, you know? He knows what it's like to run out of breath tying your shoes or to take the elevator *solely* so people don't watch you gasp for air at the top of the stairs. He should have known how embarrassing it was that my own mother wanted to send me to a boot camp to lose weight." I paused again, shaking my head. "And instead he signed right up to come along."

Dr. Munson tried to hide her smile. "Are you telling me you're upset that your best friend was supportive and came with you?"

"No, it's not like that. He comes along, and the a-hole is a born natural. He shredded twenty-two pounds his first month. Me? I can barely run the obstacle course. Seth sets a record. We were always *both* the fat kids. The bottom of the totem pole. Everyone gave us shit and together, we dealt with it; and kicked it back and forth between us to ensure we were equal."

Dr. Munson offered me tissues to dry my eyes. "Seth isn't doing this to you on purpose. He found something he's good at and he's excelling. You'll do the same thing when you find your thing."

I looked up in time to see Counselor Eric walk by. He glanced in but kept walking. Great. I'd cried in front of a counselor. I just hoped Sarge didn't happen by next.

Dr. Munson continued. "And the thing you're describing? The feeling of being on the bottom of the totem pole? That's the hierarchy of bullies, like we talked about last time. It's not just you. In every clique – do you guys still say clique?" I nodded. "We just need to find a way to help you change the pecking order, Phillip." She smiled. It was a beautiful smile, but it didn't hide the impossible weight of what she suggested. No one should have to take that full weight.

But at Fit Camp, I was taking the full brunt. Alone. Seth was getting in shape, accomplishing his goals, and making me feel bad that I couldn't find a way to get up, let alone keep up. And each week it only got worse. It wore me down. Eventually, I did the only thing I thought I could do.

I gave up.

CHAPTER 3

The sun rose over Camp Wašíču as I sat on the toilet a full seven minutes longer than I needed. I finally gave in and started making my way to find Sarge. Counselor Greg jogged by with a group of older campers. They left me plenty of room, but when you're my size, everything makes you feel crowded. I stood there, watching their feet hit the dirt in unison; completely jealous of the way they accepted what they were doing at camp and did their best to make sure they didn't have to return next year.

Something tapped my elbow. I turned quickly, surprised to see the weathered wooden cut out of a slim looking teenager holding his "fat pants" to show how much weight he'd supposedly lost. Positioned next to the Mess Hall, the sign acted like an evil subliminal message; the kind of thing you normally saw in bad infomercials. It was life-size. Worse, at his fattest, this wooden man had never been as big as me. Across the bottom, it read Camp Wašíču – Fit Camp. Well, it originally read "Fit Camp," but at some point, someone painted the "I" with red paint to make it read "FAT CAMP." The "A" sat at a slight angle. As I looked it over, the sign tapped my elbow again. It was only loosely tied down, wiggling back and forth in the light breeze. And I mean a miniscule almost non-existent breeze. I didn't know the exact temperature, but it wasn't even eight and my ball sack clung to my inner thigh like cellophane on cheese. Glancing around quickly, I reached down to straighten things out. As I removed my hand, I could smell the stench of sweat rotting on my fingertips.

The joggers were long gone by the time I took my next step. I glared at my reflection as I passed the Rec Center on the other side of the Mess Hall. There are very few things I dislike as much as looking at myself. I was glad the view broke from my own shape to the endless forest a few hundred feet away. That view changed to something way less impressive as I passed another group of joggers. Shirts clung to man boobs (moobs, as I call them). Boys dripped sweat. Shirts hung too low. Shorts rode too high. And an unending chorus of mouth breathing created the worst harmony I've ever heard attempted.

During the school year, Friday was, of course, my favorite day. It was quickly becoming my least favorite day at Camp Wašíču. With each step I took, I knew my time was running out. My fingers twisted the fabric of my basketball shorts as I attempted to hold them in place. My other hand repeatedly raised to wipe the spit from my lips. I bit my lip, swallowing repeatedly. My voice was distant, labored. "You'll be fine. It's not the end of the world. It's just a race. You're not going to die today."

As I cleared the crest of the small hill, my nemesis came into view. The oval running track did not glare the way I did but we both knew we didn't like the other. A coldness ran through my body as I stared at it. I'd "run" the mile my first week at camp and barely survived it. That was twenty pounds ago. That was before the training. Before eating better. Maybe it would be okay. I shook my head, staring at the ground. It's difficult to lie to yourself, because you know it's a lie.

My best friend Seth stood next to the sole black kid at Fit Camp, Timothy Mallick. Mallick's oversized ass waved side to side as he tied his shoe. As I approached, I heard Seth say, "I swear, I've never seen you with the same shoes twice. What's up with that?"

"Get off my dick, Jenkins. You need to be worried about getting your fat ass across that finish line, not thinking about my kicks." Seth waved as Mallick added, "And your tiny ass white feet would be swimming around in these babies."

Sarge seemed to appear out of nowhere. Weighing at over 200 pounds by the age of fourteen, I'd always had a natural aversion to PE teachers, but Sarge took that trepidation to a higher level. He wasn't some failed football star with no other career to fall back on. Gordon Stanheight was the real deal; a former Marine Drill Instructor who had also served in both the First Gulf War and Operation Enduring Freedom before leaving the military for a more peaceful life back home in Iowa. Now the head counselor at Camp Wašíču Fit Camp, Sarge took his new role of saving lives just as seriously as his last one. But that didn't mean he was nice about it.

"Look who finally decided to grace us with his presence. Did you wash your hands once you flushed your potential offspring?" I tried to respond, but nothing came out. Sarge wasn't awaiting a response anyway. "Alright you well-rounded individuals, line up. As you know, this is the second out of three times you'll run the mile while you're here… unless you run home to your mommy right after this."

"Or if I have a heart attack and drop dead right now," mumbled Timothy, as Seth giggled.

"An excellent point, Mr. Mallick," Stanheight stated, without missing a beat. "Now treat it like the opposite of the dinner table. Shut your yap unless you're gasping for air."

I took my spot. "Let's just get this over with."

Seth giggled. "That's what she said."

The world went silent as I looked out at that track. A flush crept across my cheeks as I cleared my throat. I made sure not to look anyone else in the eye. I couldn't worry about them. I hadn't even taken a step and my breathing was rushed. My heart rate increased. *It's just a race. You've lost lots of these.* My brain even attempted to play some of those races in my memory, but I fought it off. My eyes shifted, and I saw the other guys; the confidence on their faces. They had something I didn't. *They know they won't come in last.*

In my entire life, I'd never once won a race fairly. A few times in grade school, Seth was a sport and took a loss to let me win, but he could've run circles around me back then and now he was taking his weight loss more seriously than anyone else on campus, so I had a feeling he might lap me. Stanheight pulled the trigger on his cap gun, smoke wafting off it as we left the starting line in unison. The others instantly left me behind. Sarge tried to give me words of encouragement. "You're not competing with them, McCracken. You're only competing with yourself." Oh, how I wished that were true. If I was only competing with myself, I could accept a forfeit as a victory. Sarge cut in again. "Focus on the thing you want most." My brain went to a greasy, cheesy triple burger with enough bacon to kill a pig.

That image disintegrated, replaced by a gorgeous seventeen-year-old cheerleader, Emily Claussen. She was the reason my right triceps was a full inch thicker than my left. My sister's best friend, Emily had been the object of my lust and affection for the better part of two years. My gait straightened. My arms pumped smoothly. My steps per minute increased. My breathing bordered on wheezing, but that was par for the course when thinking about Emily. The pain in my side screamed like I'd been sliced with a kitchen knife, but I was more worried that my moobs might slap my face. If I'd seen a video of that run, I would've given up the small hope I had of dating Emily and this might be a very different story. Sarge yelled, "You can do it! Just push!" Then he kicked into running speed and caught up with the others before they crossed the finish line.

I watched as both Timothy and Seth crossed. Sarge recorded their times as the two-bent forward, holding their knees, catching their breath. Meanwhile, I felt like I still had almost the full mile left to run. *Just do it, Phil. You're almost there. Think how amazed Dad would be if he could – No. Don't think about Dad. Terrible idea.* I wiped a tear from my eye, focusing on the Thud! Thud! Thud! of my sneakers on the track.

Barely an inch across the finish line, I immediately dropped, my hand gripping the mound of flesh to the right of my left moob. Tightness gripped my chest, pulsating in my ears, replacing the wheezing rasp I had been listening to on repeat. My wince eventually lightened, and I opened my eyes, only to find Gordon Stanheight standing over me, with a rare smile etched on his face. "Feels astonishingly good, doesn't it, McCracken? You cut four minutes off your time from six weeks ago!" He extended his hand to me. "And you thought you couldn't do it."

CHAPTER 4

We stood on a freshly mown field watching as Counselor Jeff Halden, the resident vegetarian Hippie, put the bases out for a game of baseball. Counselor Greg dropped a large bag of equipment near home plate. I watched them with such intensity, I didn't hear Seth slide up next to me.

"What's up, secret lover?" Seth whispered.

I jumped. "I hate it when you do that. Nothing. What's up with you?"

Seth pointed at his smart watch. "Just out killing calories, my man."

"How? I'm worn out from that one run."

"No way. Not me. I'm just getting into my fat burning zone. Did you know that a single game of baseball, when played to your full capacity could burn as many as 920 calories? That includes the times you're just standing in the outfield."

"I've never seen you play baseball to your fullest potential. Ever."

Seth shrugged. "First time for everything, I suppose. Except for your sister. We're way past that."

I rolled my eyes. Seth was about to say more, but Sarge cut him off. "All right. We're gonna play some ball. You two are team captains."

Seth and I stared in disbelief. "Us?" I gulped.

Jason Kramer and Fred Hoffman, two high school defensive linemen laughed as they pushed past me. "Hardly, loser."

I'd faced one fear that morning on the track, but now I had to meet an entirely different level of punishment. I stood countless times while jock captains picked teams, always knowing I'd have my name listed last. People always seemed annoyed to have to take me, which was crazy, because it's not like they let me play anyway. Sometimes I just switched teams. It was the only way Seth and I got to be on the same team, as ninety percent of the time, we were the last two picks. Sometimes, I wondered if he hated the days I missed school. But it had always been this way, and, for the most part, I'd come to accept it; so, he probably had as well.

Then we came to Camp Wašíču and it was painful all over again. It wasn't the jocks and the popular kids picking their friends first. It was a group of other kids who were normally picked last *still* not saying my name. I hid my feelings as well as I hid the bottom of my stomach when I reached for things on the top shelf. As each name ticked off, I took another stab of disappointment. Nothing had changed. Fred and Jason proved the jocks were still the captains, instantly taking their friends Jonathon Young, Chuck Denlon, and my roommate Georgie Perkins. The only difference here was that they were defensive linemen trying to get into better shape instead of unsigned models playing quarterback. The popular kids at camp went next. Randy Waterhouse and his crew were divided between the teams quickly and soon the pile of possibilities resembled a line at a comic book convention. It was exactly like high school all over again. So why did it hurt so badly? Even Roger Tonkyn, the sole anorexic kid at Fit Camp went before anyone in my group.

But my world really crashed down when Seth was the first one in our group to be picked. I'd been through this pain a million times, but my best friend always stood at my side. But no. Seth was sorted into a team, leaving me with Timothy and Obi. Hoffman stared at the three of us as if his life really depended on his choice.

"I suppose we'll take Obi." His pronunciation made it rhyme with "hobby" instead of "Moby."

As Obi started toward them I threw my hands up. "He didn't even say your name correctly."

Obi's head bounced up and down quickly. "I'll live. See you out there, Phil."

Timothy slid over next to me. Well, as close as two people our sizes can stand. "It's not like it matters. We're all playing the game, no matter which team we're on. So, I don't know why they even bother with this whole—"

Kramer pointed to Timothy. "Give me Mallick."

Timothy's fist shot up into the air. "Oh, thank god!"

And then everyone just walked away. They literally didn't pick me at all.

So, I followed Seth. "What position are you playing, Seth?"

"Same as always."

We smiled in unison as we both said, "Outfield-Outfield."

My roommate Georgie accidentally made eye contact with me as he covered home plate. Normally he just ignored my existence, but that day, he took the time to insult me. "Heading out to the bleachers in the next town over, McCracken? Meanwhile, I'm the Frrrrraaaank Doyle."

I rolled my eyes. I was so sick of hearing about Frrrrraaaank Doyle. Doyle was a legend. The guy was the epitome of everything Camp Wašíču said they could do to help young teenagers lose weight and straighten out their lives. And the counselors never let us forget it. Frank came into camp and embraced the entire philosophy. It led to an absolute change. "And if you embraced it, you'd change instantly too." Doyle immediately started dropping weight. He was putting on muscle and still making huge strides on the scale. The second time he ran the mile, he chopped a full four minutes off it… in six weeks. Doyle went on to win every competition that year and is widely regarded as the most successful camper to ever set foot in Camp Wašíču.

Today's counselors still preach the greatness of Frank Doyle. They hold him in such high regard they literally can't just say his name. They stretch out the first name, as they did each time he won a race or track and field event. "And in first place, Frrrrraaaank Doyle!" Every single counselor at Camp Wašíču pronounces it this way at least once when they talk about him. The guy has trophies still left on the mantle in the main room of the Counselors' Quarters because he couldn't bring them all home with him. According to Sarge, Frrrrraaaank went on to be a major league catcher and World Series MVP with the Orioles. "And you can too if you put in the work and embrace this system. You can do anything if you put your mind to it."

They didn't seem to understand that I was no Frrrrraaaank Doyle. I was just Phillip McCracken and I was barely keeping up with the expectations associated with that, let alone some living legend no one could compete with.

Seth smiled. "Do you think they're gonna say my name like that after I destroy each of Frrrrraaaank's remaining records?"

"Are you serious right now?"

"Why not? I've embraced it. It shows. I'm making moves. I'm coming for you, Frrrrraaaank." I ignored him as we walked until we were past the people playing outfield. Normally we did this, so we could just talk the whole time and not pay attention to the game. But Seth wasn't content to just stand around for once. He jogged in place each of the five innings we were out there. In the final inning, they made Seth cover second base when Roger Tonkyn claimed he had to piss. I knew better. He preferred to shower alone, due to being so self-conscious over his tiny body. But Seth moved up to second base, reminding me again that a strange alien had clearly replaced my best friend at some point.

Seth once again jogged in place, but this time it cost him. The ball bounced directly between his legs and into the outfield. I froze as I watched the ball coming right toward me. I heard Seth yell, "Get it, Phil!" I reached down, grabbed the ball, pulled back, and aimed with my other hand toward Seth at second base. I launched it. The high arch brought the ball down a mere fifteen feet from me. Randy shook his head, grabbed the ball and launched it home, but the runner crossed the plate a full two seconds before the ball arrived.

Randy stared at me with his hands on his hips, shaking his head as Stanheight's voice boomed, "That's game!"

We all huddled up, as Counselor Greg started his usual pep talk. Seth slid into the circle next to me. smiling. "I didn't get the full 920 calories, but I got a lot of them. Going to have to push harder next time."

Greg's voice seemed to echo in the group as we fell silent. "All right, men. I saw some good hustle out there today. I liked that you made decent steps with fundamentals. I saw some good teamwork out there. Still, it wasn't good enough today. One problem I see is that you need to break old habits. It's not that you don't understand what your new responsibilities here are, but just the fact that you've been doing something else for an extended period of time and you're kind of used to doing it that way. It's a habit. It's a bad habit and we're going to break it. Along with a lot of other bad habits. We need to undo those sorts of things before we can even start to do something new."

I leaned over toward Obi. "What the hell is he blabbering about now?"

Obi smiled. "Who knows? Don't worry about it. Greg just likes to hear himself speak. He's one of those guys who thinks he's super important when he's really not important at all."

Greg continued. "I think there will come a day when you'll look back on your time here at Fit Camp with fondness, remembering how it truly changed your life."

"This is so bad it almost makes me miss Eric's pep talks. Almost."

Obi nodded. "That guy was the worst counselor in the history of this camp."

But Greg was right. I look back now and my time at Fit Camp truly changed my life. And made me appreciate having a life to change.

CHAPTER 5

The locker room looked like any other; featuring several showers, a few rows of lockers, some benches, and way too many overweight naked teenage boys. But the smell. My god, the smell. An exhaust pipe soaked in urine spraying fecal matter from a hog pen might be preferred. It reeked like a sulfurous wet dog's gym socks had been stuffed with rotting meat and left in the sun. And that was before you added the copious amounts of gas released by the campers. Bottles upon bottles of Old Spice body wash and Axe Body Spray did not help any more than the countless air fresheners plugged in around the room. Rows of naked teenage boys hurried to get dressed, pretending no one could see them, but all too aware that everyone could; provided anyone had been looking around the room to begin with.

As self-conscious as we all were, one kid had it worse. Roger Tonkyn -- the sole member of the group weighing less than double the suggested body weight of an average teenager -- sat on the far end of the room, hunkered down on the bench as if he believed he could camouflage into it and disappear completely. Weighing in at only ninety-six pounds, Roger struggled with bulimia but refused to engage in the act with the others around. The only thing Roger hated more than the way he looked was being reminded that only girls purge.

I had watched as he finished toweling off long before most people had the opportunity to head to the shower. The boy's extremely small frame accentuated his rib cage and pipe cleaner legs. My head nodded in his direction. "I'll never understand why he's here."

Seth's eyes narrowed as he looked up at me, careful not to look below my neckline. "It's Fit Camp, Phil. He's still got an eating disorder. It's just different than ours. Gotta try to be sensitive to that."

I nodded, walking toward the mirror to comb my hair. My eyes instinctively sought to look anywhere but my stomach, so I watched the others through the mirror.

Randy Waterhouse drew attention from several of the other boys as he threw open his locker, revealing several bottles of prescription pills. Jonathon Young grabbed his wallet, as Randy began his meticulously practiced spiel. "I'm telling you, seriously. I'm your hook up. What you want, I got it. I got Thermadrol, Phentermine, Lonamin, Bontril, Meridia, Adipex, Diethylpropion, Xenical, Cenafil, Hydroxycut, Trimspa—"

Obi cut him off, standing between Randy and the others. He waved one hand mysteriously. "These are not the roids you're looking for." Young glared at him. Obi dropped his hand and moved on.

Randy opened the next locker over. "Or, if it's more your style, I got Snickers, M&Ms, Reese's Pieces, Skittles, Laffy Taffy, Hershey's Kisses..."

I did my best to ignore all of this, opening my own locker. I locked eyes with the picture taped inside the door; Emily Clausen, the beautiful brunette cheerleader whom I'd been in love with since the first time my sister brought her home for a sleepover. I'd wandered into the basement with no idea they were there. Thank god the couch blocked their view of my boxers. Looking into Emily's eyes – even in picture form – made the world a better place.

I could ignore all the negativity around me. Besides, she was my push.

On the first day of Fit Camp, they made us stand on a stage outside, with everyone else in the audience watching. We had to introduce ourselves. Give our names, current weight, and our push; the thing that will motivate us to keep going. While most of the others found saying their weight aloud to the group to be the hard part, for me, admitting Emily was my push was way harder than quickly mumbling "405 pounds."

As the others rattled off their statistics, I pictured myself standing in front of them, "I'm doing this for a girl who barely knows I'm alive. She's a cheerleader who wouldn't be caught dead with a ginormo fat ass like me. Her name is Emily and I hope to one day have the courage to talk to her." The room would go silent as they stared at me.

At the same time, I'd promised to be true to myself while I was at camp and make a completely honest effort to lose the weight and figure out what got me all the way to a god-forbidden 405 pounds to begin with. It wore off, of course… but at that moment, I just went for it.

Staring out at all the others, I stood there, looking out, my arms crossed over my man tits as if they weren't flowing out the sides of my underarms, and said, "Name: Phillip McCracken." I paused. Sometimes there were giggles when I introduced myself in new places, like when I stupidly tried to go by "Phil" on the first day of High School. At Fit Camp Orientation there had been no giggles, but I'd braced for them just the same. It's a conditioned response. You just prepare for the bullying. "I currently weigh 405 pounds. My push is my girlfriend, Emily."

Why the hell did you just say that?

"And just to be healthier all around." Everyone clapped out of habit as they moved to the next person. I realized as I walked back down that they probably weren't listening to me any more than I'd listened to each of them.

But the truth was that whether she was really my girlfriend or not, Emily *was* my push. She was the goal. Being attractive, being able to think I'd stand a chance with her, praying to God that I could kiss her one day – That meant more than not having diabetes or fearing a heart attack ever could. The fear of death can only push you so far, but the thought of holding Emily's naked body to mine could move mountains. So, I hung pictures of her over my bed and in my locker to remind myself every single day what I was working toward. Some days, staring into her eyes for ten seconds was all the push in the right direction I needed. Some days, it still didn't help. Some days all it did was help me masturbate.

I gathered my clothes from the locker as Young walked up, carrying the Hydroxycut bottle. Fred Hoffman was right behind him, holding four snickers in his hand. Jonathon stopped, turning toward my locker. His finger pointed to Emily. "Who's the hottie, Philly?"

Jason Kramer appeared, laughing. "That's his girlfriend. Haven't you heard?" He made air quotes around the word girlfriend. Clearly, he wasn't buying it.

Jonathon's eyes narrowed. "Girlfriend? You been buying hallucinogenics from Randy over there, Philly? You expect me to think that that hot little piece of ass wants you?"

My legs planted wide, I cut Jonathon off. My eyes went cold. My lip curled. "I'm not in the mood, Young. Back off while you can."

Jonathon smirked, wiping at his nose with his index finger. "If anyone is not in the mood, it's this gorgeous bitch when she sees you." I squared up. He did as well. "So really, Philly. Which website did you download her from? Facebook? Snapchat? Pornhub?"

Spit built at the corners of my mouth. My extremities shook. "She's not imaginary, asshole. She's real."

Undeterred, Young leaned in. "I don't doubt that she's real, you fat piece of crap. I just doubt that she'd waste her time on that double chin in the back of your pants."

His arm shot out toward the picture. Mine caught his, making him miss. "Don't you freaking touch her."

Young backed off a little, laughing. "Oh, no, guys. Philly's breaking out his big boy words. Better cover your virgin ears."

"Stop *fucking* calling me Philly."

Seth's voice cut us off. He stood there, calmly, removing his ear buds. "I've seen her, Jonathon. That's his girl all right. And she can't keep her hands off him. It's actually kind of gross. Pretty sure she was rubbing one out for him under a blanket one night while I was trying to watch a movie. Very distracting."

Young pointed at Phillip. "Can't keep her hands off that?"

Seth shrugged. "Or her mouth."

Young stared at him in disbelief. "I guess that leaves the pussy for you, huh, Jenkins?"

He was still staring at Seth as his head bounced off my locker. He hadn't expected to be tackled any more than I had planned doing it. We hit a bench and the lockers echoed the impact. I threw four punches before he was able to block them. Everyone cheered me on, including Young's friends. Before they could jump in and help him, Stanheight's voice broke it up.

"What in the name of Jenny Craig is going on in here now?" As he rounded the lockers, everyone scattered.

My fist hovered over Young's face. Oh, how I wanted to get in one more punch. I leaned in. "I'm sick of bullies like you. Got it?"

Young nodded quickly, glad none of the others could see him. He pulled himself up.

I tried to stand but fell again. My eyes didn't leave Jonathon. "He just..." I paused, checking my nose for blood. The liquid on my hand was clear. "It's nothing. Nothing is going on."

"My metal lockers are dented. *METAL*. And you're telling me nothing is going on? Well, I don't give a rodent's patootie. Year after year, you kids come in here and fight among yourselves just because there's no one from the real world holding you down right now. Fight this. McCracken, get to the Mess Hall and help with supper rush. Young, you stay here and clean this whole place up. I want this locker room spotless."

"Sarge, we were just..." My shoulders paused mid-shrug, staying up longer than they should have. "I don't even know."

Sarge cut me off. "Did your momma hold you at the teat too long, McCracken? That was an order. Now rotate in that general direction." His finger was perfectly still as he stood, pointing at the door. Randy tried to quietly close his locker, praying that Sarge hadn't seen anything. I left, not looking back at Jonathon Young, but I heard that Young shook his head, smirking to his friends.

Sarge lowered his arm as I left. "I don't know what you're smiling about. You're not leaving this room until I can *eat* off these toilets."

CHAPTER 6

Walking toward the Rec Center for my punishment, I giggled to myself at the thought of Sarge laying out his lunch on the porcelain toilet seat. A lot of guys hated Sarge's style, but for the most part, I loved it. Some people thought that Sarge shouldn't curse at us like that. Maybe they were right. Maybe they weren't. At the meet and greet a week before we started camp, Jonathon Young's mother called Sarge out on it. She did it discreetly, and I wouldn't have heard it at all if Seth and I hadn't been walking from the courts to the front of the Rec Center. Passing the small office to the side, I heard Karen Young say, "It is appalling that you speak to children this way."

"Children?" Sarge responded. "With all due respect, Mrs. Young, these children, as you call them, are a year or two short of being able to ship out around the globe and die for your right to that opinion. Now, if they're too fragile to hear some word you deem inappropriate, let me tell you, they're going to have even bigger problems coming their way. The real world ain't going to coddle them."

Karen didn't let it go though. "Well, I just think your concern should be caring for these children."

I hadn't known him long, but I could feel Sarge roll his eyes. "Let me ask you, Mrs. Young. Would you prefer I spend my time getting your son to fit at the table in time for family Christmas or worrying about the words coming out of my mouth?"

Karen eventually gave up, but rumor has it by the time Sarge finished ripping her a new one, she'd dropped four pounds. The man knows what he's doing, whether you like his methods or not.

The Rec Center interior was split into two sides. The cafeteria half of the building housed the dining room, with tables, benches, and a counter to serve food. The kitchen behind it was barely visible unless you were at the counter. The large recreational center on the other side of the building had a television projector, pool tables, and several games. Almost everyone was in the cafeteria except Young, who was faithfully scrubbing toilets that exact second. The voices carried, creating a mix of conversations about weight loss, working out, sex, comic books, and insults questioning the sexual preferences of friends.

Jeff Halden watched, as any counselor would, as he listened to some light tunes on the radio. Most couldn't have heard his radio even if they were next to it, but I guess he was polite, at least.

Seth, Obi, and Timothy sat at one of the tables, near a large window. Obi was lost in thought, looking outside at the rain that started a few minutes beforehand. They were all almost finished eating before I made my way to the table with my own segmented tray. My grilled boneless, skinless chicken breast, large helping of broccoli, and side of baby carrots may not have been a triple cheeseburger with pizza for a bun, but I was too hungry to care. Plus, I was way more excited to tell them the newest gossip I'd just learned.

Timothy shrugged. "All I know is sometimes, when there's too many white people, I get nervous, you know? Oh great. Here comes another one."

I took my seat, carefully, glancing around to ensure no one could overhear what I was about to say. I leaned in. "Alright, so when I was working in the kitchen, I heard them talking. Randy had his cabin raided. They took so much stuff. Almost all his diet pills and candy bars. It's all locked up in the pantry in the kitchen now. Isn't that nuts?"

Obi turned back. His shoulders fell. "That's terrible. I'm almost out of Hydroxycut. I should've gotten some in the locker room. Does he have more in his locker still? Or did they get those too?"

Timothy kicked Obi under the table. "You serious? Forget the Hydroxycut. Let's get them Snickers." He stared at the others like they were out of their minds.

Seth wiped his face with his napkin, locking eyes on Mallick. "No offense, Timothy, but do you have *any* idea how many calories are in a Snickers? You'd be on the treadmill for years making that up." I could literally feel Seth's popularity falling. Maybe there was hope for me yet. He shrugged. "Hate on me all you want, but at the end of the summer, I'll be the only one with a girlfriend and you'll still be jerking each other off, looking at pics of your moms."

Obi smiled. "You guys do that? All this time, I've been jerking myself off like a chump."

Obi could be a bit much to take sometimes, but we'd learned to cut him some slack. Fit Camp was the one time that Obi was not required to follow his parents' grueling daily schedule. He had no practices to attend, no musical instruments to learn, no additional STEM classes or coding classes. He did not have to lock himself in his room at his desk, studying something he had little to no interest in. He could just unwind and go crazy. As such, he often took it to the next level. Still, it could wear on you after a while. Obi's overboard excitement to be a normal teenager made me semi-glad I didn't live with my friends in their cabin.

Fit Camp was the direct opposite for Timothy. At home, his parents expected very little from him, instead pacifying him with video games and takeout food. Both parents worked and neither seemed to really know how to connect with him. He never really noticed it when he was plugged in, talking smack to random guys on the internet, but at camp, he was forced to interact in the real world; or at least a moderate version of it. Timothy couldn't wait for summer to be over, while Obi would stretch it out for as long as he could.

Jonathon Young had just finished mopping the plain tile floor with mildew-darkened grout when he heard a large object clank against a locker on the other side of the area. "Hello?" His voice echoed through the empty locker room. He took a few steps forward, careful not to slip on the tile. "Hello? Is someone there?" His lower lip curled as he heard the low hiss of hot water as a shower turned on. "What the hell?" He gripped the mop handle like he intended to turn it into some of martial arts weapon.

Young's curiosity turned to terror as the room closed in. Not normally one to fear claustrophobia, Jonathon knew there was nowhere to go. The steaming shower stood between himself and the door he needed to exit. Jonathon's eyes locked on the man standing with his back to him. A dark hoodie covered the man's face, but it was the blood covered machete that held Young's attention.

"Holy shit. What are you doing?"

The Killer spun around, his face lost in the shadows; the bright fluorescent lights reflecting in the machete blade. Young turned to get away. He bumped into the bin for dirty towels. His shoe met the wet floor, squeaking loudly as it slid. Young toppled over, hitting the hard tile with a resounding fa-thud! He tried to push himself up but found no traction on the wet floor and fell again. The Killer exited the shower, allowing Jonathon to see there was something else in there. The woman's body didn't register in Young's mind right away, due to the missing head. Once it did, Young lost all feeling in his legs.

Unable to blink, his bulging eyes hurt, as he blubbered his plea; but his words were lost as he began to cry. "I won't tell anyone. Please. Don't. Please?"

The Killer stood, his head tilted to one side, almost questioningly. Jonathon's voice strained. "Please?"

The machete quickly rose and fell several times as blood splattered across the floor. Jonathon's screams echoed loudly throughout the dark locker room. Then, all at once, the screams stopped.

CHAPTER 7

Still chewing the last of my food, I went to throw my garbage away. My ears caught part of the announcement on Counselor Jeff's radio. I strained, trying to decipher the words being said over the din of the room. Lightning hit outside as Jeff turned the volume up. Amber, the local weather girl, brought us up to speed. "The satellite shows plenty of action right now. While it will be clear for much of the state, the southeastern corner should experience some heavy rains. Maybe as much as three inches in a little over an hour. We're going to see some flooding occurring in the lower elevations. Visibility will be limited. Temperatures will fall to around fifty degrees."

Jeff raised his voice quickly. "Everyone! Quiet! This is important!"

Amber continued. "We're now also getting word that a tornado was just spotted on the ground near Davenport. It appears to be traveling East at about 35 miles per hour."

Obi whispered, "That's less than an hour from here."

"Yes," I replied. "And traveling the opposite direction. We're fine, unless another one drops."

Sarge entered the Mess Hall with Counselor Greg directly in tow. "All right, you spherical wonders, there's a storm coming in and it doesn't look good. They've spotted a tornado about an hour from here, but we're not in the path. We are looking at enough rain coming down to drown a whale."

Timothy smiled, "You think he's talking about one of us?"

Sarge continued. "So, we're gonna call it a night. Head back to your cabins. It's going to start pouring any second now." Seth, Timothy, and Obi stood to go. "You ready?" I waved them off because I needed to finish cleaning up for my punishment to be over.

Seth started to say something while peering out the window next to our table. Lightning hit. The thunderclap was almost immediate. Seth let out a high-pitched shriek that would've made most girls I know jealous. Breathing heavily, he stared at me, either unaware of everyone looking at him, or despite it. "Don't tell anyone I scream like that, okay?"

My three friends headed for the door. The rain ran off the eaves creating an absolute waterfall the guys had to dodge through. At least they had one of the closest cabins. Mine was clear on the other end of the camp. Suddenly, cleaning up the Mess Hall didn't seem so bad.

I finished collecting trays, carrying dishes to the sink, pre-rinsing and loading them into the industrial dishwasher when Diane, the head cook, told me I could go. "I'll take care of the rest. The rain tapered down a little. You get to your cabin while you can."

I reached the kitchen counter and could clearly hear the counselors talking. Sarge's voice just naturally carries anyway. He said, "Do bed checks when the rain stops. Let's make sure we got everyone. With Eric not here anymore, we'll have to cover his kids too. Things might be a bit confusing for the next few days."

Greg cut him off; something I would never dream of doing. "We got this, Sarge. No problem."

They stopped talking as I walked through. I reached for the door as Sarge said, "McCracken."

My eyes closed as I took a breath before turning around. "Sir?"

"I hope you got a few good shots in. Way to stand up for yourself for once."

"Thanks, Sarge." Lightning hit again as the rain picked up. I turned to reach for the door, waiting for Stanheight to say something else, but nothing came out. I smiled as I ran out into the rain.

Let's just be honest, running has never been my strong point. I'm not fast. I'm not even slow. I'd have to work to get fast enough to be considered slow. My feet don't go where they're supposed to. Then you have the two globes I call moobs swinging like pendulums, shifting my balance with every step. My stomach? That's a whole other beast. All I know is that it seems to actively work against me. The weight makes it impossible to breathe and within five strides, I'm huffing and puffing like Darth Vader. And let's not forget the fun of holding up my pants the entire way, because if I don't, they'll be around my knees and I'll faceplant on the ground. It really must be a sight to see, but I'm glad I've never been the one to see it.

Running from the Mess Hall toward my cabin was even worse. I had to literally shuffle (more so than usual) as the dirt path was all mud. My drenched shirt clung to me like I'd been vacuum sealed into it. I slowed to a walk. The repeated *squelch-squerch* as my shoe pulled free from the mud only to slide back in on the next step became too much. The sheets of rain poured so heavily I felt like I was running through sheer curtains with every step. Lightning lit everything around me and momentarily I saw that it continued this way all the way to my cabin. Peering to my right, I could see the light in Seth's cabin was on.

As I knocked, I heard my three friends giggling. "You get it."

"You're closer."

I reached and tried the door. It opened. Timothy was right there. "What the hell? Did you fall in the toilet?"

Obi's voice called. "What the heck kind of toilet would be big enough for one of us to fall into it?"

Seth jumped up, throwing me a towel. "Holy crap. We gotta get you out of that shirt." He rummaged quickly through his closet and pulled out a shirt he'd worn every other day for the last year. It was suddenly too big for him. I hoped it wasn't too small for me.

Timothy stared at me. "I hope you brought those Snickers. If not, I'm tossing you back into the rain."

As Seth tossed me the shirt, I looked up at Timothy, "My cabin is way on the other side of this camp. I'm not going back out there. But I do know the combination to get to the Snickers if you want to go back."

Timothy nodded. "Welcome to the cabin."

CHAPTER 8

The others turned away as I pulled my shirt off, as though we didn't shower together every day. But I was glad they turned away since I was the only one who was wet this time. As I peeled the shirt away from my skin, it made a sickening sucking sound.

Seth giggled. "That's what she said."

Obi chimed in, as I tried to ignore them. "Did you ever stop and consider how strange it is that if water is on clothing it becomes a vacuum, but if water is on a surface it usually just becomes a slipping hazard? There's actually a really good reason for it." I wanted to interrupt, but I was hoping Obi's words would drown out any other grotesque sounds I might get changing my pants. He continued. "Harder surfaces get slippery because the water forms a little layer between your foot and the ground. This causes you to slide on that liquid layer. On the other hand, a wet t-shirt has a lot of surface area, which creates surface tension. That tension is relieved by sticking to your body."

Timothy slugged Obi in the arm. "No one wants to go to science class. We want to get back to roasting our good friend Phil."

I took a seat next to them on the floor, where Seth was dealing cards to everyone. He took seven more off the top of the deck and slid them to me.

"Bring it on," I smiled. "I've got a thick skin."

Timothy's mouth couldn't contain the joy about to escape it. "You know what they say, Phil? The thicker the skin, the better the roast."

Without missing a beat, Seth added, "The only roast that's going to happen is when the crematorium finally gets a hold of him and all of Phillip's bacon grease runs out on the floor."

I shook my head, with no idea what else to say. I looked around the room. I hadn't spent much time in Seth's Cabin. Much like my own cabin, there were four beds, one on each wall, and each had decorations on the wall. Seth had pictures of his family and some pictures of my sister. I tried not to question if he looked at those pics the same way I look at Emily's; unfortunately, the image was already burned into my imagination.

Timothy's wall was covered in posters from spy movies and video games. Obi's wall didn't have decorations, but he did have a bookcase filled with books that were probably above my reading comprehension. There was a fourth bed that no one had used since Scott moved out the second week of camp. I'd begged to move into the cabin, but Sarge said it would build character to live with people I wasn't used to. It had only built a distrust of others when my earbuds went missing.

We played poker for the next twenty minutes. Seth reminded us every single hand that it wasn't strip poker. "Keep your chonies on, big boys."

Timothy's stomach rumbled. "We should've grabbed some of them chocolate bars when we had the chance. I wish the rain would stop so Phil can go get us some."

"What? Why do I have to go?" I said.

Mallick shrugged. "Well, this isn't your cabin. Call it rent."

Seth stared out at the lighting. "The rain does need to stop. Otherwise, Nicole won't be able to get here tomorrow."

Mallick raised an eyebrow. "Nicole? Phil's sister? Why do you care if she can get here?"

Obi cut in, pushing his index fingers together, making kissy noises. I tried not to laugh as I said, "Because Seth is dating my sister. That's the only reason she's coming. She doesn't want to see me."

Timothy's eyes were wider than usual. "No shit, Seth? You're nailing Phil's sister?"

Seth's arms flew outward, "Dude, shut up. If the counselors find out, they'll never let her come."

Obi smiled, but I cut him off before he could say it. "He means come visit, Obi. You're in dangerous territory. Back off." Obi continued smiling, but at least he attempted to hide it.

Timothy looked from Seth to me, back to Seth. "You're both nailing cheerleaders? The last time I got a piece of ass was because my toilet paper ripped."

Obi stared at Timothy in disgust before turning his attention back to me. "Are you really dating that girl? The one in all your pictures?" *All my pictures?* As though I had hundreds of them posted everywhere. I had two. One in my locker and one by my bed.

I stumbled for words, but Seth cut in before I had to answer. "Emily. That's her name. She's gorgeous. Can't keep her hands off him, like I've said."

Obi sat upright. "Do tell. I need details."

My stomach rumbled, so I copied Timothy. "Maybe we should've grabbed those candy bars."

Timothy slapped my back. "Now you're speaking my language."

Obi shrugged. "So, let's go get them."

I stared at him. "Yeah, okay. How are we going to pull that off? If Sarge sees us…"

"He's not going to see us," Obi stated matter-of-factly. "We'll just send one person. If that person gets caught, he just says he was just trying to get out of the rain."

Seth pointed at Obi. "I think you should go. You have ninja blood."

Obi stared at the floor, sighing loudly. "For the last time, I'm Chinese."

Seth shrugged. "Fine. *Chinese* ninja blood. I'm still voting for you."

Timothy smiled. "I second that motion."

Obi stared at his friends. "What happened to Phillip going?" He winked at me. "Really, why don't we draw straws or something instead."

Seth looked around, "Do we even have straws?"

"We have the deck," Timothy said, holding up the cards.

Obi stated the obvious, "Lowest card goes." We each pulled a card, having no idea of the gravity of what we were doing.

"Why do I even have to be a part of this? I'm not going to eat the candy." Seth pouted.

"Because you're here." I said without a thought.

Obi went first, flipping a Jack. I was next, turning over a five. Seth stared at me, "Dang!" Seth pulled a nine, he looked at me, almost gloating. As Timothy reached for his card, I began to feign prayer.

Timothy laid down the three of spades. "Imagine that. The black kid's gotta go. No one saw that coming."

Seth scowled at him. "Would you just go?"

We stood at the door together, looking out at the rain. The wind whipped trees back and forth, as rain pelted the ground so hard the puddles jumped from the high-velocity drops. The heavy moisture in the air felt like a warm compress over my nose and mouth.

Timothy turned, practically begging not to go, but refusing to say the words.

Obi placed a hand on Timothy's shoulder. "Do or do not. There is no try."

"That Jedi mind shit isn't gonna work on me."

I looked over at the posters on his wall. "What would Bond do, Timothy? Bond would bring back the snacks."

"Bond would have an umbrella, you jackass bastards."

Seth's hand touched Timothy's back and shoved. As Mallick hit the mud and rain, he screamed, but it was a manly roar, not that banshee noise Seth makes. He stared back at us and then tore off running for the Mess Hall, both middle fingers in the air, telling us where we could go. I was a little jealous he didn't seem to have to hold up his pants as he ran.

As we closed the door, Seth and I made eye contact and began to laugh. "I wasn't expecting that from you, Seth. Don't you know how many calories are in a Snickers? Why are you so pushy for candy all of a sudden?"

Seth's face lit up with a smile. "280 calories. And I just *really* wanted to push someone into the mud. I would've done it to any of you."

CHAPTER 9

I think a lot about how things would have gone if I'd picked a different card. Or if Timothy had. My five was the lowest until he drew his three. But that's how life works, isn't it?

When it was my dad who died, I thought a lot about how it should've been me instead. He was such a good person. He always knew the right thing to say to people. He'd pull over and help someone change a tire. If he said he'd be somewhere, he was there. He played basketball and fixed people's cars. The guy knew everything. I knew nothing. What a waste. Why let me keep breathing instead of someone who was on the planet doing something to help others?

But I pulled a five. And Timothy pulled a three. And he's the one who was pushed into the rain. Sent on a mission to get candy bars that I shouldn't have told him were there.

Mallick ran through the camp, fingers in the air, until he was out of sight of our cabin. He made his way to the Mess Hall just around the corner. Lightning flashed several times as he ran. The wind picked up. It wasn't the level of the tornado a few towns over, but it wasn't a light breeze. Branches snapped, pushed out of their normal alignment, falling to the ground in random piles. The Fit Camp sign came untied and jiggled back and forth violently in the wind like a hand crassly waving goodbye.

Timothy threw open the Mess Hall doors and tried to dry off. The sole light in the building came from the floodlights outside and the lightning. The switches near the front door required a key, so he couldn't have turned them on if he wanted to. But it's not like he wanted to draw attention anyway. The idea was to get in and get out without anyone noticing.

As he neared the kitchen, lightning hit, allowing the other person in the room to see him. The Other pulled up the hood on his sweatshirt. He pulled on the glove he had just removed. And that glove wrapped around the narrow triple-riveted wood of a Henkles Carving Knife, almost silently removing it from the hardwood knife block. Lightning hit again. Timothy concentrated on the ground, careful not to trip, having no idea he was mere feet away from The Killer. By the third time the lightning hit, the man in the hood was directly in front of Timothy. Timothy screamed. All eight inches of the carbon steel sank directly into Mallick's chest, before he had the opportunity to fight back. Blood ran from his mouth as he looked down at the wound. He looked up, making eye contact with his murderer. Timothy fell to the ground as the knife was removed.

As The Killer turned away from his victim, lightning hit again. A silhouette of a very large overweight teenager was highlighted against the window; perfectly outlined against the lightning strike. Then everything went dark. When the lightning flashed again, there was no one at the window.

"Obi, why do you even hang on to this Star Wars crap? That's stuff my dad liked. Why can't you be into something I like?"

"Don't listen to him, Obi," I smirked. "Seth just has to run his mouth and hate anything that someone else likes. He would be a hipster if he could grow a beard."

"Hey!" Seth yelled. "I shaved last week. When did you last shave? Like four years ago? Does your mom even give you a blade in your razor?"

"Nope." I laughed. "I mainly just push shaving cream across my face."

"Not to interrupt your little love fest, but did you two know that there's actually studies on people disliking popular things?" Typical Obi. He had to take every opportunity to teach us something new. "Holding a dissenting opinion on movies or music or whatever else is one way middle-class people fight one another for status."

Seth rolled his eyes. "Please make this stop."

But Obi just kept going. "The irony is that people work so hard to run counter to the culture that it creates the next wave of culture other people will, in turn, attempt to counter."

Seth put down his cards, "So you're saying one day a group of people will try to tell me how awesome you are, Obi?"

Obi put down his cards, beating Seth. He reached for the pile of chips, but I cut him off. "Where are you trying to take my chips?" I laid down a flush.

"Are you kidding me?" Seth sighed loudly. At least there was something I could still beat him at.

We were deep into our eighth game of Texas Hold 'Em. Everyone was thinking that Timothy should've been back by then, but no one said it aloud. I pictured him passed out on the pantry floor, surrounded by empty wrappers, mouth covered in Fun Dip remains, with an IV of Mountain Dew running to his arm. Not full-blown Mountain Dew. Just the syrup in the bags at the convenience store. But I wasn't worried about him. I was pissed off he probably didn't save any for me.

And I was angry I had to listen to the insane conversations Seth and Obi always had.

Obi lay on his stomach, staring at his cards, a plastic straw hanging from his mouth, covered in bite marks. "I call it the Liquid Farts."

"Gross. Why? Why do we have to—" I tried.

"—It feels like your ass is covered in poo, but when you wipe, it's clear! Like, what is that about? Is my anus sweating?"

I threw up my hands. "Seriously? Stop."

A huge grin slid across his lips. "And why is it the consistency of warmed Jell-O?"

I laid down my hand and pulled in my chips, as Obi yelled, "Phil wins again? He's gotta be cheating. That's like his fourth in a row."

Seth laughed, "No. You just pay too much attention to what's coming out of your ass."

Obi feigned worry for his friend. "And you don't?"

Obi took the deck and started dealing. "Hey, Seth, should we be losers and have like three wild cards this round so maybe one of us can finally beat Phil?"

Seth laughed. "No way, man. I'm no Eric Schultz."

"That guy was literally the worst counselor ever." I said, tugging my pants up out of habit more than necessity. "Who teaches you to play poker like that?"

Seth nodded. "Well, I mean, the fact he was teaching us to play poker at all says a lot about the guy. I just think he was cheating. He had to be. He always took all my money."

Obi raised an eyebrow. "Think that's why he got fired?"

Seth looked at me. "He didn't get fired, did he? I thought he quit."

Obi raised a finger before I could speak. "Well, that's the rumor. That he had a big fight with Sarge about something and stormed out of the office and then Sarge called him and fired him."

I rolled my eyes. "Who did you hear that horseshit from?"

"Young told his crew. Brandon passed it on to Roger. Roger told me one day in the shower." Obi said.

Seth's eyes squeezed shut as he shook his head slowly back and forth. "Nope. Nope. And nope. I know you're lying. There's no way Roger was in the shower with another person. He's way too self-conscious about his body."

"What body?" I interjected. "Dude weighs what? 110? I think my left nut weighs more than that."

Obi smiled. "It's true. I mean about Roger. I don't know about your nut, but you should probably get that checked out."

I flipped him off. "Finish the story."

Obi lay down on his stomach on his bed, looking at us. Once he was comfortable, he said. "I had locker room clean up that day, so I was in there, waiting for Roger to finish. The way he tells it…"

Even though it was just down the hall from Dr. Munson's office, most of us had never seen Sarge's office. It was basically off limits to any camper, but the occasional screw up got to see it now and then. That day, Jonathon Young was that screw up. He'd been assigned cleaning duty in the Counselors' Quarters. Young watched as Counselor Eric Schultz sauntered down the hallway, a latte in one hand and his phone in the other.

Eric stopped in front of Sarge's office, knocking lightly, even though Stanheight could directly see him standing there through the glass door. Sarge sat at his desk, sipping a cup of coffee, black, with a double shot of espresso, but he'd deny that he knew what was in it. It was just "some damn coffee" when he ordered it. Eric closed the door and crashed into the chair opposite Sarge.

At that point, Jonathon couldn't hear anything that was said, but he could see it all through the glass window of the office. Eric jumped up, throwing his arms out wide. Sarge pointed at him repeatedly. Eric stood and threw open the door. Young dove out of view, but clearly heard Sarge say, "It doesn't have to end this way, Eric. Take a night or two off and think about which is more important to you."

Seth and I stared at Obi in disbelief as he finished. "Anyway, he was really, really mad. Furious. Or at least that's what Roger said Brandon said Jonathon thought Eric was feeling."

I laughed. "Somehow, that actually made sense to me.

Seth looked toward the window. "Anyone else wondering what the hell is taking Timothy so long?"

Obi leaned back on his bed, his fingers laced behind his head. "It's pretty simple, really. There's no one there to push him back into the rain and make him come back."

"Do you think we should go look for him?" I asked.

Seth shook his finger at me. "Are you kidding? He probably got busted by Sarge."

I stood up. "I'm the one who should've gone. Like Timothy said, it wasn't my cabin. Plus, I'm the one who knew where the snacks were. I'll go look for him."

I opened the door to the cabin. The rain was so thick I couldn't see three feet in front of the door. The rain made a glop-glop-glop-glop as it hit the mud. Lightning crashed across the clouds again, followed almost immediately by a barrage of thunder.

I closed the door. "I'm good. I probably shouldn't have any candy anyway."

CHAPTER 10

Obi rolled himself around his bed and pulled his blanket over him. "I think I'm gonna hit the sack, Phil. If you still want to stay, there's that bed over there."

"Thanks, man."

Obi was asleep in less than two minutes. Seth and I stayed up a little bit longer. I wanted to take this chance to tell him I was leaving the following day; but every time I tried, I couldn't form the words. The ideas just died in the back of my throat until I managed to regurgitate more of them.

Seth had been there through the worst times of my life. When my dad died, Seth was there. He picked the shell casings off the ground after the twenty-one-gun salute in case I wanted them. When my grandma was in the hospital, Seth stayed there with me. He even brought his Xbox, so we'd have something to do in the waiting room other than wait. Every time life got hard, Seth was there to help push me through. How was I supposed to tell him that he was part of the reason I didn't want to finish Fit Camp?

No. There was no way to just tell him.

But I couldn't *not* tell him. What was I supposed to do, just casually wave goodbye from Nicole's car as we sped off? And it's not like I could trust Nicole not to tip him off. No. I needed to find a way.

"I'm leaving tomorrow." I was horrified. It came out before I knew what I was doing.

"Excuse me? I think not!" He sat right up, staring at me. "I love you, man, but if you try to leave before I get to see Nicole, I'll kill you."

"What? No. She's coming. She'll hang out with us all day and then I'll go home with her. I just have to pack some of my stuff. I couldn't do it sooner, so they wouldn't know."

"That's ridiculous. She'll never go for that. She'll break me out of here before you."

"Okay. Come with us."

"Hell no. I'm too close to achieving history. Plus, I'm down almost thirty pounds since we arrived. That was six weeks ago, man. Do you know what I could accomplish in six more?" He paused, staring directly at my stomach. Was that disgust I sensed? "You could make a lot of progress in six weeks too, if you put in the work."

I moved my head several times, getting the pillow to line up with my neck the way I wanted. "Well, I can work on it from home too."

"That's BS and you know it." He went silent.

"I'm not asking for permission, Seth. I'm just letting you know that I'm going. And that I appreciate you coming here for me."

His head shook. "I didn't come here for you. I came here *with* you. The difference is I worked on my issues."

I rolled away, ensuring he couldn't see my reaction to that. Right when I thought he might have given up, Seth quietly said, "You're making a mistake, you know."

"How do you figure?"

"You need this place. You need the confidence it will give you. You need to embrace it and actually work at it instead of half-assing it every day."

"Are you seriously telling me what to do right now?"

"Yeah. You know why? Because someone needs to. Everyone just pussyfoots around you because your dad died." Seth held up two hands like a man talking to the police. "That came out harsh. Just hear what I'm saying. I just mean that everyone is afraid to upset you. It needs to stop."

It took me everything not to punch him in the throat.

"Phillip, all I'm saying is you can't keep going the way you have been. You've gained more weight in the last year than ever. You're gonna be dead in a couple years at this rate. That's exactly why you need to be here. So that you don't *literally* die."

I stared at him in disbelief. First, he isn't there when I needed him to listen to me. Then he became athletic and left me alone on the bottom of the pile. Now he had the audacity to not only remind me my father was dead but to try to act like my father and tell me what to do? Screw this guy. Friendship be damned.

I stood up. Seth asked me to sit back down. "Dude, I'm not trying to be a dick. I'm trying to help you."

"Really? By doing what exactly? Just bitching at me and telling me how horrible I am?"

"I'm worried about you, man."

"Oh, piss off."

"I'm serious. I don't want to lose you the way you lost your dad."

"Don't talk about my dad!" I screamed.

We both looked over as Obi woke up momentarily, adjusted his pillow and went right back to sleep. He was snoring within five seconds. We both laughed, momentarily distracted from the weight of our conversation.

He looked at me, "Can we talk about this another day when you've had time to think about what I said?" He was literally using Dr. Munson's exact words against me. She'd asked me that question repeatedly. But, I quickly noticed, framing it that way made it all okay. It was as though Dr. Munson was in the room instead of Seth; a professional instead of another screwed up kid trying to tell me what to do.

"Okay." I walked over to the empty bed. "Is it still okay if I just stay here? Or do I need to go back to my cabin?"

"You need to go, bro. And give me back my clothes. Out into the wild blue yonder with your naked ass!" He laughed even as my pillow hit his face from across the room. Why couldn't I throw a baseball that well?

Seth pulled his covers back. This time he was purposely less abrasive. "All I'm saying is you can do it too, man. Everything I've done. Every record I've set. Every pound I've dropped. I'm not doing anything you can't do. You just need to believe you can and put in the work. Don't run away, man. We've both run away from things too many times. Stay and fight."

I laughed. "What happened to talking about it another day?"

"I can't, if you're not here." He paused as he pulled his covers up. "It's going to be okay, man. I'm here for you. I'll help you through it. Just don't go, okay?"

"Okay. I'll stay."

"You promise?"

"I promise."

"You're totally lying to me."

"I know. Good night, Seth."

"Good night, man."

That was the last night I slept well for a long time.

CHAPTER 11

The storm set records in Iowa for its severity, a total of three tornadoes touched down less than ninety minutes from us but luckily, we were on the outside edge of the storm cell and mainly got rain and some flooding, but it was a ton of rain. Sarge estimated we got 3 inches in a couple hours. To say the camp was in disarray following the storm would be a lot like saying that I could stand to drop a pound or two. The place was a disaster.

The forest running along the northern edge of the camp was covered in fallen branches, crisscrossing in multiple directions, like a room filled with lasers guarding some great treasure. At least the lightning hadn't hit any of the trees. The dirt path running through the middle of the camp was an endless mud puddle, but the shallow edges allowed people to walk without slushing through the drying quagmire of sludge. Shutters hung at odd angles on cabins. The field we played baseball on the day before stood flooded. One camper a year younger than me was collecting earthworms to use as bait, seemingly unaware of the two-foot wide rut through the saturated ground, running all the way from the locker room to the Mess Hall. Even the Fit Camp sign boy – the one who had lost all his imaginary weight and couldn't stop smiling – lay damaged, hanging askew from the one cord barely still attached to the wall. It jiggled in the wind, threatening to hit the large window of the Mess Hall.

The Counselors' Quarters was worse for wear; the triple flight of wooden stairs running up the east side of the building lost a section of its handrail in the wind. Inside, Sarge met with the other counselors in the main lobby-like area. Flames grew in the fireplace, but the heat was barely noticeable even six feet away on the leather couches, where Counselors Greg and Jeff shared a bag of Cornuts. The two overnight counselors, Tony and Todd, sat on the other couch, eating candy bars they'd secured from the raid on Randy's room. Sarge paced in front of the flames, using the fire poker for a pointer.

He shot the poker out toward the window looking over the camp. "If you've looked out the windows, you already know the camp is seriously messed up. Everything from the parking lot this way is a mess. And Greg tells me the elevator is still shot, so you'll need to use the stairs." The overnight counselors groaned in unison. Sarge shot them a dirty look. "If we're gonna stand up here and preach fitness, we shouldn't be taking the easy way out either. You're not phys ed teachers. Now then, as I was saying, we need to get this place fixed up. I figure the easiest way to get it back in tip-top shape is to have the kids do it."

Greg nodded along. "That'll get 'em some exercise too. So that's a plus."

The fire poker shot out, directly aimed at Greg's chest. "Exactly. A great point. I like the way you think." Sarge pulled the fire poker back in. "With Eric gone…"

Tony shot forward on the couch, "Do we know when he's coming back?"

Trying to be as politically correct as he could get, Sarge said, "Eric will not be returning to the camp, to the best of my knowledge."

Tony smiled, "So there's an open day position?"

Sarge rolled his eyes. "Well, yeah, I guess there will be. Right now, I need you on overnights still, but if you want to help during the day, you're welcome to do so."

Todd leaned in, "Do you have any more candy, man?" Tony gave him another Snickers.

"Now, as I was saying, with Eric gone, that leaves a lot for the rest of us to cover. I had Greg draw up some printouts with everyone's new responsibilities."

Greg reached over to the glass coffee table, removing a stack of papers to pass out. Each counselor grabbed a packet as Sarge continued. "As long as we use that teamwork we're always preaching, I think this will work out with very few problems."

Before they even made it to the end of the first page, Sarge put the fire poker down against the wall and waved the counselors out the door. "Let's get to it."

For the second time in two days, I was the last person in camp to wake up. I expected Sarge in my face, running his mouth, screaming things like, "You better move your fat ass, or I'll get a forklift and move it for you." But no, he was nowhere to be found. I opened one eye because I was too lazy to open them both. Confused, I found myself in Seth's room, looking at Timothy's bed. His dresser was covered with a hodgepodge of loose change, mismatched socks, pictures of his family, and aftershave bottles. The clock radio flashed 5:14 over and over, but the sun was up, so there was no way that was correct.

Pulling myself into a seated position, I yawned, inhaling a mix of wet towels, body spray, and rotting orange peels. I could've slept another four hours. No one was going to look for me. If they checked my bed, I wouldn't be there. They'd assume I was out doing whatever everyone else was doing. I closed my eyes and leaned back down on the pillow.

Instantly sitting up, I realized Nicole was on her way and I still needed to pack. I pulled on my socks and shoes and looked out the window. I heard other campers laughing and talking, although I couldn't make out their words. Most were busy working. Some gathered branches. Others laid down mats through the mud, as if a mat was holding anyone's weight and keeping their shoes clean; well, other than Roger. But I knew it wouldn't do to try to walk through the standing water forming small pools that snaked their way throughout the camp. Up by the Mess Hall, Obi was hard at work, down on one knee, trying to secure the Fit Camp sign.

At the cabin door, my nose was assaulted with the smell of mildew from our many wet towels from the night before; so, I didn't overthink my decision to get out of the cabin. I took two steps and tried to turn to my right and head directly to my cabin to pack. Instead, I found myself face to face with Seth.

CHAPTER 12

Seth stared at me, almost suspiciously, but it's possible I was so aware of my own guilt that I imagined that. He smiled. "Hey, Sleepy Head."

I watched two bumblebees play in the rose bush in front of Seth's cabin, as I refused to make eye contact. "Why did you let me sleep so long? Am I in trouble?"

"I thought you might need to clear your head after our chat last night. Sarge volunteered everyone to do some cleaning. There's like five or six groups. Us. Those guys over there. Some down by the lake. Just all over, really. So, they have no idea where you are anyway."

Obi called from where he was, "Can you guys help me with this for a minute?"

Kneeling next to Obi, I worried about how I'd get back up. "So, what exactly are we doing with this sign?"

Seth stood there taking his pulse, as Obi and I fixed the sign. "Well, I think that's probably as good as it's gonna get. It should hold unless there's another storm."

Obi stood up. "So last year, when I was here, they were fed up with all the graffiti. They fixed this sign seriously like six times. In the bathroom stalls, they replaced a lot of the doors with dry erase boards, thinking it would encourage people to draw there instead of ruining the stall walls."

"Did it?" I asked, completely unsure how I'd gotten wrapped up in this story.

"Sort of." Obi smiled. "But it also encouraged us to think outside of the box. Suddenly, one of the older kids wiped his brown butt juices on the corner of the board. He makes an arrow. A little cartoon arrow. And he writes 'POO!' He becomes an instant celebrity. I'm talking Frrrrraaaank Doyle level of greatness. My roommate, Paulie, he decides he's going to outdo this. And he talks for a solid two days about how he's going in there late at night and he's gonna rub one out and paint the whiteboard whiter."

"That's disgusting." I said, wishing I had a way out of this conversation.

Not Seth. He was totally into it. "And did he?"

Obi leaned in, miming the action with his wrist. "He's going and going, and he knows it's about to happen. And he's holding out, trying to make it the biggest explosion possible. And he finally can't handle it anymore and he lets loose." Obi's hands slowly pantomimed a mushroom cloud, as he leaned back, eyes closed, with a huge smile on his face.

Seth laughs. "He actually did it?"

Obi's smile disappeared. "Nah. He just made a huge mess all over the floor."

Shaking my head, I said, "Can we stop? I'd rather Young, Kramer, and their crew don't see you pretending to masturbate all over me."

"You're no fun, Phil." He smiled. "Hey, that reminds me. Maybe you can settle a little debate that Seth and I were having earlier."

"About?" I asked cautiously.

Obi wiped his hands on the sides of his jeans. "Relating to the trials and tribulations of man-scaping when you're overweight."

"Pass." I said, trying to change the topic. "Have you guys seen Timothy? Like, did he come back to the cabin at all last night? What do you guys think happened to him?"

Obi shrugged. "He could be anywhere, man. He'll turn up. People don't just disappear, you know."

A smirk illuminated Seth's face. "Especially people his size."

Obi's left eyebrow raised. "You know you're bigger than he is, right?"

Matter-of-factly, Seth responded, "And I've never just disappeared. That's my point, exactly."

I love Seth, but he does some weird stuff. One of the things that makes me the craziest is when he grinds his teeth together and speaks, so no one can understand him because he's not moving his mouth… even though he's louder than usual when he does it. As Obi and I stood double checking the sign, Seth did this exact thing, grinding his teeth, and loudly saying, "COUNSELOR COMING.". I looked up to see Counselor Greg walking up, carrying a clipboard.

Greg wiped his hair out of his eyes. "Hey, guys. Sorry to interrupt, but Sarge is making us account for everyone's whereabouts last night. McCracken, your roommate says you didn't come home. Can you tell me where you were?"

"Sure. I was with these guys. In their cabin. It was the closest to the Mess Hall. I didn't feel like running in the rain all the way back to my cabin."

Greg stared at me. "Is it really that far?"

"Yeah. It's the last cabin on the left."

Greg jotted some notes on his clipboard. For all I knew, he could be writing in Morse Code. I had no idea what he was doing. Finally, he said, "Works for me." He made eye contact and held it for a second. "Provided what you said is true."

Seth cut in. "Yeah, he was there. All night."

Greg didn't look up as he made more notes. "Did anyone leave your cabin at any time?

Seth said the word "Yes" before Obi or I could stop him. We stared at him, imploring him telepathically not to sell out his friend. He stared at us, shaking his head slowly. "I'm sorry, I'm not getting in trouble for him or anyone else."

Seth looked from Obi to myself and back again. He'd already made up his mind and all this time killing certainly wasn't making the situation any better. Greg tapped his clipboard. "Do you have something to say or not, Jenkins?"

"Timothy Mallick left our cabin late last night. Middle of the storm. We haven't seen him since." The guilt hit Seth's stomach the same way a double cheeseburger hits mine; all at once. As annoyed as I should've been with him, I was glad he had more courage than I did. Someone had to figure out what happened to Timothy.

Greg scribbled some notes on his clipboard in the same manner his wife, Dr. Munson, often did during our therapy sessions. He peeked over the top rim of his glasses, "Mallick right? Black kid. Ridiculous sense of humor?"

Seth nodded quickly. "That's him."

Greg flipped pages. "Well, if this is accurate, it looks like he's supposed to be down at the lake with Jeff's crew, cleaning up branches and eating tofu and whatever else they do." I instantly felt better. Greg straightened his pages. "So other than Mallick, none of you left the cabin last night?" He glared at me, "Even if you were in the wrong cabin to begin with?"

My eyes narrowed. "He's the only one who left. I'm sorry. No one told me I had to be in exactly the right place. I didn't know we were on lockdown last night."

Greg's body relaxed as he oversold his reaction. "It's not lockdown, McCracken. You don't have to get all melodramatic." He smiled more to himself than to us. It faded. "Honestly, I just do what Sarge tells me to do. Don't want to end up unemployed like Eric, right?" I couldn't tell for sure, but I thought he giggled to himself as he walked away.

Obi waited until Greg was talking to the next group of campers, as though he half-expected the counselor to come back. "See? I told you Timothy was fine. You guys were crying like little girls for nothing." He stood up, farting loudly. "Oh. Looks like I got a turtle munching on cotton. If you'll excuse me, I need to go make a deposit at the stank bank."

Seth giggled nonstop as Obi made his way to the bathroom, but I just shook my head. "That boy is not right. Why does he insist on telling us when he has to use the bathroom?"

I jumped three feet as Sarge said, "Probably doesn't want to be alone in there." He'd appeared out of nowhere. He put one hand on the Fit Camp sign, shaking it lightly. "You did a really fine job on this, McCracken." Before I could tell him, it was mainly Obi, Sarge continued. "I just got a call from your sister, McCracken. They should be here any minute. That's probably them now." He said as a blue Ford Escape came down the road.

I watched as Nicole's car came closer. Seth instantly stood up straight, adjusting his hair, as though he wasn't covered in dirt and mud. I continued to pick up branches nearby, pretending I'd be upset to stop working. "Yup. That's her, alrighty."

Seth continued trying to clean himself off, to no avail. I rolled my eyes. It was pathetic watching him panic to impress a girl he was already dating. If she'd dealt with seeing him naked (and I liked to think she had not), I couldn't imagine she'd be that disgusted by a little mud on his jeans or dirt on his shirt. And let's face it, there was nothing Seth could do about his face. It was still going to look that way whether he washed it or not. That thought made me smile, as we started to walk toward the car together. I expected Sarge to stop Seth from going with us, but he didn't. With quick steps, we cleared the hill to the parking lot as quickly as the squirrels I sometimes saw.

Nicole's blonde hair was longer than I remembered, but it's not like I spent a lot of time looking at her. It wasn't up in a ponytail, which told me she worked way harder to look nice for Seth than he'd worked for her. Her tank top and tight shorts told me I should get in the car and leave with her now, before one of the other campers saw her and had a heart attack.

Boys are easily overwhelmed.

The passenger door opened as the color drained from my face. As Emily Clausen stood up, I felt the hair on my neck rise through the sweat. The temperature around me seemed to drop twenty degrees. She flipped her hair. My elbow stabbed into my side, causing my shoulders to tighten up. My breath burst out and then back in and back out. I couldn't have spoken; but even if I had, I wouldn't have heard it over the heartbeat pounding in my ears. She waved to me, with a smile.

Then everything came out of me at once. "Oh shit. No. No. No. NO! This cannot be happening." I wiped my eyes. My head slowly turned to the right, glaring directly at Seth as his Cheshire cat-like grin spread across his face, resembling a psycho in a horror movie who enjoyed the chaos he instilled in others. Even though I knew the answer, I blurted out, "Did you know she was coming?"

Seth nodded his head, still smiling like a psycho. I turned back to Emily. Her cropped tank top and her cutoff denim shorts were killing me. She was like a model painted into her clothes.

I turned and ran. On any other path, I would have set a record for fastest time across the camp. But no. Not me. I turned around, caught one foot on the other, and lost my balance. I bounced twice on the way down the hill and hit the mudhole at the bottom before I could even get my arms out to protect me. My left arm buckled and slid through scummy water and mucky sludge. Muddy water instantly filled my shoe. Dead leaf fragments and mud clumps hugged my wet skin. I hoped the liquid running from my neck into the back of my shirt was just sweat but knew the liquid running from my eyes all too well. Inhaling through my tears, I slowly turned to see if Emily had witnessed my tumble down the hill. Glancing up, I realized my shirt was halfway up my back. Luckily the mud covered most of it.

Hands on his hips, backlit by the bright summer sky, Sarge yelled down, "You all right, McCracken? Walk it off."

I ran faster than I ever have. I was halfway to the showers before I even knew where I was going. In a single bound, I cleared the mats placed on the marsh, running through the middle of camp.

I didn't know it at the time, but The Killer stood watching my impressive run. He also knew I would most likely be alone in the showers, and he decided to make his move.

CHAPTER 13

Nicole found the whole thing hilarious, but, of course, her favorite part was when I pulled myself out of the mud, uncovered stomach hanging down to my knees, and turned to run away with my ass crack hanging out. When Sarge realized he couldn't help me, he tried to run damage control, attempting to take their minds off it by telling them the rules of Fit Camp.

"You mean Fat Camp?" Nicole asked innocently enough, pointing to the wooden sign of the kid holding out his fat pants. She hadn't meant any disrespect, but Sarge was instantly on guard.

Sarge sighed audibly. "Honestly, I'm embarrassed you saw that. I kept cleaning it. It kept happening. After a while, you have to pick your battles and I just stopped. I would take down the whole sign, but the company paid a lot to have it made. The kid in that picture is a grown man now. Apparently, the company used to fly him out for special events and for recruitment, but over the past couple years, he started packing on the pounds again, so now they kind of steer clear of him. But yeah, no matter how much I clean it, some funny man paints it again." Sarge's chest puffed out as he went full military, giving Seth a death glare. "I want that cleaned off today."

Seth fumbled for words. "Oh. Okay. Yeah. Sure. I can do that."

"Then why are you still standing here? Go."

Seth mouthed, "I'm sorry" to Nicole and turned to leave. He couldn't stick around long anyway, or it might tip Sarge off that they weren't just my guests.

Once Seth was gone, Stanheight launched into a full description of what Camp Wašíču was meant to accomplish. He followed that with, "We aren't exactly used to having visitors. A lot of these boys are more or less abandoned here and their families don't so much as pick up a phone all summer."

"That's terrible." Emily's eyebrows squished together the way they do when she's having issues understanding the algebra homework.

"Well, you need to understand that most do it out of love. There are many mothers who cannot admit outside of here that they are part of the problem, but once their bouncing baby beluga is enrolled in Camp Wašíču, the reality sets in and they get a lot better at calling things down the middle."

Seth watched from a distance, as he gathered branches, already feeling his only allowed time with Nicole was slipping away. Of course, being Seth, that only made him work harder to finish rather than making him quit like I would have.

"Speaking of calling," Sarge began, "I have to take your cell phones. It's policy. The upper brass would probably skin me alive and toss me to the wolves if they knew I didn't take your phones as soon as you were on the property. We don't allow phones down where the boys are. At all. Part of it is that they're here for therapy, so it helps to not have the distractions. Keeps them focused on what they should be doing to lose weight, not texting all the time or Facebooking or snapping chats or whatever. I don't get it. I don't want to get it. That said, two years ago, one boy, John Walker. Weird kid. Real rednecky type with the long hair in the back and the short hair in the front like his barber was as lazy as John's left eye. He used to French kiss his soda bottle before we got rid of them. Anyway, Walker got a hold of one of the counselors' cell phones and ordered forty pizzas."

"Oh, wow. He ordered for everyone?"

Stanheight slowly shook his head no. "We found him passed out in his cabin covered in sauce and cheese and vomit." His speech rate and volume lowered as he added, "He was still eating." Sarge was quiet for a second. "But anyway, really, I'm going to need your phones. You won't get much of a signal down there anyway. It's pretty much a dead zone."

Nicole almost left right then. "You're serious?"

"Afraid so."

Nicole sent a quick text to mom, letting her know that the girls had to hand over their phones. She hit the power button and handed the phone to Sarge. Tearing up, she watched him slightly suspiciously; the same way I imagine a mom who has just given birth watches a nurse walk out of the room with the newborn.

Sarge turned to Emily, making the "gimme" motion with his hand. She stared back as though she didn't understand what he wanted. "What about you? Do you need to call anyone first?"

She shook her head, eyes wide. "Couldn't if I wanted to. I didn't bring mine."

Nicole and Sarge stared at Emily with facial expressions usually reserved for someone who tries to convince you the ceiling is the floor. Sarge looked down at the ground, sighing loudly. "What is this? 1996? You expect me to believe that a teenager, a FEMALE teenager came to a summer camp filled with creepy teenage boys with their hormones going crazy and you didn't bring your phone with you?"

Emily raised both hands in the air. "I don't know what to say. I really didn't bring it." She made eye contact with Nicole. "I'm serious. I had it plugged in at the house and I forgot to grab it. I feel totally naked without it."

Sarge rolled his eyes. "Naked? Good God in Heaven! Don't let these walking sacks of hormones hear you say stuff like that. We'll never get them out of their beds." He moved closer to her. "Are you absolutely sure you didn't bring it with you?"

Emily turned her pockets out, purposely sliding the palms of her hands down her silk-soft legs in a sexually suggestive manner. She coyly raised an eyebrow. "I suppose you can frisk me if want."

"No thank you, young lady. I happen to like my job. I'll believe you, but I catch you using one, it's gone. Do I make myself clear?"

"That will not be a problem, sir."

Stanheight smiled. "Why don't you call me 'Sarge'" He paused, smiling. "Or Gordon." He led them toward the Mess Hall to get them each a drink.

Emily's phone continued to charge on the floor of the Ford Escape.

CHAPTER 14

While they were all living it up on their tour of Camp Wašíču, I reached the locker room, still crying. My body collapsed in on itself as I fell onto the bench in front of my locker. My head bowed, shoulders curling over my chests, hitching and thrusting with each sob; my throat bobbed with each whimper. My hands clutched at my face so tightly my lip had to work to find room to tremble. My self-loathing at an all-time high, I threw open my locker expecting to find that I had no backup clothes and would need to go back out there. I teared up again when I saw them. It wasn't my best outfit, but man was I glad I hadn't taken them the day before.

I peeled off the destroyed clothing. My underwear clung to my ass cheeks like a wet washcloth. Rolling them down I wondered if I should wash the clothes or attempt to burn them. I grabbed my hygiene products and moved to find a shower. The first one reeked like rotten meat. I supposed that many overweight boys washing who knows what off themselves would give you that unpleasant aroma. I picked the shower at the opposite end, which did not smell as strongly, even though it was used much more often. I had to crap first, so I sat down on the elongated toilet seat and tried to hurry it along. The last thing I needed was to come out of the stall and have someone see my mud-covered clothes and assume I'd shit all over myself.

Now, I know what you're probably thinking, dear reader, but just because I was almost 400 pounds doesn't mean things are that different. So, the answer to your burning question is that I wipe my butt the same way you probably do. I reach back there, and I wipe it. I don't require any special tools or a sidekick who I call over at the right time like a three-year-old. Just because I'm fat doesn't mean my arms don't work.

Showers? Same thing. I use a normal shower scrubby-dubby, as my young cousin calls them. I like a handheld showerhead, but that wasn't exactly an option at Camp Wašíču. Again, my arms work well, so I can reach everything just fine and get clean. I mean, sure, a couple times, I've sprayed the walls of the shower with soap and rubbed my back against it, but it's not that I couldn't reach. It's that I can't give myself a massage and that's the best way I've found to do it. I lifted my leg on the side of the shower and got the shower poof down there, scrubbing the deep dark recesses of my sweaty taint. Soon it was shining like I planned to auction it off on eBay. Well, I assume it was, I might be able to reach down there, but I can't see down there.

Although, Sarge seems to think I'm flexible enough to fit my entire head in my ass.

I think I knew beforehand that I wasn't alone. Sometimes you can just feel it. I don't necessarily believe that the human body has some built-in Spidey-sense by any means. You don't always know when someone is watching you. But sometimes, you feel it. And sometimes, that feeling is right. Maybe it's something in your peripheral vision; like your brain sees something out of the ordinary. Maybe you subconsciously notice a change in the sounds you hear. Maybe you see the face in the shadows pointed at you, but don't register what it is.

CRRRCHT!

A sound like static ripped through the air.

Crrcht! Again, but quieter, as though it faded from existence as it hit.

Looking around carefully I didn't see anyone. "Hello?" I called; quickly realizing I didn't need to let anyone else know I was there. I needed to get out. I toweled off as fast as I could, but by the time I reached my locker, the desire to flee and my overreaction to whatever the sound was had basically faded.

If that wasn't bad enough, I saw my reflection in the mirror. For once, I looked at it. Normally, I avoided it like eye contact on public transportation. For whatever reason, I thought that was a great time to really look at my body. I had a hard time believing that's what I looked like *after* losing some weight. What did I look like before? I inspected the topographical map on my stomach made up of hair, stray pimples, and stretch marks; or as I called them, the track marks of addicts who can't stop abusing food. I turned to my locker and found myself face to face with a picture of a woman who I knew would never want to look at what I'd just been staring at.

The humiliation of falling in the mud flooded back into my mind. That feeling had not washed down the drain with the soap after all. *Why did she have to show up?* But, I quickly realized I couldn't blame Emily. It was my problem. I'd brought it on myself. I'd taken that picture at my sister's graduation party only a few months ago. I told Emily I was taking pictures of everyone, but I was just trying to get a picture of her. She was eating at the time, so she wiped her face off, and sat upright.

"How's my hair? Do I look okay?"

"You look amazing." I somehow managed to say. I snapped three pictures of her, but I was shaking so badly only the one came out well. "Thank you."

She smiled. "Sure. Are you excited that it'll be us next year?"

"What? Us?"

Emily's eyebrows rose, widening her eyes, making her even more beautiful. "Graduating? Next year. It will be our class."

"Oh, yeah. I can't wait."

"Me either. I'm so jealous that Nicole is going to college. At least I can still go to the parties with her, right?" She laughed.

The thought of Emily at a fraternity party caused a burning sensation in my chest. My stomach seemed to harden. I recovered quickly though. "Well, don't get too far ahead of yourself. Gotta enjoy Senior year, right?"

"Oh yeah. It's going to be a good year, I think."

Nicole appeared next to Emily. "Oh. My. God. You have to come outside with me. You're never going to believe this." She stopped, her face scrunching up as she looked at me. "You feeling all right?"

"What? Yeah. Yeah. I'm great."

"Okay, weirdo." Nicole pulled Emily out of the small reception hall by her arm. Emily didn't look back once, but that didn't stop me from assuming she wanted to do so. I was never good at telling myself that Emily wasn't perfect. As far as I was concerned she probably shit Snickers and pissed lemonade.

And I still felt that way, looking at her picture in my locker. "I can't believe you're here." I said aloud. "A little warning would have been nice, so this wasn't so incredibly awkward."

I closed my locker, to find Roger Tonkyn, in just a towel. "I didn't know you were here or I would have given you a warning."

"Holy shit!" I screamed. Quickly recovering, I apologized to Roger. I'm sure, given our size difference, he'd been intimidated enough without me yelling at him. "Jesus, Roger. Don't do that." I pulled on clothes as he gathered his hygiene products. We were both very careful not to look in the other's direction.

"I'm really sorry, Phil. I'm not used to other people being down here this time of day. I just figured everyone was busy with clean up, so I could probably shower in peace. That way no one else – you know – like watches and stuff."

Pulling on my gym shoes, I tossed my mud-covered sneakers into the locker. I'd deal with them later. "Well, you don't have to worry about me. I was just leaving.:

Roger walked to the first shower as I gathered the couple items I needed. I heard him say, "Oh my god. What died in here?" He made his way to the shower I had just used. I left unaware that we weren't the only two in the locker room.

Sometime after I left, The Killer stood right outside of the shower, as Roger inevitably sang to himself, eyes closed. Roger didn't like looking at his body any more than I liked looking at mine. He leaned back to get the shampoo out of his hair, making his neck a larger target.

CHAPTER 15

Everything looked better than it had when I went into the shower. I was clean and so was the world. I didn't know how I'd ever live down what had happened, but I would accept it and own it as best I could. The trees on the edge of the forest looked a brighter green following the rain, but it might have been my imagination. The sky itself was now clear; the blue specks of sky in the leaves reminded me of Dr. Munson's eyes. The sole cloud I saw might as well have been on the other side of the earth. I walked toward my cabin, unsure if Nicole and Emily were there or in the Mess Hall.

Just play it cool. Everything will be fine. I told myself. Maybe you won't even have to talk to Emily. That hurt, as much as it made me feel a little better.

But when I looked up from the still-muddy path, my eyes met Emily's. Walking right toward me, she waved slowly, purposefully. When she finally reached me, she quietly said, "Hey, Phillip."

"Hey. Where is everyone else?"

She took a drink out of her water bottle. Judging by the logo, she'd gotten it in the Mess Hall and somehow made it out without being mobbed by other campers.

Hands on her hips, Emily twisted back to look behind her. She looked back. "Obi and that Counselor went to keep cleaning. Seth was cleaning. Now he and Nicole are… they're… I mean…"

"They're in Seth's cabin getting naked?"

She tried not to laugh but couldn't help it. "Your cabin. But yeah, possibly. I left when they were just kissing." Her eyes met mine again. "Sorry."

"For what?"

"You're her brother. He's your best friend."

"We don't really have the normal brother/sister relationship going on. And Seth is so far out of his league I can't take this away from him."

We both laughed. As she stopped, Emily leaned in. "Is there a reason people are watching us?"

As I looked around, I now noticed several other campers watching from a distance. I smirked, "They're definitely not checking me out." I turned away from her. "Come on. We're going to have to brave seeing them naked, but we'll do it together."

She laughed as I held my cabin door open for her. "McCracken!" I turned to see Counselor Greg jogging up. "Can I have a word?"

I let the door close as I walked toward him. "What's up?"

"Is there a reason you left your guests unattended?"

"I had to clean up. Sarge told me to take a shower." I lied, saying, "I was covered in mud at the time. I thought he was still showing them around."

"Well, okay. But don't let it happen again. Especially when your guests look like that." Said the guy with the most gorgeous wife I'd ever seen. As he walked away, I thought about how great it must be to come home to Dr. Munson every night.

But I forgot that feeling as soon as I opened my cabin door. That next image will live forever in my mind. It's the kind of thing I imagine I'll remember when I'm forty, late at night, when my wife and kid are in bed sleeping. I'll think back to the feeling when I saw

Emily Clausen in my bed; her cut-offs sliding down as she leaned forward, laughing. Her low-cut tank top allowing glimpses of taboo flesh. The horror of the mud incident was gone. The embarrassment disappeared. There was only beauty and hope as I stood there.

Until I remembered the photo of Emily on the wall directly behind her.

I certainly wasn't going to mention it, but I could see no way she hadn't noticed it. As I entered, Emily looked away from me, focusing on her shoelace which was perfectly tied, but suddenly needed retying. Seth leaned back in the open bed, his arm around Nicole. "What's up, Moon Pie? You doing okay?"

"Yeah... I just.... I don't know what happened."

Nicole smiled. "So, whose bed is this?"

"It's open." I said, leaning awkwardly against the wall so Emily wouldn't feel uncomfortable if I sat on my bed. "It belonged to Orlando, but he washed out the second week of camp and went home." This was my chance. I went for it. "A lot of people don't make it all the way through. I don't see any real shame in it. I think if you know it's not working—"

Nicole laughed. "No worries, Big Little Brother. I'll take you home with us. Seth already brought us up to speed. I'm surprised you're not packed through."

I stared at Seth in absolute disbelief. He shrugged. "Someone had to talk you out of it."

"She literally just said she'd take me home." I replied, both arms out.

"How was I supposed to know she'd take your side?"

Nicole sat up. "I tried to convince Seth to leave too and come home, but he wants to stay."

Seth's hands locked behind his head. "I'm killing it here. I'm the record breaker. I'm not leaving now." His left arm shot out, pointing at me.

"And you shouldn't either. You should work your ass off and stay here and enjoy the benefits like I am."

Emily suddenly moved from my bed to the one Seth and Nicole were on. She held her own hand out to offer me my bed. Her eyes locked on the picture of her I had on the wall. I sat directly in front of it. "How are you, Emily?"

She stared at me. "Good."

"Awesome."

We all sat in silence for the next thirty seconds until the door opened. My roommate Georgie Perkins entered. Don't let the fact that they call him Georgie throw you off. He was huge. 6'1" and almost weighed as much as me. His arms were gigantic. He spent all of his time at the gym lifting and almost never did any cardio. Georgie came to camp willingly. He wanted to get in shape heading into Senior year, so more schools would notice him. He could've already used the offers he had to wallpaper his side of the room. Perkins did not need the money. He came from old money; some of the oldest in Iowa. His father owned several big-name hotels and the biggest publishing company in Des Moines.

Georgie ignored me as he stared at Seth. "Jenkins, what the hell are you doing in my cabin? Get out. Now. And take your friend with you."

"They're Phillip's guests." Seth shot back.

"I wasn't talking about them. These gorgeous Chicas can stay. I meant you and that fatso over there need to get out of here." Georgie's index finger pointed right at my head even though he hadn't once looked at me.

"Let's get out of here." Seth said.

Georgie held out his hand to Nicole. "Hi. I'm Georgie. Perkins. As in the hotels. And you must be Nikki, because Philly doesn't have a pic of you near his cum rag." He turned to Emily. "And, there's the infamous Emily. I hear your name in my dreams. Mostly because Philly won't stop calling it out when he's touching himself."

That did it. I was in his face. "Back off, Perkins. Didn't you get enough pussy rubbing up on Young and Kramer in the shower?"

"Keep running your mouth, McCracken. I'm gonna be running your girl's mouth over my body here in a few minutes."

"You can either leave or you can shut your mouth, Perkins." I heard myself say from like 200 yards away. I tried to run toward my body. Tried to tell myself to stop. I screamed, "He's balling up his fist." But whoever was in control of my body couldn't hear me.

His fist came up fast. It was huge; bigger than a softball. It stopped so close to my face I could feel his knuckles on my cheek. He laughed, flipping his head to get his hair out of his eyes. "Two for flinching, McCracken." He tapped my arm twice, lightly, but his eyes told me he wanted to do a lot more damage. He turned to the others. "Just giving you guys shit."

"We were just leaving anyway," Nicole scowled.

The four of us left. As I closed the door, I looked back. Georgie pointed at me. Then he gave me a thumbs-up.

CHAPTER 16

I went to catch up with the others and Nicole fell back to wait for me. When I reached her, she quietly said, "I need some alone time with Seth. Is there, like, a place?" I stared at her. She rolled her eyes. "Where do you guys normally take girls when they're here?"

"No one ever comes here, but definitely not girls." She looked around and saw this was true. Other campers stopped anything they were doing to ogle two real-life cheerleaders.

"What about his cabin? Or are his roommates as terrible as yours?"

"They might Stanley and Waldorf you, but otherwise, you'll be fine."

"Thank you!" Nicole jogged up to Emily and gave her a rundown of our conversation. I couldn't hear their words, but Emily took some convincing, but Nicole got the job done.

"I owe you." I heard Nicole say.

Emily looked right at me as she said, "Big time."

We stood there awkwardly as Nicole and Seth disappeared into his cabin.

"We should probably go somewhere." I finally said.

"How about we just walk around?"

"That's fine, but we need to be out of sight of Sarge. If he sees we're all separated, he'll probably revoke your visitor passes and make you guys leave."

"Isn't that what you want?" She shaded her eyes. "Aren't you trying to leave?"

"I mean, I don't know."

"I think it's shitty." She said straight out. "I mean, you've made some big strides already. You're way thinner than the last time I saw you. Whatever you're doing, it's working."

"Seth is the one doing great. I'm just here." I deflected. I've never been good at taking compliments.

She started walking toward the Mess Hall. "Exactly. You're here. Take advantage of it."

"Maybe you're right. I'll think it over."

As we walked, my arms swung lightly, but not as much as usual. I was extremely careful not to touch her, although it was killing me not to. She seemed just as uneasy. Her eyes were wide, her gazed unfocused, bouncing all around the camp and the different people still watching us. She wore a false smile, talking too quickly. She shook her head quickly, moving her hair out of her face and her chin rose, opening her neck more.

"So… how did Nicole get you to spend your weekend here of all places?"

"She asked, and I came."

"To Fit Camp… to spend your day surrounded by overweight boys who haven't showered? I find that difficult to believe."

Emily laughed. "I just broke up with my boyfriend and I thought…"

She trailed off, so I helped. "And this was the best place you could think of to find another one? Are you crazy? I know most of these guys and they're terrible choices."

She laughed again. "No. No more boys. Not for a long, long time. I just needed to get away and do something other than sit in my room and mope. She wanted to see Seth, so I figured, why not?" She paused, "Oh, and you."

"What?"

"She wanted to see you, too."

I nodded playfully. "Sure, she did. You know we haven't said a single word since she arrived, right?"

"You're the one who ran away." She joked, but instantly saw the pain flashing on my face like a neon sign in a dive bar window. "Sorry, I was just kidding."

"It's fine. I was just hoping you hadn't noticed me scream like a girl, fall down a hill, land in a mudpuddle and run across the camp."

"If it helps, you were really fast."

"It doesn't." I lied. No one had ever told me I was fast before.

"So, it doesn't bother you?"

"Falling absolutely bothered me."

"Oh, no. Sorry. I meant your sister and your best friend. That doesn't bother you?"

We reached the edge of the camp, where the lake was roped off to keep us on the property, even though no one swam in this area. "I guess when dad died last year, everyone dealt with it differently. I dealt with it by eating anything and everything I could get my hands on. Nicole just got angry. She used to punch walls. Put a dent in her car and broke her power locks one day. Crazy stuff like that."

"I was there for that one." Emily said, staring at the water, running her hand through the dirt.

I nodded. "And she used to get in fights. I'm sure you've noticed. That sort of stuff."

Emily looked me in the eyes for the first time. Her brown eyes sparkled as she defended her friend. "She hasn't gotten into a fight in a long time now."

"Actually, that's exactly my point. It's only since Seth came along. He makes her happy. When they started seeing each other, I was furious. I felt sort of betrayed by each of them. He's been my best friend since a field trip in second grade. So, it sucked. I assumed if they broke up, I wouldn't be able to hang out with him anymore. I couldn't pick between him and my sister. He's like a brother to me. Which makes it more disgusting."

I knelt on one knee, the sun-heated earth was warm to the touch. Placing my hand in the water, it surprised me how warm the water was following the storm the previous night. Looking back at Emily, I added, "Then I noticed she couldn't stop smiling. That's why I helped sneak her into camp. I was worried about what she was like at home. Without him. I didn't want her reverting to her old ways just because we were gone, if that makes sense."

She stared directly at me, no longer distracted by everything around her. I had the full, undivided attention of the most beautiful girl I'd ever met. It gave me the confidence to continue. The same way Dr. Munson's interactions allowed me to get things off my chest, Emily's interest allowed me to tell someone the good of Seth's relationships without coating it in guy talk. "Wow. You are a way better brother than Michael is to me. He probably couldn't tell you what color my eyes are." *Brown.* "Or even whether I wear glasses or contacts or not." *Contacts, always clear.* "He definitely doesn't know important stuff like which part I had in the play last year or things like that."

"Helena."

"How do you remember that?"

"I was in the play with you."

Her eyes narrowed, as she looked left, biting her lip. "You were?" Before I could answer she snapped her fingers, pointed at me, and smiled. "That's right! You were on the crew!"

"I was!" I smiled.

Emily looked back over her shoulder. "Did we get boring?" I followed her gaze. There were no other campers around now. It was just the two of us.

"They probably expected us to start making out and we didn't,
so they left." I tried to backtrack. "I just meant… that that's
probably what they were thinking. Not that it's what I was thinking.
I wasn't thinking that at all." I questioned if it was too soon to try
running away again.

Emily just laughed. "It's okay. I get it. Gordon said you guys
don't get a lot of girls here."

"Who's Gordon?"

"That crazy counselor who tried to take my phone."

"Oh, Sarge!" My eyes doubled in size, which is not an easy
thing for the eyes of a fat kid to do. "He let you call him by his first
name?"

"Yeah. Is that not normal?"

"My mom doesn't even get to call him that when she calls."

We sat silently. I picked through the pinecones and acorns
scattered on the ground to find a skipping stone. My fingers found a
larger triangular stone. I'd look at her and then look away. I've been
conditioned not to keep looking at a good-looking woman for very
long. It makes them uncomfortable. But she never averted her eyes
from me. "Can I ask – Sorry if I shouldn't. How about your mom?
How does she deal with your dad being gone?"

I scoffed, as I pulled back and released. The rock left my hand,
skipping three times across the lake's surface before I lost track of it.
"She doesn't. She deals with it by not dealing with it. She just sort of
ignores that Dad was ever there."

"Oh my god. I'm sorry. That would make me crazy. I'm
definitely a daddy's girl."

"I've learned that if I shove food in my mouth, I can't say
anything I'll regret. Can't talk if your mouth is full." I forced a
smile, but I know she didn't buy it.

Emily stood, stretching. We had no idea that The Killer was a mere fifteen feet from us, staring directly at her cut-offs. She held out her hand to me. I got up on my own. Her hand was still outstretched. Eventually, I understood I was supposed to hold it.

She didn't let go the entire walk back.

CHAPTER 17

I treasured every second Emily held my hand, as I had no way of knowing when it would end. As Brandon Katz stomped toward us, I had a feeling that time was coming. "Are you really his girlfriend? Because that's what he keeps telling everyone."

My eyes sank closed. I exhaled through my teeth as I bit into my lip, trying to come up with any explanation, but knowing how futile that was. I gave up and went with honesty. I turned to say something, as Emily shot back. "Dude. Not so loud. Do you want him to get in trouble for me being here?"

Katz's eyes grew. "You're serious? You two?"

"Why else would I be here? Do you guys get a lot of visits from girls who aren't related to or dating people here?"

Katz scratched the back of his head. "I mean, we just sort of figured he cut you out of a magazine or downloaded you off some website." He smiled, standing up straight in a failed attempt at appearing taller. "You're way too hot to waste it with him."

His hand slapped me on the shoulder twice as he passed me. "Good work, McCracken. Sorry I doubted you, but…. You know."

Shaking my head, I watched him walk about fifteen feet away before flipping around, "Hey, Cheerleader! If you get sick of him, I'm in Cabin number 12."

"I have a name you know." Emily responded.

"So, do I. You'll be screaming it tonight." He wandered off, laughing to himself.

The right side of Emily's face scrunched up. "What a douche. Why do guys never have good pickup lines?"

"I have no idea."

"Do you have any?" She asked as we started a third lap around the camp.

"Not me. No. I don't."

She stared at me in disbelief. "None?"

"None that I've ever tried."

Emily turned, pulling me into her with the hand she was still holding. She let go, looking deep into my eyes. "Try. What would you say to pick me up?"

I shrugged. "I have no idea."

"Try."

"I guess that I've been in love with you since the moment I saw you and I would give anything to just—"

"Too strong. Try again."

I paused, fumbling for words. I found her eyes again. "That you have the most mesmerizing eyes?"

"Great word choice, but no confidence and too overdone."

"I love the way you—"

"Nope. You used love again. You're just meeting the girl. You can't start with love."

I shrugged. "This isn't exactly something I'm good at. What would you do? Like what would you say?"

She raised an eyebrow. "If I was trying to pick you up?"

The smirk slid across my face before I could catch it. "You can't pick me up. I weigh like five times as much as you."

Her lip curled around her open mouth., her tongue pushing slightly forward as her nose wrinkled. She looked away from me for the first time. "You need to stop talking badly about yourself or no girl is going to want you."

"Sorry."

She regrouped, taking two steps forward, until she was mere millimeters from me. "Now then, I would lean in, super close, like this. I'd put my mouth next to your ear, like so." The speed of her speech slowed dramatically. "And I would almost whisper, but not quite. And I'd say, 'Hey, Phillip? Do you have any Pledge? I'd reeeeeeally like to polish your wood." The breath exiting her mouth warmed my ear.

I eventually shook it off, but let's just say for once I was very glad my stomach hangs out so far, so Emily wouldn't know how not as far out other parts of my body were sticking. We walked slowly, as she took my hand again. "So yeah. See? Boys need to learn how to do that instead of making us do all the work."

She stopped, looking at my face again. "Are you okay, Phillip?"

Trying to deflect from what I really wanted to say I thought back to Katz running his mouth. "Yeah, I'm just trying to figure out why you covered with me when Brandon said that."

She raised her shoulders slightly. "What do you mean?"

"You just lied to him. For me. Why?"

"Because you don't need to take his shit, Phillip. Besides, it's not like anyone I know will ever talk to him. Let him think whatever he wants to think."

Her fingers tightened on mine, reminding me the girl I'd been in love with forever was here, in real life, holding my hand. "You're like a superhero."

Emily scoffed. "What? What does that mean?"

"You got the bully to leave me alone."

She let go of my hand without thinking about it. "He bullies you?"

"Him and like twenty other people. And that's just here at camp. But yeah… the number grows exponentially outside of here."

"Wow. I didn't know…. Or I mean, I just figured since he's here… that…. I don't know."

"Because they're fat too? Yeah, it surprises a lot of people. That's the Hierarchy for you."

She stared at me like I was speaking Klingon through a Vader voice changer. "The what?"

"The Hierarchy of Bullies. It's a theory I learned about in therapy. It's really helped me deal with things."

The sleek hardwood of the hall gave way to the carpeted floor as I entered Dr. Munson's office. She wasn't there yet, but Counselor Jeff had shown me in any way. The soft lighting illuminated the small plants on her desk, making them look even more green. Taking a tissue from the box near her chair, I wiped my eyes, before dropping it into the small wastebasket. I don't even remember who had said what exactly, but I was sick of it. I wanted to be done with bullying. I took a seat in the plush leather chair, unconsciously enjoying the smell of it, and glanced at the many pads of paper, pens, and other knickknacks on her desk. Her coffee mug read, "You've cat to be kitten me right meow." It made me smile, so that's something.

Muffled voices in the hall told me she was almost there. There weren't many females at Camp Wašíču, so it was relatively easy to make out her voice, even when you couldn't hear her words. She entered, and my day instantly brightened. She held a single finger up as she finished her phone call, her cell phone tucked between her ear and her left shoulder. "Perfect. I'll see you next Wednesday. Have a great evening, Dr. Landis."

As she set the phone down, her concerned smile told me she was aware why I was there without a scheduled appointment. I laid it out for her anyway, as her pen scratched across a pad of paper.

Tears trickled down the back of my throat as I picked at my cuticles and replayed the events of the day. She listened attentively to everything before pretty much repeating it back to me. I didn't let her hold eye contact, but she never stopped trying.

"Phillip, let me tell you a little bit about my thesis, because this is a topic of such importance to me. I'm going to try my best not to drown it in fancy words and hyperbole, but the basics of it are that bullying happens in every aspect of society. It never goes away based on age or socioeconomic status or anything else. Humans work hard to sort themselves and they create a ladder of sorts. The super popular ones are up here, the extremely unpopular ones—"

"Like me"

"-are down here. There are many tiers in between. Well, let's just look at it as a high school system. You usually have the popular kids like jocks and cheerleaders, then there's the less popular athletes, the kids who could have been athletes but aren't, maybe the art kids or the stoners or whatever and then down here, you have the intellectuals."

"The Nerds. The Geeks. The Virgins."

Dr. Munson laughed, even though she didn't want to. "I wouldn't use most of those words, but I suppose so, yes. But that's not the part I want you to concentrate on, Phillip. I want you to hear me out on this next part."

Staring into her gorgeous green eyes with their flecks of blue, I would have agreed to anything; so, I listened to the rest.

Emily bought into the theory faster than I did, which surprisingly helped me understand how true it is. Seth and Nicole walked up behind us, but Emily waved them away, so she could hear the end of what I was saying. "But," I continued, "even within each clique, there's an established order as to who gets made fun of.

In the group that is picked on the most, there's usually one that the group picks on. Like I was saying earlier when you didn't know why Katz was picking on me."

Emily looked at the ground, wounded.

"It's nothing to be ashamed of. I don't understand your level any more than you understand mine. So, like I said, in each group, there's usually one or two who get picked on. It's true on the bottom, and it's true on the top. The Hierarchy of Bullies is everywhere, really."

"What about the super popular kids?"

"Same thing. One gets singled out to be made fun of, like—"

Emily coyly smiled. "Like how Melissa makes fun of me?"

I held out my hands sarcastically, "Well, she *is* the top of the pyramid."

Emily laughed. "So, who do you pick on?"

"Privately, we pick on the super popular kids. Just not to their faces, because we like breathing. But in our group? I pick on Seth."

"But he's your best friend."

"Well yeah, it's easiest to pick on your best friend. Way more ammo."

We both laughed at that as we made yet another lap around the camp. At least I was burning calories for once. "Really though, I don't know where I'd be without him. When Dad died, Seth was the one who kept me sane. Don't get me wrong, he also drove me to the Pizza Hut buffet every day and helped me wind up here, but if it wasn't for him, there's no telling how I would've turned out."

Emily spun, standing directly in front of me. She held both of my hands, although I had no idea when that had happened. She leaned in, her mouth near my ear. "I think you turned out pretty great." She closed her eyes and leaned in more, toward my mouth.

Looking around, I saw several campers watching us, including Seth and Nicole. Seth motioned for me to kiss her. I went for it. I didn't close my eyes, out of fear I would miss, but I leaned, pushing my lips into hers. To my surprise, Emily Clausen kissed me back.

CHAPTER 18

The chattering of squirrels in the distance was the only thing reminding me this moment was real. The second I'd dreamed of for years had come true. Emily Clausen's lips were pushed against mine and it wasn't because I had to give her CPR. She opened her eyes and pushed her forehead against mine. "There," she whispered. "That should get them talking."

Emily let go of my hand and skipped over to Nicole. Seth stood nearby with a huge grin on his face. I watched her for a second before she called over her shoulder, "Are you coming or what?" Following the three of them, I smiled.

It's weird how things in our lives can line up to set up events for our futures and we can't see them at the time. As I said before, Seth was at my father's funeral and he was there for me when I was the most vulnerable I'd ever been. But it wasn't just me. At the time, my sister Nicole barely acknowledged Seth's existence, but that changed at the funeral. I was with some cousins I hadn't seen in a couple years, and for the first time in a month, I was laughing. It probably had something to do with the fact that my oldest cousin JT brought a small flask with him and I was midway through my first buzz. Seth was clearly uncomfortable but hung in like a friend should.

Until Nicole offered him an out, by accident.

My sister isn't the kind of person to show when she's hurting if she can help it, so she tends to disappear, have a meltdown, and then return, hoping no one is any wiser. She wanted me to go on mental time out with her, but I knew I was too buzzed to walk straight and told her I was going to sit with my cousins a while longer, but I'd run interference if anyone asked where she was. She wasn't impressed that my plan was to explain she's extremely lactose intolerant and to claim she was in the bathroom painting the porcelain walls brown. Before she could comment, Seth volunteered himself.

"If you want someone to go with you, I'll go, Nicole. I could use some fresh air."

As much as she didn't want to take my overweight pimple-faced best friend with her, Nicole saw that her options were limited, and she didn't want to be alone, so she said yes.

They were gone for a very long time, but I didn't notice at the time. Between the Kentucky Bourbon ripping through my chest, my own despair at having just lost my father, and my mom's endless tales of how dad screwed up her life, I was too far gone to care where Nicole was.

At some point, my stomach kicked in. At first, I thought I was going to have the dookie from hell, but then it reversed course and I knew I was going to puke. I stood quickly, which only made it worse, but somehow managed to make it outside the reception hall before it happened. Doubled over, hacking up the excessive amount of food and the little bit of whiskey I'd had, I finally lost it. If you've ever continued to puke while bawling your eyes out, you'll know that it's not the best feeling in the world. I wiped my mouth across the wrist of my dress shirt and everything suddenly felt better.

That's when I saw them, coming back. I had no idea how long they'd been gone or where they had been, but Seth and Nicole walked hand in hand, talking like old friends. They didn't see me from where I was, even though I'd tried to wave them down. They were lost in one another. And when she pulled him close and kissed him, I understood everything had just changed.

I wasn't a fan of it at the time. It took a while for the idea to grow on me. But walking into the Rec Center, I was all for it. Without those two becoming an item, I would've missed out on the kiss I'd waited years for.

Emily held the scratched metal door open for me and I jogged the last five steps. I stopped for a quick drink of water from the fountains and glanced up at the corkboard filled with announcements. No one ever took them down. They just stapled new ones on top of the outdated ones. There were advertisements for dances that had long since ended, reminders for scholarships, healthy recipes, and even a piece of paper that only said, "OBEY" in all capital letters. The top group of papers rustled in the breeze each time someone opened the door.

Seth pointed out the public restrooms for the girls. "Cleanest bathrooms you'll find on this campus. And with the nurse and the cook gone already, they're all yours." He wasn't joking. Diane, the cook, was about the only person who ever used the women's bathroom. If a male camper was caught attempting to use it, they were forced to clean the whole room with just a toothbrush and then were stuck on dish duty for a month. None of us had seen this happen, but we'd been told those were the consequences and that was enough for us. Have you ever cleaned dishes for fifty overweight teenage boys? I'd rather fill my pants with the brown goo than deal with that.

I pointed down one of the halls to take the girls on a tour of the gym and the multipurpose room but found myself pointing directly at Sarge. He stood in the middle of the hall, arms crossed. "McCracken, last time I saw you, you were six feet under the wet dirt. Glad you found a way to rise from the dead and keep going. Jenkins, what the hell are you doing here? These aren't your guests. Get out there and help with the rest of clean up. Jeff's got a crew down at the lake. Greg's got some guys fixing up the cabins. Pick one."

Seth bowed out, quickly mouthing "Sorry" to Nicole, but she just waved him off, as she didn't want to get him in trouble.

As the metal door slammed shut behind Seth, Sarge began the tour no one asked him for; but it kept me from having to do it. "Cafeteria is over that way." He said, pointing at the bench seating at the long tables. The smell of gravy drifted toward me, reminding me I'd missed breakfast. *Should've grabbed them candy bars,* Timothy said in my mind.

Sarge smiled, "I'll be honest, it's delicious food. Small portions, but that's the idea, right? Kitchen is behind there. We're standing in the multipurpose room." Emily looked around at the tables and chairs and well-worn couches. The couches were still relatively new, but when you have teens weighing several hundred pounds flopping onto them every day, they wear out quick. "Down this hall, we have some old offices from before they built the Counselors' Quarters. Now we use them for some group and individual therapy if needed or just for therapeutic family visits." He ran his hand across the cold cinder block wall, before turning and continuing down the hall.

Sarge's keys jingled as he walked. His walkie-talkie bounced with each step. *Crrcht!* "Greg to Sarge, come in."

"Sarge here." He said, holding the walkie sideways.

"Just making sure everything is okay. Haven't seen you in a while."

"Giving a tour to McCracken's family right now."

"Sounds good. We're gonna finish up this last cabin and then probably try to clean off the parking lot some more."

"Good call. Sarge out." He hooked his walkie-talkie to his belt. "Further down here, we have an indoor basketball court. We prefer the guys play outside. The fresh air does wonders for you." As he opened the door to the gym, I heard sneakers squeaking and a ball bouncing. "These two were the first ones awake today. Worked their asses off. Now they get to unwind and have some fun."

Sarge led the way back to the front door of the building. "I'm gonna take you up to the Counselors' Quarters next. That's where you'll be spending the night tonight." He paused. "You're staying the night, right? That's what your mother said."

Emily stuttered through her response. "Well, I mean. We'll see how late it's getting and then make a decision but…"

Nicole interjected. "Yeah, we're staying." She turned to me, "Is one more day okay with you?"

I would have agreed to anything right then. I was enjoying watching her lips and reliving the moment I kissed them. But I knew full well that the best way for me to win over Emily was to stay at camp one more night, so I agreed.

We followed Stanheight out to the parking lot. "You ladies grab whatever you think you'll need from the car and I'll take you up there. The duffel bags the girls grabbed from the car read Vonnegut High Canaries, with pompoms next to each girl's name printed on the bag below our school logo. Staring down at the cracked blacktop, analyzing the faded paint marks, I almost missed Sarge's cue that we were taking the bags for the girls. Emily tried to carry her own, but reluctantly gave in when she saw Sarge's face.

As we started away from the car, a group of other campers came toward the parking lot, to sweep the debris and trash off the ground from the storm. Obi was in the group. He gave me a head nod as he walked by and started working on the bushes framing the parking lot. The horn beeped twice quickly, and I jumped. Nicole laughed. "Sorry about that, Phil."

Emily started back toward the car. "Wait a minute, Nikki. Can you open it again? I need my makeup bag." As she bent over on the passenger side of the car, I tried not to stare, but that was like asking my dog not to chase a tennis ball.

"Makeup bag?" Stanheight muttered. "I'm glad I got a twig and berries. How about you, McCracken?"

My eyes outlined the small curve in Emily's back, visible between her tank and her cut-offs. "More than ever."

With both of us distracted, Emily unplugged her cell phone and slid it into her makeup bag. She pulled several tampons out of the glove box and threw them on top to ensure we wouldn't sneak a peek inside. Closing the door, Emily smiled brightly. "Lead the way!"

CHAPTER 19

Another one of the things people don't understand about being almost 400 pounds is that sometimes we run out of breath by thinking about the fact that we could run out of breath. It's like any other time you think about your breathing. It immediately changes. You can't keep your normal breathing pattern when you focus on it. Something about doing so automatically changes everything. You can breathe, of course, but it's not the same. When you're my weight, you know at some point – a point coming much faster than it would if you cut half your weight – you will be a mouth breathing air gasper. And the fear of thinking about it makes it happen even sooner.

Crossing the campus usually winded me as it was. It's almost a quarter mile stretch from the parking lot to the Counselors' Quarters; and it's not like it's level. It's a very hilly area, as you may remember from my mud bath. So, the slight elevation changes wear on my lungs quickly. That's without carrying anyone's bags, but I was hauling Emily's cheerleading duffel bag, which she'd apparently filled with rocks and padlocks, judging by its increasing weight. I stared out at our destination, still half the camp away.

The Counselors' Quarters were gaudy compared to the rest of the camp. It sat on the top of the highest hill in the area. A three-flight staircase ran from the camp to the front door of the building, with two landings along the way featuring decorative benches as though people would just sit there, just sipping coffee or something. When Kane H. Perkins donated the money to have it built, his family expected to use the building the rest of the year as an upscale

Bed and Breakfast. Everyone laughed. No one thought it would work. But apparently, everyone was wrong. The Perkins family made enough money every year off the Bed and Breakfast they had paid off the building in less than three years.

I only knew this because my roommate, Georgie Perkins never shut up about his family history. I was only thinking about it in the moment to keep from crying. My eyes were scratchy, and my vision blurred slightly. I'm sure they were bloodshot from holding in the screams, but I had no way to know for sure. Neither Sarge nor the girls seemed the slightest bit bothered by the walk.

As we reached the bottom of the hill the Counselors' Quarters sat on, Sarge paused for a second to switch hands he carried my sister's duffel bag with. I kept going, knowing if I stopped for even a second my momentum might bottom out and I was pretty sure I'd never move again after that. I glanced over at the wooden stairs and kept going toward the far side of the building.

Sarge stared at me, "McCracken. Where are you going?"

"Elevator? I just figured—" I knew instantly what I had just done. I saw it in his face.

"How do you know there's an elevator over there?"

"I had to bring food up a few times with the kitchen crew." I lied. But my roommate Georgie had done so and didn't shut up about that either. And it's not like I could tell him the truth. Dr. Munson always let me ride in the elevator after a tough session instead of having to take the stairs. I wasn't about to get her in trouble though.

"Well, good thinking, McCracken." I smiled, until he added. "Unfortunately, the power outage last night did something to the elevator and we can't use it right now. Greg already scheduled a technician, but they can't be out here until Monday. So, for now..."

Sarge trailed off, turning toward the stairs. The girls followed right away.

You remember when I told you that if I think about breathing it changes how I breathe? Did you know that your brain tells your body not to breathe when you're climbing stairs? Yup. It's true. That's why even marathon runners will often be short of breath when they reach the top of a couple flights of stairs. Dr. Munson told me it's called the "Concentration Program," and basically humans are hard-wired to stop breathing as we focus on a specific task.

"Imagine," she said, "if someone tried to make a surgical incision or throw a dart or even thread a needle. By reducing or even stopping our breathing, we decrease the background movements of our bodies, and achieve better accuracy in the performance of our planned actions."

So, there I was, staring at the three flights of wooden planks leading to the almighty Counselors' Quarters paying attention to my breathing, knowing it was about to get worse, carrying a duffel bag in addition to my own 400 pounds. You can probably guess how this turns out.

Whether they were being nice or also needed to stop for air didn't matter to me. What mattered was that the girls stopped on each landing to look out at the camp. I glanced at the bench on the second landing and considered stopping to "tie my shoe" to gain a few more seconds of downtime, but I realized that bending forward wouldn't help me catch my breath and I'd lost enough momentum already. One flight of stairs was all that stood in my way. Thirteen little steps. It was totally doable in those terms. Three flights of stairs sound like a lot in my head. Thirty-nine steps doesn't sound as bad.

As my feet touched the top level, I found my confidence. I did it. I was out of breath and I was wheezing a little, but I did it and it wasn't as bad as I'd expected. Sarge held the door open for the three of us and we walked into the lobby area of the Counselors' Quarters. I dropped Emily's bag next to Nicole's and sat down on the nearest couch. Emily sat next to me; not touching, but not a full cushion away either. I'd succeeded twice in the last five minutes.

"Well," Sarge said, "This is the Counselors' Quarters. Your room is down this way. Do you want me to show you?" Nicole agreed, but Emily stayed with me. The other two returned not even thirty seconds later. Sarge smiled. "McCracken, I'm going to head back down to help finish the cleanup efforts. Don't get too crazy up here. The overnight counselors are probably still sleeping. You wake them up and you'll be running laps until the next time you get visitors."

"Sir. Yes, Sir." I smiled.

"One of these days, I'm gonna pull your head out of your ass for you, McCracken. But I don't have the time or the energy today, so you're on your own." He was gone without another word.

CHAPTER 20

The room was illuminated by the large floor to ceiling windows, each framed by heavy blackout curtains. The overstuffed leather couches begged to be used, throw pillows carefully placed by each armrest, each one a deep red that almost perfectly matched the lamps carefully positioned on the end tables. The area rug held tints of the same dark red. Nicole walked to the fireplace to inspect the memorabilia on the mantle; two small trophies (belonging to Frrrrraaaank Doyle, if there was any doubt), two picture frames (probably pictures of that asshole Doyle, but I had no way of knowing), and a small floral arrangement. Her eyes moved from the mantle to the shovel and poker near the pile of logs in the hearth and onward to the small rug under her; marked with scorch marks from sparks popping out of the fire. She detected leftover hints of wood smoke and ash.

Emily and I sat quietly watching her, only inches from one another. Emily's hand lightly touched my leg. I pulled away, thinking I'd accidentally touched her. "You okay?" She asked.

"Yeah. Why?"

Before she could answer, Nicole said, "Would you guys mind if I go grab a shower really fast?"

I glared at her. "Why didn't you take one before you got here?"

"I did!"

Emily smirked, not making eye contact with either of us. "And then she got all dirty again."

"Oh gross." I grimaced. "Go. Take your shower. Whatever gets us to stop talking about this."

Both girls laughed as Nicole left the room. She called from the hallway, "I'll be right back."

Emily turned toward me on the couch, her legs tucked under her. Her hand landed on my thigh. "I'm sorry. I really couldn't resist the dirty comment."

"It was actually pretty funny," I conceded.

Emily sat staring at me, her upper teeth sliding across her lower lip several times. But she didn't consider that I was new to this whole dating thing and had no idea she was trying to make out with me. So, we sat in an awkward silence until she said, "Well… Gordon seems pleasant."

"Sarge? Oh, he's not bad. He tries to appear way worse than he is. He just picks on us because it's his job. Deep down, I'm pretty sure he kind of likes us."

Her eyes narrowed in a playful manner. "The Hierarchy again?"

I shook my head. "Nah, not like that. This one is more like he's just trying to push us to our potential. He and Greg are both kind of like that. Jeff is the only counselor who's all laid back and happy and always trying to make us look at the bright side of life."

Emily's lips pouted and separated. "You better watch out. It's the nice ones you gotta look out for."

"Is that what you think? That the nice ones will end up hurting you more?"

Her fingers twirled through her hair. "I don't know. I don't have a lot of experience with the nice ones. Would you like to teach me about the nice ones?"

"What makes you think I'm not dangerous?"

She smiled. "I think it's a chance I'm willing to take."

Nicole flushed the toilet in one of the guest bathrooms and looked at herself in the mirror. She checked her teeth to ensure she didn't have anything stuck in them, even though she hadn't had anything to eat since grabbing McDonald's right before they arrived at Camp Wašíču. Even though it was no one's personal bathroom, she couldn't help but open the medicine cabinet. She was surprised to find it empty. She jumped as the deodorizer sprayed from above the cabinet. A fine mist fell through the air next to her, the hints of lilac taking over the area around the sink.

She reached into the shower and turned on the water. It was the perfect temperature almost instantly, with no pipes shaking or gurgling in the walls. "Wow. I need this at home." She moved onto the small rug and took off her clothes. She unfastened her bra and inspected the hickey Seth gave her less than two hours beforehand. Sliding the shower door open, Nicole stepped inside. The shampoo scented steam quickly overtook the frosted glass doors.

She didn't see the door handle jostle and slowly turn. She didn't hear the door creak open. Washing the shampoo out of her hair, Nicole felt the light breeze from the open door. She tried to focus on the sounds being mostly drowned out by the consistent drum of the shower, as she pushed her hands under the water to remove the creamy lather on them. Turning slowly to her left, she saw the outline of a person in the shower. She inhaled deeply, steam invading her lungs as she weighed her options. She called out, "Emily?"

"Yeah?"

"You scared me."

"Did you think that counselor was coming to watch you?"

Nicole shook her head. "I don't know what I thought. What are you doing in here?"

"I just needed to use the bathroom."

"Okay, but don't flush." Emily checked herself out in the mirror, rearranging individual strands of hair, as Nicole said, "My brother isn't giving you too many problems, is he? I know he can be a little much to handle sometimes."

Emily smiled to herself. "No. He's okay. I mean, he worships the ground I walk on. Who wouldn't like that? And he's pretty funny. And brave! Did you see how he stood up for me with that Georgie kid?

"Are we talking about the same guy?"

Emily laughed. "Yeah. I don't know. He makes me smile. He's been a great distraction. I've barely thought about Chris dumping me at all."

"I was going to ask how you're doing, but I didn't want to bring it up. I figured if you're making out with my brother you can't be doing that well."

Emily shot a dirty look through the glass door, but Nicole couldn't see it. "Something about the way they were all judging him. And being jerks to him. It just reminded me of how Chris and his friends treated me." She paused. "Plus, it was kind of nice. I might do it again."

Nicole grimaced, almost cutting herself with the razor as she shaved her legs. "Eeeeew. He probably drooled on you like you were a slice of pizza."

Emily sat down on the toilet, situating herself in a way that Nicole wouldn't be able to see anything if she looked out. "So enough about me, give me the details. Did Seth get you off?"

"We didn't do it."

"Why? Is it your time of the month? I brought extra tampons. They're in my makeup case."

Nicole laughed. "No. It's not that. It's Seth... he hasn't... you know... before."

"Ever?"

"Ever. But, with any luck, maybe tonight!"

"Here?" Emily's toes curled as her nose wrinkled. "At camp?"

The razor slid across Nicole's left calf as she said, "Not just camp. Like up here. You know this is an expensive bed and breakfast the rest of the year, right? People pay a lot of money to have sex here. Why not do it for free while I can?"

Emily laughed, reaching for the toilet paper. "Makes sense to me. Go get it, girl."

The Killer stood in the shadows watching as I paced in front of the fireplace. He saw me pick up one of Frank Doyle's trophies and read it. He watched as I straightened the throw pillow where I'd been sitting. And he withdrew into the shadows without any indication he had been there. My mind was solely on the girls, who hadn't returned. Part of me figured they were in there talking about me. Either that or Emily was "Taking the Browns to the Superbowl," as Obi would say. I returned to the fireplace, picking up the fire poker and placing it in its proper position. As I did so, I heard a scream.

"Emily!" I gasped.

Sprinting down the large hallway, past the random paintings and the potted plants, I threw open the door to the first bedroom and ran to the next door. Fumbling with the door handle, I realized it was locked. As my fist pounded on the door, I heard giggling.

Giggling?

I called through the door, "Are you okay?"

"Phillip?" Emily replied through her laughter. "We're fine. I just flushed when I wasn't supposed to."

I stared at the ceiling. "Don't do that to me." Emily opened the door. I saw Nicole's body outlined through the frosted glass window. I swiftly turned away. "Oh man."

"Sorry. Didn't take that into consideration."

"Emily!" Nicole called. "Close the freakin' door. It's freezing out there."

Emily pulled it closed behind her.

"I was so scared—"

Emily killed that thought by grabbing my face with both hands and kissing me. When she pulled away smiling, I said, "Wow. What was that for? No one's watching or anything."

Her smile was gone. "Does someone have to be watching?"

"Well, I just thought… I thought that's why you kissed me outside…"

"Phillip, I kissed you because I wanted to kiss you." She smiled. "I might even want to kiss you again later, too, so you should probably try to get used to it."

For once, I didn't feel like a 400-pound person standing next to a cheerleader. I was just me and I was with her. "I think I can get used to that."

"Good. You should probably head back and get ready for our date tonight."

"Date?" I didn't wait for Emily to kiss me again. I wrapped my arms around her and pulled her into me. I kissed Emily Clausen.

And she loved it.

Light as a feather on my feet, I made it down all three flights of stairs and back to the cabin without so much as a single wheeze.

CHAPTER 21

Randy Waterhouse was the man who was always for sale. Anything you needed done, anything you needed smuggled into camp, anything you had the money for, Randy had a price. And he lived in the cabin right next to mine. I cashed in some birthday money to have him iron Seth's shirt, my shirt and my jeans. I didn't know if people normally ironed jeans, but I figured it was better to have no wrinkles than to worry about how much sense any of this made. Let's face it… Emily Clausen was kissing me, so NONE of this made sense.

While Randy took care of our clothes, Seth begged me for sex advice; which, let's be honest, was a lot like having a priest walk you through your feelings following a divorce. I didn't know what the hell I was talking about. Worse, I didn't want to talk about it at all. He was talking about my *sister*. I continually deflected. I paced. I dodged. I literally walked out of the room twice.

Finally, Seth stood with both hands on my shoulders, trying to force me to look him directly in the eyes. "I need this."

Glancing around his cabin, I refused to hold his gaze. "Why can't you talk to Obi about it?"

"Because he's not my best friend. You are. I'm just asking you to be my bro for a minute instead of her actual brother. I need this. I can't do this without you."

"You can't hook up with my sister without me? Do you see how this sounds?"

"Would you just hear me out?" He didn't blink. Hadn't the whole time. It was creeping me out.

"I'll listen, but I won't guarantee that I'll help you or even let you finish if you get gross." I pushed his hands away lightly. "And you need to stop touching me."

Seth paced. "So, I just... can't. Like she wants to. Really bad."

"And I'm out." I turned away.

"Come on." He was weak. Vulnerable. *Real.* That was the part that bothered me. For the first time in a long time, Seth needed me.

"I'm sorry. I was joking. Go ahead."

"I can't take off my clothes. I just... feel... gross. Like she won't want me anymore."

I plopped down on my bed. After ensuring it was still standing, I said, "Seth, Nicole really likes you. She might even love you. I don't know. We don't talk about that kind of stuff. But what I do know is that when she talks about you to other people and I eavesdrop, it's always about *you*; you know, the person inside of there. Not the shell. Not the body. Not your weight. Not your hair. Not your clothes. *You.* She's going to like whatever you're hiding under that shirt. Which, at the rate you've been dropping poundage is probably just skin anyway."

"But what if—"

"What does Dr. Munson say about What-ifs?" I shot back out of nowhere. The authority in my voice was met with instant recognition in Seth's eyes. No wonder Sarge spoke in this manner all the time. "And what does she say about speaking about yourself that way?"

She'd stood before us all in the rec center gym one day, for group therapy. Her tight jeans were the same miraculously bright white as the shirt she wore; her hair wrapped in a loose ponytail she'd tied together with more hair. "There's an old saying that if you repeat a lie enough, people will believe it. In Domestic Violence situations, when a victim is told repeatedly that she's ugly, that she doesn't matter, that she's nothing without him, that she doesn't deserve to live… when she hears that enough, she believes it. When a high school kid is told he's fat, he's ugly, he's worthless, he's never going to amount to anything. He learns to believe it."

She paused, letting that hang in the air. "I can look around this room and I know how many of you have been bullied. I know how many of you have probably bullied others. And that sucks. Bullies suck." She reached back, adjusting her ponytail and pulling it over her left shoulder, before crossing her arms. "You know what's worse? Self-bullying. And we all do it. We do it every single day."

She paced in front of us as she spoke. I peeled my skin away from the metal bleacher, wishing I could grab a couple of the gym mats to make my seat more comfortable.

"You all do it. I do it. We look in the mirror and we're so negative. We say things like, 'Holy crap I'm overweight.' Or we concentrate on pimples, freckles, the way our clothes fit. And we're horrible and we say the worst things we can think of. And you might think that doesn't matter. You might think you're 'being honest' (she made air quotes). You may think it's true, so it doesn't matter. But that energy that you're putting out affects where the rest of your life goes. When you tell yourself every day that you're not worthy or you're not capable or you're not loved and when you hear those words over and over, you're setting yourself up for failure."

She stopped dead center, in the middle of the gym, facing all of us. "I'm giving each of you the same homework. I'll know whether you did it or not. It won't be because you tell me or because your bunkmate rats you out. I'll know by how your life is going. I'll know by the smile on your face as you walk through camp; or the lack there of. Your homework, should you choose to accept it, is to spend time looking at yourself in a mirror and talking about the things you like about yourself. I don't care how small it is."

That drew giggles. She shook her head and moved on, trying to ignore it.

"Pick anything. Tell yourself about the weight you've lost and how hard you've worked. Or maybe you like your eyes. Tell yourself you have nice eyes. Maybe you are good at whatever video game you guys play these days. Anything. Pick anything."

Roger Tonkyn's hand went up. His eyes tripled in size when he realized the amount of attention he'd just pulled onto himself. "Yes, Roger?" She said, adjusting her ponytail again.

It took him two tries, but Roger asked, "What if there's nothing? Nothing we like about ourselves at all?"

She walked over to him, her gray velvet ankle boots clicking on the hardwood floor with each step. She took a knee next to Roger and looked directly in his eyes. "First, I would hope one day you can see all the good things in yourself that I see in you. And, second, if you can't? If you absolutely can't? Lie to yourself. Tell yourself how great you are. And if you say those lies enough times, you'll believe them."

I stared at Seth. "Look, man, it doesn't make me happy that you wanna hook up with my sister. I always imagined you and me in college, sitting in bars, picking up random hotties. Dating my sister makes that weird. Like we can't be gross guys when we talk about it because the person you're talking about is important to me."

Before I could say anything else, there was a knock at the door. Randy brought in our shirts and my pants. I paid him the other half of the money (half up front). Randy wished us luck and left.

Standing in front of the mirror on my wall, I combed my hair a total of eight different ways, which should have been impossible, given how short my hair was. I finally added a little gel and decided for a messy look.

We looked each other over, pulling little pieces of lint off one another. There was another knock at the door. Our dates had arrived.

CHAPTER 22

I opened the door, expecting to see the girls all dressed up, ready for a fun night. Instead, they were each in cut-offs and T-Shirts. "Oh, man." Emily put her hands to her mouth. "I didn't know we were supposed to dress up."

Nicole pushed me out of the way, wrapping her arms around Seth's neck. "You look amazing!"

Emily closed the door and kissed me as well. "I'm so sorry."

"Does this mean I can change?" I joked.

"Yes."

"NO!" Nicole yelled. Then she looked at me. "Well, yeah, you can. But not Seth. You look sexy as hell, babe."

Seth's lips turned up in a small smirk. "I was just telling myself the same thing.

As we entered the Mess Hall, the girls were, of course, the center of attention. It didn't matter what they were wearing. The other campers would have given them just as much, if not more attention, even if they wore nothing at all. We each grabbed our trays and stood in line. Emily went first, then me, then Nicole, then Seth. We thought that way no one would realize Nicole wasn't spending much time with me, but as I look back, like most things teenagers attempt to get away with, we were probably paying way too much attention to the details no one else even thought about.

I stared at my chicken, broccoli, cottage cheese, and tea. Again. It was like déjà vu. How many more times could I eat this meal? *As many times as you need to in order to get in shape to keep this girl?* It was as good an answer as any.

Emily looked at her food. "This is awesome. Do you always eat this well?"

"Here." I shrugged. "Not so much on the outside."

Nicole loved hers as well. Apparently, when you didn't view eating healthy as a punishment, it was a lot more appealing. Dr. Munson told us once that food is just fuel and if you can learn to view it that way, you'd want the best fuel. You don't want gunk clogging up your engines. She said when you stop eating food for the flavor and you eat it as the fuel you need to get through the day, it becomes incredibly easy to eat the same thing every day. Maybe that was true, but I had a long way to go to get there.

We sat in our normal booth, next to the window. Obi had only been three people behind Seth in line. He brought his tray over. "I see how it is. I've been replaced by people who are way hotter than me." He laughed, pulling up a chair.

Seth pointed to Obi. "This is Pavlo. He's really ugly, isn't he? Don't be afraid to say so. He can't understand you anyway. He speaks only Romanian." Obi flipped Seth the bird but quickly jumped into conversations and interacted with the girls like they were all old friends. It made me jealous of him in a brand-new way. Was I the only person at Camp Wašíču suffering from being incapable of doing anything easily? Before long, all five of us were lost in conversation and laughing excitedly at Obi's crazy stories.

Twenty minutes later, we were each finished eating, but still talking when we heard the main doors slam shut. I looked up just in time to watch Sarge kick some mud off his black combat boots. He exchanged pleasantries with a few other campers as he made his way to our table, but I never had any doubt where he was heading as soon as he walked in. "Did you ladies decide if you're spending the night or not? I only ask because the cutoff time to leave the camp is 8 PM and some of the events we have planned tonight will run much later than that."

Nicole made eye contact with Seth. "Yeah, we're staying."

Stanheight pulled a sheet of notebook paper from his pocket and unfolded it. "So, we have dinner now." He looked at our plates. "I guess we can check that off the list. Then next we have a campfire ghost story exchange. We'll be making s'mores, of course. There's a cornhole tournament going on in the parking lot. They have movie night right over here in the multipurpose room," he added, pointing over his shoulder awkwardly. "And there will be popcorn and snacks and whatnot. Most of the guys earned it with all the calories they burned cleaning up the camp today."

Emily smiled as she finished her chicken. "That all sounds amazing."

Sarge continued, "And then tomorrow morning, we have sunrise yoga and a church service for anyone who wants to attend. The service is up in the Counselors' Quarters. Hopefully, it doesn't bother you if you ladies are late risers."

"We'll be just fine, Gordon, but thank you so much." Emily responded in the most professional manner. I wanted to laugh but knew I couldn't.

Before Sarge could continue, Greg entered the main doors, by the bathroom and quickly made his way over to our table. "Hey, man. I figured you might need a refresher."

Sarge took the thing Greg held out to him. It wasn't until Sarge popped the back off his walkie-talkie that I realized it was a battery pack. Sarge smiled, "Good thinking. I kept meaning to go up and get another one, but I haven't had time."

"Always looking out for you, Sarge."

Seth held up a finger as he finished chewing. "Question. Have any of you seen Timothy Mallick? We haven't seen him since last night and it's not like him to be this far away from the Mess Hall this late in the day."

Sarge rolled his eyes. "Like any of you are ever very far from the Mess Hall. I'll find out."

Stanheight grabbed his walkie, but Greg cut him off. "He's down at the lake with Jeff and some of the others. Kramer, Denlon Perkins, Young. The usual crew."

"Why is he with them?" Seth asked, confused. "He hates them. Well, really they hate him."

"I have no idea, Jenkins. Just going off what Jeff told me when I was out that way earlier."

Seth shook his head. "Poor guy. They sent him out with the Bully Crew? I'd rather die than deal with that all day."

"So, you saw him?" I asked, ignoring Seth.

"Well, no. I guess not. I didn't go all the way out there. I just met Jeff halfway down the path, so I could give him a battery pack as well. We've all been using our walkies a lot today. I didn't think to do a headcount." He turned to Sarge. "Anyway, if it's all the same to you, I wouldn't mind running up to the CQ and taking a shower."

"Take your time, Greg. I got this handled down here. Everything is just fine."

But nothing was fine. Nothing at all. And we were about to be face to face with that reality, very soon.

CHAPTER 23

After a long day of picking up branches and burning them, the most popular of all the kids at Camp Wašíču went down to the lake for a late afternoon swim. Fred Hoffman led the way, his long brown hair flowing in the wind. Jason Kramer followed, rubbing his left arm, which still hurt from picking up debris all day. "At least it's not my throwing arm." He tried to sound like he wasn't worried. Their good friend, Chuck Denlon was three steps behind them.

Counselor Jeff brought up the rear, nibbling on one of his homemade vegan power bars. "You guys sure you wanna do this? You don't want to head back to camp and get something to eat?"

"I'm still full from the burgers you made while we were cleaning." Denlon said.

"Yeah, we earned a quick swim." Hoffman added.

Counselor Jeff smiled, "You definitely did. Chuck, that's my personal recipe. That's why. A lot of veggie-burgers, while delicious, are pretty lacking in protein. Sure, a Portobello mushroom can masquerade as a juicy burger when cooked properly, but it doesn't have nearly as much protein as an actual cut of beef."

Kramer smiled. "I'll be honest, if someone told me that a Vegan could make one of the best burgers I've ever had, I would have punched them in the throat, but that was great."

"Vegetarian," Jeff smiled. "Vegans wouldn't use the egg I used."

Kramer pointed at him. "Either way. I would've said it was impossible. I usually need meat for my protein."

Hoffman tapped his friend on the back. "I got some meat you can suck on. I'll make you a nice protein shake right now."

Jeff shook his head, trying to ignore the comments and stay on the topic of his burgers. "So, what I do, to keep the protein, is I use black beans and quick oats. Chop up some red pepper, scallions, cilantro, garlic. Throw in some cumin, some salt, and a little bit of my homemade hot sauce. And the egg, which is what makes it vegetarian instead of vegan."

He could see no one was listening to him, but he kept going anyway. "If you make your burgers with beans or vegetables, they'll also contain much more fiber than a meat-based burger, which is another nutrient that's great for satiety."

As they reached the clearing, the lake came into view; waves lapping the edge, the wooden boat dock standing silently against the setting sun. A chair and blanket caught Hoffman's eye before he started running toward the water. "Oh shit! Georgie's here! It's a party now!"

"Been a party for the last twenty minutes. You jerks are just crashing it." Georgie called back.

Kramer and Hoffman leaned against different sections of the old black walnut trees bowing out over the lake, casting their dark reflections over the gently moving water; a stark contrast to the colorful echoes of the sunset glittering off the surface. The two football players stripped down to just their boxers, their stomachs hanging over their front waistbands. "Let's go, Chuck."

Denlon had not mimicked his friends, instead looking around at the beauty of nature around him, in an effort to ignore the expectations. "I didn't bring a suit."

"Neither did we, dill hole. Just strip down to your lady panties and let's do this."

"You guys go ahead."

"For shit's sake, Denlon. Let's go."

"Fine." Chuck slowly removed his clothes until he stood in his own boxers and his white t-shirt. By the time he finished, the others were in the water already. Jeff was near the path, talking to someone on his walkie-talkie. Denlon looked around, as though there might be hidden cameras somewhere and finally walked toward the lake.

"Shirt!" Hoffman yelled.

"I'm not taking off my shirt."

"Dude, really! Get over it." Kramer shot back. "You know once it's wet we can still see everything anyway, right?"

"No one wants to stare at your pretty titties. I promise." Georgie added.

"That's right. Mine are way nicer." Hoffman laughed.

"It's not that, guys." Denlon said, holding his stomach. "My stomach is still a little jacked up from lunch."

"The beans'll do that." Counselor Jeff mumbled as he walked toward the trail.

Kramer splashed water at Denlon. "Chucky, you coming or what?"

"Just give me a minute. I think I gotta. Oh, Jesus. Yeah. I'll be back." Denlon clenched his stomach as it rumbled. He reached into his backpack and removed a pack of wet wipes.

Kramer turned to Hoffman. "I'm pretty sure that's code for needing to drop a deuce."

"I think it might be," Hoffman retorted.

As Chuck disappeared to their right, Counselor Jeff went further left, toward the trail. "I'll be right back, guys."

Georgie smiled to the others. "Great. Now, who's going to save us?"

"We won't drown." Hoffman smiled. "We're fat. We all float, Georgie!"

Jeff responded again to his walkie-talkie radio and began to walk quickly up the trail. He stopped to look at something on the ground. Maybe a frog or some other animal. Maybe someone littered. Whatever it was, Jeff bent over, unaware that The Killer was directly behind him. The machete sliced straight through his back and out his front. It pulled back out before Jeff had the opportunity to see it. He crumpled to the ground. The Killer reached down, pulling Jeff's long ponytail to lift his head. Gripping the back of the counselor's head, The Killer lifted Jeff and slammed his face into a nearby large rock. The thud echoed as bones smashed and teeth shattered in unison. The second thud was harder. The third shot didn't hit the rock straight on, but it no longer mattered.

The Killer reached down, picking up his machete and Jeff's walkie-talkie in one swoop. He stood silently next to the body, listening to his surroundings. The talking and laughter of the friends swimming played over the gentle lap of water hitting the shoreline. The buzz and whine of a winged insect barely registered on his senses. He moved toward the water, close enough to hear the others. Far enough he was lost in the shadows.

Kramer called out, "Denlon! Did you find a hole yet? You can dig a hole. This isn't Yosemite. It will be okay to bury it."

Georgie followed suit. "Just make sure it's at least six inches deep."

"Yeah. Use your dick to measure. Then triple it." Hoffman yelled. The three boys laughed nonstop.

The Killer saw Chuck in the distance, moving away from the group. Alone. He moved ever further away from the water. The Killer watched all of this as he listened to the black walnut trees creak in the wind.

Chuck had found a spot. The earth was loose. Good for digging. He planned to hollow out a little area, fill it up, and cover it, as he'd done many times growing up. But growing up, he hadn't had to listen to his so-called friends ragging on him and talking him through squeezing one out. Denlon continued walking until he couldn't hear them remind him to "bury his snake eggs" or whatever they were going on about now.

Soon the only sounds were the wind rustling through the leaves and the crunch of dead pine needles and twigs underfoot. He found a place and did what he came to do. With his pants down, squatting over the small hole he'd dug, Chuck Denlon unloaded. A wave of noxious odor bubbled up around him, but Denlon had built up a tolerance to that particular brand of poison. He finished, used more wet wipes than he needed, and covered it up. He continued to kick rocks at the pile, like a cat that can't tell when to stop moving litter.

He took one deep breath and turned.

Walking back to the lake, Chuck Denlon wore the biggest smirk he'd dawned in weeks. "Hey, Kramer! I buried it. You happy now?" No reaction. Only silence. "You guys think you're pretty funny, don't you?" There was still no response as he neared the clearing to the lake. He mumbled to himself, "If those assholes left me out here alone…"

Denlon stopped for a second and yelled, "You better not have taken my pants!"

Chuck screamed louder than he ever had or would again. Jason Kramer lay on the ground, his throat slashed, chest covered in blood. His right arm lay a full three feet from his body. The open eyes would've haunted anyone's dreams for years. His best friend, Fred Hoffman, had been stabbed in the chest repeatedly. He'd died watching his roommate bleed out.

Chuck tried desperately to run but couldn't move. And where would he go anyway? He realized he was still screaming, but it no longer sounded like him. He turned away but found himself face to face with the man with the machete. Before he could say a word, the metal ripped through his trachea and his carotid artery. Chuck Denlon was dead before he hit the ground.

CHAPTER 24

The fire was fully rolling when the sun hadn't even set yet. There were twelve others around it when we got there. Emily, Nicole, Seth and I took our seats just as Obi began his horror story. We'd only missed one before it. Emily's leg pushed up against mine as she leaned into my left side. I wanted to wrap my arm around her but couldn't out of fear of which counselor might walk up behind us.

Obi raised his hand for silence and began his story, while rolling a long skinny stick into the campfire and playing with the flames.

Not far from this spot, there was once a very poor village. This is back in the day before even electricity. A man sat, starving, unable to fend for himself let alone his own dog. Watching his dog sleep, the man sharpened a knife, wondering what his pet would taste like. He moved closer to the dog, ready to do the deed. It needed to happen while the beast was asleep. The man could not stand the thought of looking into his pet's eyes as he ran the knife across the dog's throat.

But he couldn't bring himself to do it. Part of it was the fact that the dog was scrawny and wouldn't provide meat anyway, but somewhere, deep inside, he loved that dog. Still, he could not afford to feed the dog, so he walked the dog into the woods and left him there.

The dog didn't know the man had left him there because he didn't want to kill him. The dog only knew he'd been abandoned and that he never wished to see the man again. Walking in the opposite direction, the dog eventually came to another village. Searching for food, the dog ripped through the trash piles and occasionally attempted to make his way into the homes of the locals. They didn't know if he was rabid or wild and the locals drove him away, hitting the dog with brooms, yelling at him, or throwing small objects. But never food. Just once, the dog wished they would throw day old bread his way. He eventually gave up and returned to the forest.

As the dog wandered into the trees this time, he saw something he had not seen before. Smoke billowed out of the chimney of a cabin in the distance. The dog ran toward the house, praying for food as his stomach rumbled. Arriving, he found himself at the back of the cabin. But not just any cabin. This thing appeared to be sitting on hundreds of chicken legs. The low glow of candlelight inside gave the appearance that the two back windows were eyes, staring at the dog.

A blood-curdling screech echoed through the woods. Worse, it came from the house itself. The home creaked and groaned as the chicken legs each moved in a counterclockwise motion and the entire house turned in the dog's direction. The screams, groans, and creaks ceased as the front door lined up with the dog and the house lowered itself down on its chicken legs. The door crashed open violently, ricocheting slightly off the forest floor.

Feeling he had no choice, the dog proceeded into the hut. He was greeted by a very overweight grotesque woman with a huge nose. "Well, hello, doggy. Did you come here of your own free will or did someone send you to me?"

The dog barked.

"Yes, yes, of course. You're a dog. Hang on." The woman quickly concocted a potion and poured it into a bowl. Having had nothing else in his stomach, the dog lapped it up quickly. He turned to the woman and said, "Thank you. That was delici — " suddenly aware of the fact he could speak.

The fat old woman laughed. "So, what brings you here?"

"Hunger. Dogs are not treated well. I have been repeatedly driven from the surrounding villages."

Mixing several bottles of colorful liquids, the woman cackled. "I can help you. You seem like a good soul. But I warn you it won't help you forever."

"Help me how?"

"I can make you one of them. You can walk among the humans and work and earn food and be happy."

"I'll take it."

"Not so quickly. You need to understand that my powers are finite. Every now and again, the moon will reveal the truth and all of your animalistic tendencies will pour forth at once." She held eye contact with the dog for the first time since his arrival. "I beg you to ensure you are nowhere near the others when this happens."

The dog agreed, neither understanding the woman's words fully nor caring about their implications. He again lapped up the potion she poured into the bowl. By the time the purple liquid was finished, a naked grown man knelt where the dog had once been. The woman offered him clothing, which did not fit his gaunt frame well, but he accepted them anyway and began his trek into the village.

A real people pleaser, Doug quickly fit in with other townspeople. They listened in awe to the tales of his many travels and how robbers left him with only these rags to wear. They treated him well and helped him find shelter and better fitting clothing. Even his old owner (whose name, he learned, was Robert Stuart) treated Doug much better than he'd ever treated him when Doug was a dog. But the joy of living as a human in the small village was short lived. As two weeks later, the full moon arrived.

Doug awoke the following morning, believing he'd slept the full night. The village was in an uproar. Robert Stuart was brutally murdered the night before. Some said they'd seen an oversized wolf in his home. Others stated that they'd heard growls and screams but didn't have the courage to see what was occurring. Still, everyone agreed the aftermath – the very way the body was left – could've only been the result of an animal attack.

Robert Stuart had been eaten.

Returning to his own home, Doug found his clothing ripped to shreds on the floor. And he noticed that for the first time, maybe ever, his stomach was more than full.

For several weeks, Doug tried to find another explanation, but one never came. He knew what he had done, and he knew he would do it again. Just hours before the moon would rise again, Doug made his way to the forest. The familiar smoke plume in the distance assured him the fat old woman's hut was still there. As he came closer, Doug saw the small house was now surrounded by a fence, which appeared to be made of bones. Each fence post was topped with a small woodland creature's skull; the blazing eye sockets of each illuminating the coming darkness as the sun set.

The windows looked Doug over several times before the hut once again turned in his direction. The screams and groans were just as loud and grating even when he expected them. The thud of the door hitting the forest floor echoed, but he strode toward it with a new confidence.

The fat old woman sat, whittling a piece of wood as Doug told her the full story. When he finished she looked him in the eye and said, "It's much worse than I'd expected. I tried to warn you to stay away. This needs to be stopped." She set down the piece of wood and began to mix potions. "This will undo everything. You'll be a dog again."

Doug nodded and waited. As the overweight witch handed it to him, Doug smiled. His grip loosened. The antidote crashed to the floor. The old woman was the only one who knew all his secrets. And as the moon rose in the distance and Doug's body began to change, he stared into her eyes, knowing she'd never tell anyone.

He was going to eat very well, indeed.

Obi threw out his arms and brought them back in a celebratory gesture as everyone around the fire oohed and aahed his story.

Obi pointed to his roommate, sitting next to me. "I nominate Seeeeeeth Jenkins." Obi said it like a game show host, but all I heard was the modern-day equivalent of Frrrrraaaank Doyle.

Seth held out his hand. "Challenge accepted."

Emily stood up. "Sorry, Seth, but I need to go grab a bottle of water or two. Anyone else need one?" No one did, but I still used it as an excuse to go with Emily.

CHAPTER 25

As we walked away from the others, I watched Emily's tan legs with each stride toward the Rec Center. My eyes moved to her arm as she rubbed her stomach, lifting her shirt slightly higher than her belly button. The soft contours of her abdomen were the direct opposite of mine. Emily displayed the beginning outlines of a six-pack while I had a full whiskey barrel under my shirt.

It doesn't matter what you think. I heard Dr. Munson say in my head. *She's with you. She wants to be with you. Enjoy it.* Picking up the pace a little, I walked next to Emily. To my surprise, she reached out her hand to hold mine. I knew what would happen if Sarge saw it, but I didn't care. Our fingers wrapped around one another as our arms swung lightly in unison. As we passed the picnic tables holding plastic and paper plates and cups, condiments hot dogs and buns, and several bags of extra-large marshmallows, the smell of the firewood was slowly replaced with the odor of citronella candles and bug spray. For a fat kid, it's normally hard not to stare at stuff like that, but with Emily next to me my attention was focused on her face instead.

"So, do you have a horror story to tell?" I asked, casually.

"Just ones from my dating life." She laughed. She stopped and grimaced, her teeth pushing together, and her lips stretched outward. "Sorry. It was just a joke. Mostly."

"You're fine. Don't worry about it. I just hope I don't become another tale in your storytelling repertoire." I smiled back.

She reached out, taking my hand. The clouds lit from below, absorbing the colors of the sky; a beautiful juxtaposition to the silhouettes of the trees below them. The sun's hue shifted to deeper pinks, purples, and oranges. The large glass windows of the Rec Center in front of us glowed with the sun's reflection; as did Emily's skin.

She licked her lips. "Actually, I know *one* horror story. My dad always tells it when we go camping, like we haven't heard it a hundred times." She shook her head. "It's basically about this hiker who is on a 300-mile trek through the Superior Hiking Trail in Minnesota. This massive rainstorm breaks out and he seeks shelter in a cabin. Inside, he finds no one home, but there are terrible paintings on the wall. Grotesque things that are basically human faces, only ripped off and framed, so they're all flattened out."

"Sounds awesome." I said, completely intrigued in her story

"The worst part is that there are six faces on the wall and then there's a seventh frame, which is completely black."

"I like where this is going."

"Let me finish." Emily tightened her grip on my hand. "He finally falls asleep in the cabin, after purposely facing away from the dreadful paintings."

"What? Who could fall asleep with those things?"

"Shut up. Let me finish. He finally falls asleep in the cabin, facing away from the paintings. When he wakes up, light is streaming through the cabin and the storm is over. He remembers the paintings on the wall and he mentally prepares himself before turning toward them."

Emily's feet stopped moving. Her hand tightened on my own, as she turned on her right foot, locking eyes with me. "Only, he finds there were never any paintings. There were only windows."

A shudder ran down my spine as I stared at the beautiful girl who just told me my own ghost story. "Wow. That's a good one. You *have* to tell that story at the campfire."

"You think so? Maybe I didn't want to go back to the campfire tonight. Maybe I had another idea." Emily tugged my arm; not hard, but in a confident manner. I spun toward her.

"Yes?" She motioned to the side of the trail; near the entrance to the forest. "I thought you needed water," I said, pointing at the Rec Center.

Stepping closer, she bit her bottom lip ever so slightly. "I'll get it in a bit. I just want to spend more time with you first."

"I don't know." I said nervously. "We'd miss Seth's story. How will I know what to make fun of now?" I watched her face and I immediately apologized.

She laughed it off. "The Hierarchy of Bullies rears its ugly head again, huh?"

"Always!" I said.

"Why do you think people form cliques with the people that they do?"

I looked at her questioningly but thought I knew how to answer. "I would assume because you find people you have stuff in common with. For instance, I wouldn't be able to talk football with Mark Baxter. And he probably wouldn't understand the humor of half of my t-shirts."

"Do you think it's possible to belong to separate cliques and hang out with different types of people?"

I shrugged. "I mean, it would depend on your own strengths, what kind of people you identify with, and even how important it is to you to stay on your level of the ladder." She moved closer, inches from my mouth. "Among other things."

"What if we start our own level? A place for the two of us?"

I almost told her that wasn't possible. That you can't just invent new levels to the Hierarchy, but I wanted nothing more than to have something that just belonged to me and Emily. I closed my eyes and I joined her. Her lips tapping mine twice, before I grabbed the side of her head, her hair lightly brushing my hand as I held her neck in place, my tongue dancing with hers.

As she released, her lips tapped mine one more time; a tease of what she had planned. But as she pulled away, smiling, Georgie Perkins broke through the trees at that exact second, unleashing the most inhuman crying noise I've ever heard. His right arm hung from his body at multiple grotesque angles. His breathing was erratic, gurgling, as blood filled his lungs. He repeatedly attempted to scream, instead spraying blood across my face and shirt before he fell into Emily's awaiting arms.

<u>CHAPTER 26</u>

The Killer stood listening to the laughter of the three swimming in the lake as he stared down at Counselor Jeff's body and knew what had to be done. At some point, Camp Wašíču would realize the level of danger they were truly in and either fight or run.

He made his way to the lake. To his surprise, the three football players were out of the water. Kramer called out. "This isn't Yosemite. It will be okay to bury it." Hoffman followed suit with insults of his own.

Listening to the black walnut trees creak in the wind, The Killer watched as Chuck moved further off away from the lake. He was getting away, which wasn't ideal, but he was not on a path to find Jeff's body and kick this whole thing into overdrive. He decided to deal with the three at the lake first, then find Chuck. He didn't attempt to hide, just quickly walking up to the three boys. Hoffman was the closest to him and saw him first. "Oh, hey! Man, I thought you were—"

The machete rose above Hoffman's head before slamming into his chest. The Killer slid it out in one clean shot and buried it in a different section of Hoffman's chest.

Screaming like a little girl, Georgie turned, running the opposite way, opting to save only himself. Kramer ran at The Killer, his fist pulled back, ready to throw a punch, but the machete whooshed through the air. Kramer's right arm dropped to the ground with a nauseating thump. He screamed through his tears. Hoffman lay on the ground, bleeding out, reaching out for his friend. The machete cut through the tendons in Kramer's neck even easier than his arm. Blood poured down his bare chest and into and around his wet boxers.

The Killer kicked Kramer's body twice to double check, as Hoffman attempted to turn himself over and crawl to the water. He made it halfway onto his side, but no further. A large boot stomped on Hoffman's shoulder, pushing him onto his back. The machete slid directly into his heart. The Killer removed the blade, wiped the excess blood on Hoffman's shorts, and started to follow Georgie.

He took two steps when he heard, "You better not have taken my pants!" Chuck Denlon was on his way back to the lake. Pushing himself against the black walnut trees, he waited with the glee of a young teen waiting to fill his first doe tag. Chuck stood before his fallen friends, screaming. The Killer stood directly behind him.

As Chuck's body fell on top of Jason Kramer's, The Killer turned his attention back to Georgie Perkins, hoping he hadn't gotten far. Trudging down a side trail, he was amazed to find that Georgie hadn't been smart enough to run all the way back to camp. He'd cowered; tried to hide; wanted to survive but didn't put in the work to do so. Balled up at the base of a moss-covered white oak, Georgie Perkins sat crying, chewing fingernails for his last meal. Slowing, The Killer's boots took on a rhythmic quality as he stepped toward the kid who had been led to believe he'd one day own the land around him.

A twig snapped under The Killer's boot. Georgie took off like Frank Doyle hearing a gunshot. The Killer followed at the same pace.

He had something Georgie didn't have. He'd been jogging these trails for years. The fading light left behind shadows and dark patches as the wind wailed between distorted trunks, carrying the sickly stink of wood rot. But The Killer continued closing in. Ten feet away. Seven. Five.

Georgie stopped suddenly, twisting around with a high kick. He knocked the machete to the ground. Incensed, The Killer fought back, tackling Georgie. The two traded blows. Rolling on the uneven ground pitted with rocks and roots, Georgie got up and threw a punch. His opponent dodged it and Georgie connected with the rough, cracked ridges of tree bark, dead on. With five distinctly audible cracks, his ring finger and middle finger splintered instantly against the great White Oak. The combat boot came up fast, connecting with Georgie's elbow; the sick sound as the bone snapped echoed in both of their ears, as the Perkins boy screamed louder than he ever had. The Killer went back for his machete, intent to finish the fight. Picking it up from the ground, he was surprised to see Georgie running down the trail away from him; right arm bouncing with every step, pain coursing through each breath.

Georgie's pain was so intense he was unfazed as branches slapped and cut his face. His assailant didn't have the same luxury, consistently slowing down to avoid losing an eye. Finally, only feet from the edge of the trees, The Killer's sweat-soaked glove wrapped around Georgie's shoulder, pulling him firmly with that hand while the other drove the machete through Georgie's back. Georgie continued to run, even if he wasn't aware he was doing so. The machete ripped out of his back as Georgie tried to scream. Blood sprayed all over me as Georgie fell into Emily's open arms.

As Emily screamed, Georgie continuously repeated one word:
"Sleeves."

"GET HELP!" Emily screamed. I ran toward the Rec Center, screaming for help, pulling my pants up as I went.

Sarge hobbled outside as though he thought a wild animal was out there. "What the hell are you out here yelling—"

"It's Georgie. Georgie Perkins. He's bleeding. And his arm."

Sarge ran to the body. "Holy shit. What happened to him?" He pulled out his walkie-talkie, hit the button and confidently stated, "We have a 402 on the east side of the cabins, near the entrance to the Rec Center. All hands. Repeat—" He stared at the walkie. "Son of a bitch is dead."

Emily stared at Sarge in disbelief.

"I meant the radio—"

Before Sarge had to explain any further, Seth and Nicole, Obi, and a few other campers ran up. Seth reached us first. "Georgie? Is he going to be okay?"

Sarge pointed at Seth without taking his own eyes off Georgie. "Jenkins, call an ambulance."

Counselor Greg ran out of the Rec Center doors. "It's useless, Sarge. All the phones are down."

"Down? That's impossible. What do you mean all the phones are down?"

"I've been tracing it. Looks like a severed cord. I was trying to call the police because my tires were slashed." He swallowed hard. "I think everyone's are."

Sarge stood up, hands on his hips, looking around. Georgie spit out more blood. Sarge said, "Greg, grab me anything you can that you think will help."

"I don't know if there's much of a point, Sarge."

Sarge stared at Greg like he stares at fat kids who make excuses on the obstacle course. "I said get me anything you think will help. Now." Greg bit his own lip as he turned and went back into the Rec Center.

Emily's hand slid into the pocket of her cutoffs and she pulled out her cell phone. Staring at the empty service bars, she repeated, "Come on. Come on."

Sarge shook his head in disbelief and frustration. "Normally, I'd be pissed, but right now, I'm just glad that you have it. Are you getting any signal at all?" Emily furiously shook her brunette locks. "I told you." Sarge said. "It's a dead zone down here. You keep trying though."

He looked directly at Seth. "We still have cell phones up at the Counselors' Quarters. Run up there, find one, and call the paramedics. I need to stay here." He handed his keys to Seth. Seth might as well have received the Holy Eucharist based on his reaction and careful handling of the keys. Sarge barked, "You make sure you call as soon as you have the phones. You're not gonna get reception down here. There's no point in bringing them back. Call from up there."

Emily nodded. "He's not kidding. I can't get a single bar."

Seth started toward the Counselors' Quarters. Nicole called, "I'm going with you."

Sarge yelled, "My office. My desk. Bottom drawer. It's the key with the red cover. Go. Go now."

Another cup of blood sprayed through the air like the world's worst sprinkler system. Emily held Georgie's hand. "You're going to be just fine. Help is on the way."

Greg returned from the Rec Center, holding a pile of towels, four bottles of water, and a first aid kit. He ran directly to Sarge, but shot up, staring at Emily. "You… you have a cell phone. Did you reach anyone?"

Emily's brunette hair swung left to right as she shook her head. "No, I can't get any reception down here. I should have given the phone to Seth."

Georgie's eyes opened. He reached out for Greg; blood bubbling from his mouth.

Greg did not respond as he and Sarge worked to stop the bleeding, knowing it was a lost cause. Georgie hacked twice, loudly. He dry-heaved twice. Each time the counselors backed up slightly. Then it happened. His throat buckled, as bright red blood-laced vomit exploded from his mouth; the splatters on the ground echoing around us. Georgie's head fell sideways at an irregular angle.

"NO! NO!" Sarge shouted. But it was too late. He knelt forward, his legs tucked under him, his fingers clutching his pant legs in anguish. A single tear streamed down his left cheek. "I don't understand."

Greg attempted to comfort him. "I'm sure you did everything you could, Sarge."

Sarge stared into Greg's eyes. "We need to make sure we take care of everyone else. Something very bad is happening. We need an immediate headcount. I'll start in the Rec Center."

Greg counted those of us still out there. "You guys search around here. Get everyone in the Rec Center or the Mess Hall. I'm going to head down to the lake and find out where the rest of Jeff's group is. I don't think any of them have returned."

Sarge wiped at his face with both hands. "Jesus, I hadn't even thought of that."

Greg started toward the trees; almost exactly where Georgie had come through. He turned, motioning to Emily. "Why don't you come with me? Sometimes you can get a signal down by the lake."

Emily walked over, inspecting Georgie's body as she got closer. She handed her phone to Greg. "I'm staying with Phillip, but if you can get a signal, do it!" Greg was clearly annoyed but took the phone and placed it in his pocket.

I looked at Emily, "Maybe it will be okay. Hopefully, Seth and Nicole made it to Sarge's office and they got the other cell phones. Emergency Services are probably already on their way." I tried to sound reassuring as I watched Greg disappear into the trees.

CHAPTER 27

Seth and Nicole climbed the three flights of wooden stairs outside the Counselors' Quarters. He was ahead of her and not nearly as winded. Nicole was still able to speak, however. "Hey, Seth?"

"Yeah?"

"I just wanted to say thank you for bringing Phillip here."

"Your mom brought Phillip here. I just came along."

She smiled. "That's what I mean. I think he would've washed out right away if you weren't here."

Seth looked back. "You think so? I don't. I think Phil just needs to believe in himself. I keep telling him he's more than capable of doing these things. Honestly, I think he uses me as a crutch. I might be slowing him down."

They reached the second landing but didn't stop moving. "Almost there!" Nicole said.

Seth felt a twinge of guilt as he said, "Plus, some of it is my fault."

"What do you mean?"

"I used to sneak him out at night. Take him to Village Inn. We'd eat enough for six people and I'd bring him back. I broke him out of school a couple times and took him to Golden Corral."

They reached the top landing and tried the door. It opened. Seth continued. "I took him to the Chinese Buffet the afternoon we were coming here. It was like two junkies overdosing right before heading to rehab. Well, really, that's exactly what it was." They walked into the main lobby area. Seth pointed down one hall as he continued. "If anything, I owe Phil a huge thank you. If it wasn't for him, I wouldn't be here… and this place has helped me change everything. They climbed the stairs to the second floor. "We're almost there."

"Have you been to Gordon's office a lot?"

"No. Never. But this is the way to my therapist's office and that's just down the hall from Sarge."

Nicole's nose scrunched up. "You go to therapy?" They rounded the corner heading to Sarge's office.

"We all do. Every camper here." Seth pulled the keys out of his pocket, reading each name plaque. Dr. Munson, the Dietician, the Nurse, Gorden Stanheight, Head Counselor. Nicole tried to grab the keys, but Seth pulled them away from her. "You know I can't give you the keys, right, babe? These are Sarge's. I can't let anything happen to them."

Seth pulled out the key Sarge was holding when he gave them to Seth. The handle turned right away. They were in. Seth slid behind Sarges's oversize L-Shaped desk and found the locked drawer where the phones were supposed to be kept. Fumbling through all the keys, Seth found the one with a red cover and leaned down to unlock the drawer; but found it was already open.

And it was empty.

"Great. Now what?"

Nicole scanned the room and pointed to the landline telephone. "I know the others aren't working, but what about that one? Maybe they work up here."

Seth nodded, slowly reaching out his hand. With his fingers almost touching the receiver, the phone rang. Seth jumped, again releasing a high pitched feminine scream. Recovering, he stared at Nicole. "Don't tell anyone I scream like that."

"Would you answer the phone?"

Seth pulled the phone to his ear, not sure what to expect. "Hello?"

"Jenkins? Is that you? It's Greg. The Counselor. I'm so glad to know the phones up there are working. So, it must just be down at the camp. Did you get the cell phones?"

"They're not here."

"So, you haven't called anyone?"

"No, we just got here." Seth said.

"I got a signal on that girl's phone down here at the lake. I called the EMTs. They're on their way. Listen, Jenkins. What I'm about to tell you isn't good, but I need to be honest with you."

The Killer looked through one of the floor to ceiling windows in the lobby downstairs, as Greg continued. "Jenkins, I'm down at the lake. It's bad. I found four bodies. They're so mutilated I can't tell who they even are."

"Holy shit," Seth exhaled.

"Jenkins, there's no way to know who did this or where they are now, but I want you to stay there until I get there. I'm on my way up there. Do not leave until I'm there."

"Okay, but be careful, Greg. The killer could be where you are."

Nicole's face contorted. "Killer? What the fuck?"

Greg tried to sound reassuring. "Don't worry about me, Jenkins. The line went dead. Seth almost dropped the phone trying to put it on the hook as his hands shook. Tears broke free and ran down his face as he said, "We need to find the other counselors."

After bringing Nicole up to speed, Seth led the way down the dark hallway of doors. Nicole was one step behind him and would've bumped into him at any time if Seth stopped moving. "What's in all these rooms?"

"I'm not totally sure. I've never been this far. I think it's where they sleep, but I don't know." His hand reached out to one of the doors at random. His fingers closed tight around the handle. Turning it very slowly, Seth prayed they'd find something that could help them. As the door opened, a body threw itself at Seth, falling directly onto his chest. Mouth wide open, eyes shut, the torso had no arms, no lower half. It hit him full force. Seth screamed again. The CPR dummy hit the carpeted floor with a softened thud as Seth tried to regain his composure.

Nicole picked it up. "It's just a dummy, dummy."

"Can you—"

"—I get it. You scream weird. I won't tell anyone. Please stop."

Seth started to reach for the next door, but Nicole cut him off. "I got this one." Turning the knob, Nicole opened a doorway to a good-sized bedroom. Counselor Todd, one of the overnight staff, appeared to be asleep in the bed.

Seth cupped his hands over his mouth, "Counselor! Counselor! We need you!" He stared at Nicole. "I don't know his name. They work at night and I never see them." Turning his attention back to the man in the bed, Seth repeated, "Counselor!"

Nicole found the light switch and just turned it on. This time she screamed with Seth. Todd lay in the middle of the bed, covered in blood. He'd been stabbed through the stomach while he slept. His eyes were wide open but could no longer see.

The teenagers ran out of the room. Turning the corner, Seth slammed directly into Counselor Tony, the other overnight counselor. Tony wore only a towel, having just gotten out of the shower. "How did you get a girl up here?"

"You have to help us!" Seth begged.

"I'm not helping you stash a girl."

"No, save us. From the killer."

Nicole tried to explain, "The other counselor is dead."

Tony looked past them into the dark hallway. "What are you talking about?"

Nicole grabbed Tony's hand, trying to pull him down the hallways. "The other counselor! He's been mur—" The machete exploded out of the middle of Tony's chest, sending pieces of flesh and blood in every direction. Some splattered Nicole's face. Blood pooled in the corner of Tony's mouth, before running down his chin. The Killer pulled the machete out and Tony fell to the floor.

Seth grabbed Nicole's hand, yanking her down the hallway, away from The Killer. The Killer smiled to himself, wiping the blood from the machete on his own pants. His black boots hit the carpet in a slow, rhythmic fashion as he followed.

CHAPTER 28

It had to be right about then that Sarge came out of the Rec Center, holding a battery pack for his walkie-talkie. His voice caught me off guard, echoing into the night. "McCracken! Clausen! You two are with me." Emily didn't even question it. Even she could tell that no one says no when Sarge uses that tone. He slammed the new battery pack onto his radio. "We just changed it, too. These things do not last."

Sarge ensured the walkie was on and held it sideways to his mouth. "Anyone out there with a radio who can still hear me: We are missing at least eleven campers and possibly two counselors. Radio check back if you hear me, so I know I'm not alone out here. Also, Tony and Todd, I need you down here at the Rec Center ASAP. Copy if you hear me."

Seth and Nicole ran down the stairs toward the main lobby, but as they arrived, they were surprised to see The Killer was already there, waiting for them. Standing by the large glass table near the door, The Killer blocked the only way out. Seth knew this but didn't want to scare Nicole any more than necessary. He needed a plan to save her instead. Staring toward The Killer, Seth could not make out the face under the hood, but he knew the sweatshirt. The sleeves had been sliced off right above the elbows. Suddenly, Georgie's dying words made sense to Seth. Only one counselor wore them that way; Eric Schultz. Seth tried to formulate a way in which he could use this information to momentarily distract Eric and he and Nicole could run.

Before he could, Nicole made a move. Not four feet from The Killer, she stopped, as he held out the machete. There wasn't enough room to charge him. There was nothing in the immediate vicinity Seth thought he could use as a weapon. So, he played the only card he had. "Eric! No! Take me. Let her go. She doesn't know anything about you. She doesn't know how to turn you in. She doesn't even know your last name."

The machete withdrew as The Killer considered this. Nicole took the opportunity to move to the middle of the room, with the couch between herself and the man with the machete. His boots echoed with each click as they hit the hardwood floor. The Killer moved closer to Seth, opening the doorway for Nicole. Seth knew he just had to get the Killer on the other side of the room. Even if he couldn't make it out, Nicole could save herself and warn the others. The Killer's hood never moved as he stalked toward Seth. The machete rotated in his hands several times, as he grew ever closer to his target.

Sarge's voice echoed through the room, "Anyone out there with a radio who can still hear me: We are missing at least eleven campers and possibly two counselors. Radio check back if you hear me, so I know I'm not alone out here. Also, Tony and Todd, I need you down here at the Rec Center ASAP. Copy if you hear me."

Halfway through this message, The Killer reached down, trying to adjust the walkie-talkie he was carrying. Nicole seized her opportunity. Seth watched as she ran straight at the two of them. Seth steadied himself to grab the machete, thinking it would be knocked loose as soon as Nicole hit The Killer from the back. Turning just in time, The Killer realized Nicole was there, but she was never aiming for him.

Nicole bowed low, tucked her head, and wrapped her arm around Seth's body. Her momentum drove the two of them through the floor to ceiling window. With glass raining down on them, the duo landed on the grass outside. "Get up!" Nicole yelled.

Seth quickly pulled himself up, "That was a hell of a tackle."

"Three years of lacrosse!" Nicole responded as they ran down the hill toward the camp.

The Killer carefully crawled out of the window, following behind them.

"We need to move!" Nicole said, absentmindedly pulling glass dust out of her arm. The Killer gained ground as the duo tried to hurry down the hill, but Seth lost his footing, sliding down the hill. Nicole raced after him.

At the bottom of the hill, Nicole grabbed a rock the size of her fist. She turned, facing The Killer. Her left arm pointed directly at him as her right arm pulled back. She launched it, screaming, "SUCK THAT!" which only made Seth love her more. The rock didn't arc high, but the aim was true. The Killer immediately fell over.

"Holy shit!" exclaimed Seth. "Let me guess, three years of softball?"

"Seriously?" Nicole asked. "Try thirteen."

Emily and I went cabin to cabin with Sarge, completing a headcount and looking for people. I was more worried than ever about having not seen Timothy since the night before. I didn't know a good way to bring it up, so I just didn't. Part of me knew. And part of me thought that if I never said it out loud it wouldn't be real, and I wouldn't have to deal with it. Timothy would just come back.

We reached the cabin right before mine. Randy Waterhouse was in the cabin, pulling his bed away from the wall. He quickly pushed it back as we entered. "Waterhouse! You best not be hiding more candy behind your bunk."

"Sir. No, sir. I was simply looking for a sock I lost."

Sarge couldn't resist, even in a time like this. It's one of the things I'll always admire him for. "I don't suppose it was a crusty sock you keep by your bed all the time. Don't you know if you never wash them you'll get maggots? You want maggots eating your unborn children, Waterhouse?"

"Kinda. That's pretty awesome."

Sarge shook his head. "Can it, Waterhouse. Where are your roommates, any clue?"

"Roger hasn't been seen since he went to take a shower, if he actually went there, Sarge. The other two are in the Mess Hall."

Oh, Roger Tonkyn had been there, all right. I talked to him when I thought the worst part of my day would be that I was covered in mud and needed to shower. He'd scared the hell out of me while I was apologizing to a picture of a cheerleader. And I'd left him alone there. Did something happen to him? Did he end up like Georgie? Is that what had happened to Timothy as well? Sarge led the way out of the cabin before I could ask questions or think too much about it.

As we cleared the rosebushes in front of Randy's cabin, I realized there was only one left to check. "Hey, Sarge?"

"Yes, McCracken?"

"We don't really need to check mine. We both know where I am... and we both know where Georgie is."

"Could be stragglers." He said, trying not to show emotion. It didn't work. He reached out to open my cabin door and it swung open on its own. Seth stood there, screaming that scream he screams. Before he could so much as say, *Don't tell anyone I scream like that,* Sarge cut him off. "Jenkins? I thought that was the girl screaming."

Nicole stared at me. "Thank god we found you guys."

Sarge said, "Thank god we found you."

I smiled at Seth, "I thought I'd never see your fat ass again."

Seth started crying, his hands repeatedly wiping away his tears. "That guy that killed Georgie? He was up there. He killed the other Counselors. He tried to kill us."

"Who did? What do you mean the other counselors?"

"The night counselors. They're both dead. He killed one right in front of us." Nicole screamed.

Sarge grabbed her. "You saw him? You saw who's doing this?" He paused, collecting himself. "Sorry. Tell me exactly what happened."

Tears fell down Seth's face as he said, "We tried to wake up one of the counselors, but he was dead. Just slaughtered in his bed."

"Holy hell," Stanheight whispered.

"And then the other one, he asked me how I got a girl up there and then the machete just stabbed him right through the back. And the blood. And then he chased us. And we could've been next."

Nicole added, "I don't think we would've gotten away if you hadn't distracted him coming over the radio like that."

Sarge's eyes narrowed. "Radio? Like a walkie-talkie? You're saying he had one of these?" Both teens nodded. "Well, he shouldn't have. Only Counselors, the Nurse, and Dr. Munson have one of these."

"Unless he killed someone and took theirs." I said, before I realized the words were coming out. "I'm sorry."

Sarge nodded. "You're right. That is a possibility we have to accept. We need to get the police here and get this taken care of. How long until we can expect them, Jenkins?"

"I'm not sure," Seth said.

"Didn't you call them?"

"No. Greg did. He said he got a hold of them and they were on their way." Seth said, rubbing his arm.

"Where's Greg now?" Sarge said, looking out at the camp.

"I'm not sure," Seth said, slowly. "He said he was still by the lake when he called us."

"Called?" Sarge shot a look at Nicole. "You got another cell phone?"

Nicole shook her head. "Just the one you already took. And I'm starting to think I won't see it again. All the others are gone."

"The other what? Cell phones?"

Seth stepped in. "Yeah, Sarge. None of them were in your office. That bottom drawer was open, and everything was cleared out."

"If there were no phones, how did Greg reach you?" Sarge asked.

"He just called the phone in your office and I picked up."

Sarge's face lit up. "You said the phone in my office still works? I gotta get up there then."

Seth's confidence returned. There was no longer any sign of his tears. "It's Eric Schultz."

Sarge flipped around. "What did you just say?"

"I know how it sounds, but I know it's him. It's Eric Schultz. He's the one doing this. The Killer's sleeves are cut. Remember Eric's hoodies? He always cuts the sleeves off them. They end around the elbows. That's how the Killer wears them. It's gotta be Eric."

Sarge slid up against the wall right inside the door of my cabin, his face buried in his elbow. "It's my fault. This is all my fault."

CHAPTER 29

Sarge paced the floor of my cabin, his stare was a million miles away as he launched into the story.

"Eric knocked on my office door, but he didn't wait too long for an answer. He just sauntered in, carrying a latte in one hand and his cell phone in the other. He didn't even look up at me. He knew the rules. Don't have your phones out where the campers can see them. It's not fair. But Eric always thought he was the exception to the rule. It was bad enough I had to schedule a meeting with him in the middle of the day to address some things I'd been hearing and talk to him about his unprofessional behavior, but to show up like that? That was just a sign of complete disrespect in my eyes.

"He slid into the chair between myself and the door, stuck his latte straight on my desk, and kept scrolling through his social media nonsense without so much as a head nod. Finally finished updating his status or whatever and he looks up and goes, 'So what's up, Sarge? I hear you had a complaint about me?'

"I addressed the most concerning issue and then talked about some of the other apprehensions I'd been having. That's all the details you need. There's a little thing called human decency that keeps me from airing everyone's dirty laundry out in public like that anyway. He got a little heated. Ran his mouth like usual. Made excuses. That's my biggest pet peeve in the world, if you've never noticed. So, at that point, I'd about had enough. I told him he should take a couple days off. Think it over. Decide if the thing I'd heard he did that he didn't deny doing was worth his job or if he'd like to be a man, own up to his mistakes, and make it right. He basically just left, and I haven't seen him since.

"Now, no one else knows this part – I hadn't even told the other counselors, really – but when I went into my office yesterday morning, there was an envelope on the floor; having been slid under my door, I'm guessing. I opened it and found Eric's resignation letter."

Stanheight snapped back and looked me in the eyes. "And, typical Eric, he didn't even bother to sign it."

Nicole shook her head. "I don't see how that makes any of this your fault. You did your job as a supervisor."

Sarge's index finger pointed straight at her. "I appreciate it, but you're wrong. I should've been a better leader and been honest with my counselors up front. I thought I could change Eric's mind. I thought I could bring him back and this would eventually all blow over. I didn't tell anyone. So, they didn't think anything of it when he was walking around in the Counselors' Quarters. I didn't warn you guys, so he was able to walk up to any camper and use the trust they placed in him. He was able to get right up to them. No one was prepared. That's on me."

I stood up. "So, let's warn people now. Let's save as many people as we can."

Sarge stared at me. "You guys do that. I'm heading up the hill. I'm gonna find him and make sure he doesn't hurt anyone else."

"With all due respect," Seth began, before Sarge interrupted.

"You think I'm old and can't handle him? You think that Eric is a lot younger and in shape and that I won't be able to keep up, is that it? Well, let me tell you something, Jenkins. I'm in better shape at my age than—"

"—I was just saying, he might not be up there anymore. We've been in here a long time. We need to get back out there."

Sarge popped up. "You're right. You guys go to the Rec Center, bring them up to date. Tell them everything we know. I'm going to head up to the Counselors' Quarters and look for him."

I stood in Sarge's way. "That's literally the exact same plan. I can't let you do that. You're going to the Rec Center. The four of us will go up to the Counselors' Quarters. If we're splitting up, we're doing it in larger numbers."

Sarge stared at me in disbelief and said, "I'm not letting anyone who isn't armed go after this guy. You're all going to the Rec Center and that's final."

Seth got a huge smile on his face. "I think we should all go to the Rec Center. I'll explain on the way."

At first, Randy's defenses were off the charts. He denied any knowledge of, or ability to get, weapons of any kind onto Camp Wašíču property without being caught. Sarge finally cut his ability to make excuses. "You won't be held accountable for any of it. You have my word. We need people to have a way to defend themselves. Do you have anything or not?"

Randy stared at each of us in turn before he smiled. "Alright. I'll trust you. Follow me."

Randy went right back to the side of his bed; the same place he was standing when Sarge and Emily and I completed the headcount. "I was actually going to grab a weapon earlier. When I saw what happened to Georgie, I didn't really feel safe, but then you guys showed up and I couldn't grab anything." He turned back as he moved the bed. "This little collection started as a joke, but now I'm glad I have it."

As the top mattress slid out of the way, we found that Randy's bed spring was hollowed out, leaving plenty of room for random items. One corner was filled with candy. I wanted to reach over and grab a Snickers, but that instantly reminded me of Timothy and my face fell. Another corner appeared to be filled with extra fluffy pillows. Now I knew how Georgie had gotten the pillow he'd been issued. I'd always assumed it came from having his last name and being given anything he wanted... but no. He had to wheel and deal just like the lowest person on the rungs.

It was the far side of the bed that interested me most, however. I saw so much sporting equipment. I don't think Sarge understood what Randy was saying at first, but after years of being relentlessly tortured by jocks, I knew exactly what level of weapon we were looking at. Randy knew he had some explaining to do. "Basically, you guys have some shit sports equipment, so we bring in better stuff."

He wasn't lying. Just from where I stood, I could see Bear Archery Brave 3 bow sets with Safety Glass vaned arrows, Grays GX10000 field hockey sticks, and Easton, DeMarini and Louisville Slugger bats. Randy removed several kettlebells, free weights, and dumbbells. "And there's this beauty." Randy removed a small metal baseball bat, painted pink and black. On the side, it read, "GIRL POWER." He smiled. "Nothing would make me happier than to beat this guy's ass with this bat. You guys are welcome to anything else." He hit the bat against his hand. "This one is mine."

Stanheight quickly went through the inventory. "This is all you got? No actual weapons? No guns? No chainsaws, kitchen knives, machetes, no harpoons?"

Randy shook his head. "I was just trying to run a business that would help people gain an advantage in the sports we play and maybe reach their weight loss goals faster. I wasn't really planning on arming the camp for World War III."

"No cell phones?" I said, in disbelief. "You got all this shit and no cell phones?"

"None. Sorry." Randy said, hanging his head a bit.

"That would be my fault. We raided the locker where he kept them." Sarge said, before turning to Randy and extending his hand. "You did good, Waterhouse. You may have just saved some lives." Turning to the rest of us, Sarge bellowed, "Grab whatever you need to stay alive. This night is far from over."

CHAPTER 30

The remaining campers and counselors gathered in the Mess Hall side of the Rec Center. Sarge stood before them. "I don't know any way to say this aside from it appears that what is happening right now is my fault. I tried to keep it under wraps, but Counselor Eric Schultz was disciplined for some things and eventually relieved of his duties here at Camp Wašíču. It appears that Eric is behind the attacks. I'm accepting responsibility for what's already occurred, but I will be damned if you think I'm going to let him continue without us fighting back. We may not have guns, knives, or chainsaws, but we do have sports equipment."

As Randy started handing some out, one kid I didn't know yelled, "Can we use the sports equipment we normally have for working out and save this stuff for the next time we play?" The other campers laughed nervously, but we all knew how serious this situation was. Almost everyone had seen Georgie's body. There was no doubt among any of us what was out there. The doubt was with whether or not we could survive it.

Counselor Greg Munson stepped forward. "I think a good majority of you know my wife. She's not here tonight, because she went to visit family, but if I learned anything at all from her, it's that you must stand up to bullies. I know this isn't the same level as someone calling you fat or homosexual or whatever things you guys say about one another these days; but the idea behind it is the same. I, for one, am not going to let some asshole take everything from me. I'm going to put up a hell of a fight to ensure that doesn't happen."

Sarge smiled. "Thank you, Greg. Guys, it comes down to this. I'm not encouraging anyone to go out there and stalk this bastard down and fight him head-on. I just want you to have a way to protect yourselves if need be. To me, the way that makes the most sense is if we all stay in the Rec Center for the night. There is strength in numbers and there's a hell of a lot of us in this building right now."

Emily stood up, "Why don't we just leave?"

Sarge stared at her. "It's five miles to the nearest town. Six miles to the nearest gas station. Where would you like us to go?"

"To that town."

"All the cars have their tires slashed. We'd have to walk." Greg interjected.

"So, we walk." Emily said.

Sarge waved his hands to calm everyone, as the room exploded into a hundred mini conversations. "By the time we got there, it would be past midnight. Besides that, we have no idea what would be waiting for us out there. Eric was a trained military man. He might have guns ready to plow us down if we present ourselves as targets."

"Wouldn't he have already—" Emily tried.

"—The point is we're safer right here, at least until morning. But if you guys want to take a vote, you're more than welcome. Anyone else in favor of walking the five miles uphill to Burlington?" He stood, looking around the room, his hands on his hips. No one else raised their hands. "There you go. We stay here."

Emily shot Sarge one of the worst looks I've ever seen. "You stay here. I'm going."

She stormed out the door. I followed as quickly as I could, attempting to pull my pants up in the process. Nicole followed behind me with Seth behind her. Emily reached the parking lot and stopped moving, allowing me to catch up with her. Leaning over the front of the Ford Escape, she hid her tears behind her hands. "This is absolutely ridiculous, guys. We can't stay here. We'll just get killed."

Nicole said, "I don't know. Maybe it's safer to stay. Like Sarge said—"

Emily's face emerged from her hands, the tears instantly replaced with anger. "Are you kidding me right now? You think it's safer to stay in the place where someone is literally stabbing people with a machete? I'm going."

As Emily crossed the parking lot, the three of us were completely lost, with no idea what to do. "WAIT!" A voice yelled. Counselor Greg came up the hill to the parking lot. "Emily, please. Don't leave yet."

"What?"

Greg jogged over until he was standing next to her. He spoke quietly, but I could make some of it out. "I'm not kidding. I can't keep them in the Rec Center without you. But two cheerleaders? Those guys are going anywhere you go." Except for a walk, apparently. "Stay here to keep them here so they're safe." As Emily looked around, trying to decide what to do, Greg added, "I will personally make sure nothing happens to you. Just please don't go. It'll be chaos, otherwise."

Two hours passed as we all just hung out with the sporting equipment weapons we'd picked. Sarge unlocked the knives, but most people didn't want them. A knife meant being too close. A field hockey stick or a baseball bat allowed for some distance from The Killer. Most of us knew if we were close enough to use any of these weapons, it might be too late for us, but we still took the longer reach weapons over the short; and we sat holding them or playing with them or at least had them within arm's reach while we watched a movie in the multipurpose room. Other kids went to the gym to play ball or stretched out on the bleachers.

Greg returned from the gym area, walking over to Sarge. "Why don't you try to get to some sleep? We're gonna be here all night and at least one of us needs to be awake for it."

Sarge yawned. "I just don't understand where the Sheriff is."

Greg smiled, trying to make a joke. "Come on, Sarge. You know he probably got stopped by one of the Hochstein sisters and can't get her to shut up long enough for him to leave." Sarge didn't break. "Maybe Sir Robert of the Lake got him?" Nothing "Tough crowd. But really, it's a town the size of my big toe. If I was the sole cop on duty tonight, I wouldn't want to blast in here with a killer either. I'd wait till backup arrived from county."

"Something smells off."

"Sarge, a bunch of the kids entrusted into our care are dead. They're not coming back. And I know you don't want to think about that right now, but that's what smells off. All we can do is take care of as many of these other kids as we can." Sarge nodded, trying not to show any emotion. Greg leaned in. "Go take a nap, Sarge. I got this."

Sarge made eye contact with Greg. "What do you think? Am I making the right choice? Maybe we should make the walk to Burlington?"

Greg looked around, trying to ensure people like me weren't listening before he answered. "Absolutely not. I think that's the fastest way to have a larger pile of bodies."

Sarge clapped Greg on the shoulder. "You're a good man, Munson."

Sarge went down the hall. Obi yelled to Greg, "What's Sir Robert of the Lake?"

Greg waved him off. "It's just a dumb old legend."

Obi's smile spread wide. "Do tell!"

Greg sat down on the arm of the couch. "Well, I mean, I don't know if there's a lot to tell. It's something campers used to tell here twenty-five years ago when I was a kid and came here for summer camp."

"You were fat?" Seth asked.

Greg smiled. "I was overweight. Yes. I came to tune it up some before the season started. Focus. Get my mind on track. Anyway, the legend says there's an old hermit that lives around here. No one's ever seen his house or any evidence of where he goes. He doesn't talk much when you do see him. He's the real grumpy, loner type. Nobody knows his past or his life story. Hell, I think he probably works hard to keep it that way. That's what happens when you reach that age. You decide not to tell anyone anything. My cabinmate when I lived here claimed to have seen Sir Robert out by the lake, fishing. Only he uses his cane instead of a pole or net. My cabinmate tried to help him, but Old Sir Robert would sooner hit you with the cane than let you help him. Sir Robert swung that cane but lost his balance and fell into the lake. My cabinmate wanted to jump in, but Robert wouldn't have it. The old man went under and came back up repeatedly. And that's how he earned his other nickname."

"Which is?" Obi asked, sucked into the story.

Greg smiled with too many teeth. "Sir Robert the Bob."

Obi swung the throw pillow, hitting Greg in the shoulder as the two laughed. "That's a horrible joke."

"I'll be right back. I need to whiz." Greg stood up and disappeared around the corner as Obi repeated, "Sir Robert the Bob…"

Finding a chair in an empty office, Sarge slumped into it and said a little prayer. He hadn't more than closed his eyes for five minutes when The Killer made his presence known.

CHAPTER 31

Using a brand-new basketball that they'd gotten from Randy's never-ending supply of sports equipment, four much younger kids I didn't know had taken to the gym. Kyle Messineo was the largest of the four and constantly had to adjust his pants while trying to dribble. The boys were lined up for a jump ball for their 2 on 2 game after they'd finally scored a third basket. Kyle's partner, Vincent Alesio dribbled the ball on the outdated painted logo on the floor. The large dragon on the hardwood hadn't represented the local high school team in over twenty years, since they built the new complex in Burlington. A glass case, empty of its trophies and other awards, stood against the cinder block wall at the far end of the gym; the multiple layers of dust a reminder of just how long ago that had been.

Kyle and his friends repeatedly checked the multiple double doors, on the off chance The Killer they'd heard so much about decided to make an entrance, but they failed to notice when he entered through a single door just off the right side of the curtained stage. Passing old audio equipment left over from past school programs, the man holding the machete looked out at the four kids, smiling as they failed at basketball one last time. He dropped from the stage area onto a small pile of wrestling mats, briefly losing his balance. That momentary window was their only hope of escape, but the boys were too busy arguing over whether an elbow to the side had been intentional or not. By the time they heard his boots clanking on the floor in a rhythmic fashion, it was too late.

Dr. Munson told me once that most people talk about flight or fight. But she had a third. Freezing. She sat in front of me, without the desk between us. Her perfect legs framed by a white skirt which was tight, but not uncomfortably so. It made some of my clothes more uncomfortable, but that's neither here nor there.

"We've already discussed fight and flight. But what you're currently describing is freezing. It's the Third F." My cousin in college lived by three f's, but they were very different. "When confronted with sudden danger, most people's instinctive response is not to fight or to run away. The very first response is stop moving and stay absolutely still. Often, people who think they know exactly what they would do in such a situation often find themselves stuck, even for an instant. It's pretty fascinating, really. It is the result of a survival skill needed in prehistoric times, when freezing was the best choice. Large predators lose interest in prey that isn't moving. If you can't beat up a saber-toothed tiger with your fists and you can't outrun him, your best option is to play dead and that's exactly what our ancestors did. Today, we make the mistake of still doing this. It's ingrained in our DNA at this point. They say it can feel pleasant. Instead of panic, one might experience comfort. Warm fuzzies. Possible even the sensation of floating."

Kyle and his friends felt none of that. They were filled with fear. Eduardo was unable to run at all, but the other three at least attempted to move toward the door. The machete ripped through Eduardo's midsection before he could scream. The Killer was fast, no longer walking in a rhythmic fashion, but instead catching Kyle's other friends right away. Logan's head didn't come all the way off, but hung from his neck in a sick fashion, only snapping free as his body bounced off the shiny hardwood, coating the worn Dragons logo in a new coat of deep red.

Vincent's sneakers squeaked as he ran into the boys' bathroom; his flopping shoe string bounced back and forth as he went. Kyle tried to follow his friend, but a gloved hand caught his arm, yanking him backward.

Kyle tried to fight, jumping up, planting both feet into the attacker's knee. The Killer released his grip for a second, allowing Kyle to turn away; but he caught Kyle's shirt, pulling him back. He gripped the back of Kyle's head, slamming him full force into the drinking fountain. Fragments of teeth fell from each corner of his mouth. His orbital bone exploded; his face instantly drooping like that of a stroke victim. As he hit the floor, Kyle's only solace was that he couldn't see the machete heading for his chest.

Even all these years later, the small bathroom/locker room mix reeked of sweat, feet, and warm bodies. Vincent searched the room frantically for a way out but found none. The fourteen-year-old climbed onto one of the stools, holding the sides of the stall for stability. An ache in his back burned as the stress tightened his muscles. Breaths tore in and out of his chest as he attempted to get them under control.

The black boots connected with the linoleum tile in the same rhythmic fashion they'd hit the shiny hardwood with in the gymnasium. Vincent's chubby fingers clenched, his nails digging into the powder-coated steel frames of the stall, as he tried to maintain his balance.

A single line of sweat dripped from the back of his neck down the center of Vincent's shirt. He closed his eyes, trying to recite the Lord's Prayer, but getting no further than "forgive those who trespass against us" when the echoing steps stopped. The Killer was on the opposite side of the room. For a second, Vincent thought he could make it. He'd jump down, open the door and run to the exit.

He'd clear the gym doors and out to the multipurpose room with so many others. But The Killer started walking again. And this time didn't stop until his heels clicked together directly in front of Vincent's stall door.

The Killer flung the door open, but Vincent was ready. Steadying himself against the steel walls, the fourteen-year-old kicked the door as hard as he could, momentarily stunning the man with the machete. As the door opened again, Vincent dove off the toilet, driving his knee into The Killer's face. The two fell to the floor. The kid was up first, pivoting toward the door. The gloved hand shot out, barely missing Vincent. The flopping shoelace slapped against the ground with every step, but Vincent didn't notice as he turned toward the double doors of the gym for a second attempt at escaping his death. He threw the door open, screaming for help. The Killer ducked back into the bathroom, furious with himself for letting the kid get away. Sarge's voice echoed from the hall.

He hadn't even realized he'd dozed off until the screams woke him. The Alesio kid threw open the double door with a clang, screaming for help. Sarge grabbed the Louisville Slugger next to him and ran into the hallway. The vision of the three mutilated bodies in the gym sent Sarge's mind back to Iraq. Throwing one arm around Vincent, Sarge carried him toward the Multipurpose room. With no idea who touched him, Vincent threw two elbows at Sarge's chest before realizing he wasn't The Killer.

"Everyone remain calm—" Sarge yelled from the hallway, but it was too late.

The Multipurpose stood mostly empty. Over half the campers had panicked and run. Through the windows, Sarge saw, to his horror, the residents of Camp Wašíču running in all different directions. And he knew whatever little hope he'd had of protecting them was gone.

CHAPTER 32

Sarge stared at me. "Why would they do that? Why would they just run?"

"I tried to stop them. It didn't work. They heard the screams and just bolted." I stood, holding another bat. Glancing around, Nicole held a field hockey stick and Seth had a third bat. I checked to make sure Emily still had her hockey stick, but she was nowhere to be found. "Where's Emily?"

The others looked around, but before anyone could say anything, he was on us. Bolting down the hallway, The Killer swung wildly, stabbing Jared in the shoulder blade. Jared fell to the floor more to get away than anything. The machete swung directly at Sarge, but the bat came up in time to stop it. "Run!" Sarge yelled to the rest of us. Most of the campers still in the Rec Center left, but Seth and Nicole and I stayed. I swung the bat; barely missing The Killer, but I'd also almost hit Sarge. Nicole's hockey stick connected with The Killer's gut. The hooded killer bent forward. She brought the stick down on his back. He recoiled, yelping loudly in pain. As she brought the stick down again, The Killer caught it with one hand, yanked it out of hers, and turned it on her. The thin side of the butt end cracked down on her wrist. Nicole grabbed her arm, instantly crying out in pain.

Sarge and I fought until The Killer was literally backed against the wall. Sarge screamed, "We got him!"

We didn't. The Killer slid across the wall in my direction and powered past me. His boot hit my shin, missing my right knee by mere inches, but the pain was incredible. He ran out the front door. Sarge followed.

In a moment I'm not proud of at all, I sank to the floor, crying. "We need to go. Emily was right. We need to get you to a hospital."

Nicole shot back. "I'm fine."

"You're fine?"

"Light swelling. Total discoloration. Can't feel my hand. Yeah. Sure. I'm good."

"Stop screwing around, Nicole. We need to go."

"We can't go!" She shouted back. "I'm not leaving here without Emily."

I threw my arms out. "We'll probably find her on the way. There's no way she stayed here. She's on the highway walking to town."

My anger subsided as tears streamed down her face. "It's broken, Phillip. He broke my fucking wrist."

Seth helped her sit down on the couch. He looked at her wrist. "Yeah, that's broken. Phillip, can you help her? I need to help Jared."

In acts that made him more of a legend than Frank Doyle could ever wish to be, Seth helped four kids recover from their injuries. He made tourniquets to stop bleeding. He got ice. He helped Jared clean out his shoulder. I saw a side of my friend I'd never seen, and while my sister had a broken wrist, she could handle that herself while Seth taught me how to help the others.

Obi ran with the others, but not to get away. He followed Emily. When she went out the door in the group, he saw Seth and I were distracted and just instinctively went with her. Emily ran almost a full football length before flipping around, "Are you going to follow me all the way to Burlington?"

He shook his head. "Not if you keep running this way. Burlington is behind us."

Emily stopped, looking up at the moon. "You're right. What was I thinking?"

"Can we at least go get the others first? There's safety in numbers."

Emily's arms stretched as far as they could go as her hair hung in her face. "You guys keep saying that, but that dude with the machete just murdered a bunch of kids. And guess what? They were together."

"Let's at least move out of the main area so we're harder to find." Obi pointed toward the archery range.

They crossed into the unlit open field. The green grass was slightly damp from the sprinklers, which had only recently turned off. The flags barely flapped, indicating almost no wind in the moment. Obi pointed to the hay bales, inhaling their fragrance. "We could hide behind those."

"In an area filled with bow racks and hangers? Are you nuts?"

Obi scanned the area, looking at the concrete shooting pads behind the shooting line, the picnic tables, and the hangers themselves. "Actually, yes. We can get weapons."

"I'm not good at archery." Emily said.

"You don't have to be. Metal-tipped arrows can do a lot of damage even if you don't know how to fire them at someone." The wind picked up, sliding through the long grass as they moved toward the bow hangers. Obi didn't bother with the actual compound bows hanging at eye level. He grabbed six arrows for himself and six for Emily. "With any luck, he'll never be close enough to us to need to try this."

She shook her head. "I know me. I'll get injured faster carrying those."

The two walked in silence. Emily followed with no idea where Obi was taking her; not realizing he wasn't sure either. When screams erupted from the nearby forest, Obi and Emily ran the distance to his cabin.

The sprinklers turned on in the fields surrounding the forest. Shirts suctioned to moobs. The grass became a slippery mess. The sporting equipment some kids still held became harder to control and many potential weapons were left behind as the campers disappeared into the forest.

But The Killer knew the forest better than anyone and used it to his advantage. Most of his victims in the next few minutes were kids I'd either never seen or didn't know well. Many I had never even heard their names before that point. We didn't have a lot of interaction with the younger kids. Blame the Hierarchy of Bullies again.

I can't tell you a lot of their names, but I can tell you that it didn't take long for the machete to find each one and put an end to an additional nine lives between the trees that night.

CHAPTER 33

Obi stared out the cabin window with Emily right behind him. She paced back and forth. "This isn't helpful. We need to get out of here. How? How can we get out of here?"

"If I knew that, we wouldn't be here."

"What if we change the tires on the car?"

"Do you have four spares?" Obi asked, without turning around to look at her.

"No, of course not. But there are what? Ten cars in the parking lot? If we take spares from some of the others and change them, we can get out."

"Have you ever changed a tire?" Emily stared at the floor, but Obi knew the answer. "Yeah, me neither. Plus, we don't have keys to the other cars to get the spare tires. Not to mention I doubt you have keys to Nicole's car anyway." He flipped around. "Wait, *do* you have keys to her car?"

"No."

"Let's get them. So, the tires are sliced. Who cares? We can still get a little way. I bet we could drive into town even without tires."

"Do you know that we could or are you hoping we could?"

"I don't have any idea."

Emily smiled. "I'm in. Let's just get out of here."

Obi stood up, striking a superhero pose. "To the Rec Center."

"For what?"

"To get the keys, remember?" Obi was amazed at her seemingly deteriorating memory.

"How do we know if Nicole is still there?" Emily asked, as they stepped onto the porch of the cabin, the door closing behind them.

"Man, I wish you would've asked me that before we came outside." Obi scanned the area and started his mission to get Emily to the Rec Center safely.

"Obi. Thank god. Someone else is still alive." Obi's head turned so fast his neck popped. Randy Waterhouse held his Girl Power bat. "I'm going with you guys. Wherever you're going." Obi nodded and led the way to the Rec Center.

Sarge, Seth, Nicole and I left the Rec Center in a group, the males with their weapons drawn. Nicole continued to nurse her injury. Seth said, "What if we head for the locker room? There are a lot of places to hide if we need to."

Sarge didn't make eye contact as he said, "I think that's a good plan for the ladies, Jenkins. Why don't you take them there and make sure they're safe? I'm going to put an end to this."

"What about me?" I asked.

Sarge looked me in the eye. "I figured you're ready to make your own decisions."

Before I could say another word, we heard Obi's whistle. Two tones, the first low, the second higher. But it echoed like he was next to us. Then I saw Obi, Randy, and Emily running toward us. Obi pointed toward the Rec Center.

"Where are you going?" I asked.

"To the parking lot. We're gonna try to drive the car out of here." Emily replied.

"It doesn't have tires."

"It will still drive." She said, staring into my soul.

"You can't be serious. Mom would kill us." Nicole responded.

Randy's head moved like a bobblehead as he said, "There's a guy who's going to literally kill us if we don't find a way out of here."

Sarge stared at us all in disbelief. "What do they teach you in school? You can't do that. You can take a flat tire about 200 yards before you'll do horrific damage. We are five grueling uphill miles from Burlington. You would destroy the car. And you won't get away. On top of that, you'll become his top priority. You think he's letting anyone leave this place?"

"Back to the Rec Center then," I said.

Seth shook his head emphatically. "The locker rooms. I'm telling you, we can hide there. Plus, we'll throw him off and go in the girls' locker room."

Obi and I stared in awe. "The girls' locker room?" I said.

Obi was stunned. "We have a girls' locker room?"

"See? He'll never look for us there. Let's go."

We walked through the cabins on our way to the locker rooms. Halfway through, he appeared, standing dead center, in the middle of the dirt path, between my cabin and the one across from it. The machete rotated in his hand as he invited us to come closer. I looked behind us, trying to analyze how much room we had and whether we could escape. As I looked back, I realized he was getting closer. We quickly huddled up. Sarge said, "Scatter."

"Scatter?" we all said.

"I know what I've said. Just do it. You all know where you're going. I'll provide a distraction. Just get each other to safety." Before we could say another word, Sarge turned, readying his Louisville Slugger. But Randy and Obi had already gone. They were halfway to The Killer when Sarge yelled back to us, "Run. Now. Save each other." And we did.

Randy reached him first, swinging the Girl Power bat. The Killer caught it instantly with his right hand; the machete fell from his left stabbing vertically into the ground like a lawn dart. The bat ripped from Randy's hands. Randy tried to back up, but The Killer took one swing. The sound of the metal against Randy's skull echoed.

Obi saw this had been a mistake and backed away slowly. Holding the metal-tipped arrows behind him, he bunched them together. He would only get one shot. He knew that. "What do you say we just call it a draw and go home? He who fights and runs away lives to fight another day?" The Killer pulled the machete out of the ground, moving closer to Obi. With nowhere to go, Obi said, "If you strike me down, I shall become more power—"

The machete lodged in Obi's skull, separating his eyes. His hand relaxed. The arrows cascaded to the ground. He slumped to his left side, dead before he hit the ground. The Killer pulled on the machete, but it wouldn't budge. Using a sawing motion, he finally got it free, but this added moment provided Sarge the time he needed to escape as well.

Even in the chaos, Seth smiled to himself as he crossed an accomplishment off his bucket list. He entered a girl's locker room with real high school cheerleaders in it. I arrived fourth, but took my time, wondering if anyone was there yet. I tried to emulate Obi's whistle as Seth waved me in. Emily grabbed me instantly. Wrapping her arms around me, she buried her head in my chest. "I was so scared that you wouldn't make it."

My hand cupped the small of her back as she looked up. Wiping a tear from her eye, I leaned in and kissed her.

"Teenagers." Sarge's voice called. "We're gonna be killed and you're over here making out." We laughed, but Sarge didn't. He didn't even make eye contact with me. "Alright, Jenkins, what's next?"

"We'll wait for Randy and Obi and we'll—"

We all fell silent as Sarge broke down into tears.

CHAPTER 34

Cuddled together in the women's bathroom, Seth and the two girls stayed mostly silent. Nicole dozed off here and there. Emily worked hard not to. Seth was too concerned about Nicole's hand to fall asleep. He made sure it was always placed somewhere it wasn't likely to get injured.

CRRRCHT!

Sarge reached for his walkie, turning it way down as Greg Munson's voice came over the walkie. "This is Counselor Greg Munson. If anyone can hear this, please respond." Sarge sat silently for a second, staring at the walkie. "Repeat. This is Counselor Greg Munson. If anyone can hear this, please respond." It was silent for several seconds. "To anyone who can hear this, I need help. I am alone. I believe I may be the only counselor left at Camp Wašíču. Most of my coworkers and many of the children who were here have been brutally murdered. We need assistance. The phone lines are down. All vehicles have been put out of order. Repeat. We need help at—". There was a loud noise in the background and then it sounded like massive amounts of wind.

"He's running." Sarge said, mostly to himself. "He's not going to make it either."

"Eric! No. Stop. We can talk about this. Eric! ERIC!" The walkie-talkie went dead after that. There was no further sound.

Sarge looked around the room at us. "We can't keep sitting here. The ladies were right. We need to chance it. We need to head to Burlington. It's the only way. This isn't going to end, otherwise."

Nicole pointed at the radio. "Aren't you going to respond to him?"

Sarge stared at the floor, embarrassed. "No. I don't know who else is listening. You've said before The Killer has a walkie. I can't take the chance he figures out where we are based on that.

As if on cue, the metal door of the men's locker room in the other half of the building clanged loudly, reverberating through the otherwise silent building. Sarge held one finger to his mouth to tell us all to be quiet. Seth moved to turn off the lights, but I motioned him not to. Pulling him close, I whispered directly in his ear, "They're always on. If we turn them off now, he'll notice." But my bigger concern was that we couldn't win in the dark.

We waited for what seemed like an eternity as The Killer stalked through the boys' locker room, opening the stalls and checking showers. He eventually stopped. We heard his boots tap the wooden floor in the open area that was once a half-court gymnasium. As I looked at Nicole, holding her wrist, fighting back the pain, my stomach churned with hot fury. I was done running from him. I grabbed my baseball bat and walked out without a word to the others.

I heard Nicole mumble, "What the f…" but I knew Seth held her back.

As I exited the girls' locker room, The Killer stood ten feet away, facing the other direction. I ran at him, faster than I'd ever run for anything. I lowered my head and extended my arm, hitting the most picture-perfect tackle of my life. I knocked him to the ground, the machete bouncing on the old hardwood. I rolled on top of him, punching him in the face. My fist reverberated off the hard-plastic mask. So, I punched him full force in the throat. The Killer rolled hard, grabbing his neck in pain, knocking me off in the process. Rolling to my right, I grabbed for the machete. He grabbed the bat I'd dropped.

The two of us circled one another. I stopped moving as I realized I was the only person standing between him and the girls' locker room. I couldn't let him get to the others. Staring at one another, we each gripped the other's weapon. "You really are a fat piece of crap." He said.

"Yeah, I had terrible counselors and never figured out how to lose weight."

"Always blaming someone else, McCracken. Do you ever accept responsibility for what you did?"

The words wounded me, but I tried to blow it off like they didn't. "Cut the crap, Eric. This is over. Greg called the police. They're on their way. Sarge got the girls out of here. Everyone's going to know what you did."

"I'm not worried about a couple of teenage sluts. And your little friend Greg won't be calling anyone anymore." He circled again. "You know you can't win."

"You're the one who isn't going to win." I said, calmly. "I'm sick of being bullied. I'm sick of watching my friends be bullied. I've spent my entire life being pushed around by your type. I'm not doing it anymore. I'm sick of being ashamed of who I am because you don't approve. I am fat. I do jack off constantly. And you know what? I don't give a shit what you think about that."

I swung the machete, but he knocked it out of my hand with the bat. He swung the bat and somehow missed me. I dove at his legs, hitting his knee straight on. The bat fell out of his hand, hitting me in the back. Pain soared through my lumbar region, but I managed to get to my feet. As I did, he launched at me, machete pointed straight at my heart. There was nothing I could do. Nowhere to go.

Sarge appeared between us, having run out of the girl's locker room. The blade sank into Sarge's shoulder as he grabbed me, eyes wide. "Run!"

"But—"

"—Run, Goddamn it."

And I did.

Blood ran from Sarge's shoulder to the floor as he threw punch after punch, connecting with The Killer's chest. He swung for the stomach, but The Killer dodged. The machete zipped through the air twice, but Sarge managed to escape it. He kicked The Killer's shin. His opponent lunged forward with the machete, but Sarge wrapped his arms around The Killer, who went dead weight, forcing both men to the floor. Trying to lock The Killer in a choke hold, Sarge sat on the ground with his feet extended. The man with the machete tried to fight it off.

I'd run into the girls' locker room, but I had no intention of leaving. Emily ran toward me, but I stopped her. "You guys need to get out of here. Now."

"So, let's go." Emily said, barely audibly.

"I'm not coming with you."

Nicole slapped me on the arm with her good hand as each word came out. "You're being ridiculous."

"I have to stay and help Sarge. Someone needs to stop him."

"How are *you* going to stop him?" Nicole said what every fiber in my body had been screaming for the last hour. I had no idea. I just knew it was right. And I knew I was the most expendable if it didn't work out.

"One of us needs to make it home, Nicole. I told you, mom can't handle—"

"—Don't lay this on mom. You always blame her, but she did fine with Dad's death. She took care of everything else. She planned the funeral and she paid the bills and she made sure everything was taken care of and the *only* thing she didn't do was comfort you. So, don't you dare."

"I love you, Nicole. You guys need to go." I pointed at the metal exit door that led to the woods.

"Phillip…. Please."

I turned away. "Seth. Get her out of here."

CHAPTER 35

As I entered the old gym, Sarge had his legs wrapped around The Killer's throat as the two splashed around on the laminated wood like wrestlers jockeying for position at a state championship meet. Sarge leaned back, grimacing with concentration as his legs worked to choke out his opponent. The Killer's arm reached out as far as possible, his hand desperately opening and closing, searching for a way out. As his fingers found the machete handle, he'd found his exit.

My own fingers wrapped around the handle of my bat as I grabbed it from the floor. I stood just as the machete cut into Sarge's upper leg. Howling with pain, Sarge released the choke hold. The Killer slid free and was on his feet in seconds. The machete point sat directly between Sarge's eyes as the Killer hissed, "Suffer."

I swung the bat. The Killer dodged it and ran toward the far door, calling, "You can't save him and stop me." Now at a safe distance, The Killer pointed his blade at me as he taunted, "I'd sure hate for you to spend your life thinking you could have saved your second father." The words formed a brick wall, stunning me in my tracks. I couldn't move.

I was back in Dr. Munson's office. That day I'd been holding the tissue box and hadn't stopped crying. It was the anniversary of my dad's death and she'd made extra time to see me. Telling her stories about my dad and his weird habits and sayings made me laugh which only made me cry more. Dr. Munson asked if I felt I'd ever find another role model.

"I'm not sure. To me, your parents are your role models. Everyone else is just a hero; someone you look up to and you hope to emulate, but you probably fall short, no matter how hard you try." I paused before adding. "Maybe Sarge. I hate him the same way I hated my dad some days. They both made me feel like I could do anything while making me do things I knew I couldn't do. Dad made me work on cars. I still don't understand them at all. Sarge makes me run the obstacle course and I can't see over my stomach enough to not trip. Maybe that's not the same."

She smiled. "I don't think it matters if it's the same thing. I think it matters how it makes you feel."

It made me feel uncomfortable. I stayed away from Sarge as much as possible after I made the connection.

Now, as he lay bleeding, possibly dying, I saw my dad in him even more. Everything from the grunts of pain to his insistence he was just fine, and no one needed to help. The difference was that I couldn't stop cancer. I could possibly stop the bleeding.

I gathered towels from the locker rooms. Sarge turned them into tourniquets. As I helped, I prayed silently that my friends had made it out of camp before The Killer made it out of the building. The vision of the three of them lying right outside the front door, sliced to pieces, their heads centered on their mutilated carcasses was too clear to unsee.

His walkie-talkie pulled me back to reality.

Crrcht! "If anyone can hear me, please help."

"He's alive!" I said, spinning around to Sarge. He waved at me to be quiet.

Counselor Greg continued. "Honey, if you're listening and you can hear this, run. Don't stay here. Don't try to find me or save me. It's too late for me. Save yourself."

My eyes grew, picturing Dr. Munson hiding somewhere trying to escape The Killer. My fist clenched as I imagined her, impaled on his machete, blood running out of her chest. Staring at Sarge, I whispered. "I'll find her."

"The hell you will. You take your friends and you go. Right now. If Munson is still alive, she's doing fine on her own. If she's not, you're wasting your time." He pushed harder on his leg to stop the bleeding.

Greg cut in again. "Honey, I love you. Please run. He's here. He's coming." His fear escalated. "I'm not going to make it. Run, babe. You're our only hope now." The walkie cut out and didn't come back on.

Sarge shook his head slowly. "That was the last counselor." Looking me square in the eyes, Sarge bit his lower lip. "You're in charge now, McCracken. Get them outta here. Wait. Here. Take this." He held out his walkie-talkie to me. "Don't ever talk on it. Use it solely to hear if anyone else is talking on it. Eric could be listening to anything."

"You need to keep that, Sarge."

"What do you think I'm gonna do with it?" Before I could respond, he said, "McCracken, I know what you think I think of you. But you could not be more incorrect. You're one of the best campers we've ever had at this camp. I want you to know that. You can do anything if you just start believing in yourself. I wish you could see what I see, Son."

Never good at taking compliments, I deflected. "I'm no Frrrrraaaank Doyle, Sarge."

"No one is. There is no Frank Doyle."

I piled wrestling mats under his arms to help him hold his position. "What? What do you mean?"

"We made him up. Well, not even me. The counselors before me. He's just a story we use to inspire you guys. We set realistic records a kid could break if he tried hard enough. Frank's just a motivator. And sometimes he works and sometimes he doesn't." I stared in disbelief. Sarge held eye contact with me. "McCracken, if I make it out of this, I have someone I can actually tell kids about next year. If there is a next year. You're the real deal, kid. Now get out of here."

I shook my head. "What about you? I can't just leave you alone."

"You can, and you will. I'll be just fine."

My eyes met his again. "What if he comes back for you?"

Sarge shrugged. "Then at least he's not with you guys. You did good, McCracken." He pointed at the door. "Now get the fuck outta here."

CHAPTER 36

I knew something was wrong. I was only fifteen, but I knew. I ignored it like most things. I may have been 280 pounds, but I was still a normal, angsty teenager who was too cool for my parents and my sister. My family didn't fight a lot or anything like that, but we all lived our own lives. Nicole had just gotten her driver's license and was gone more often than she was home. I spent my time in my room on the net or listening to music with deep, haunting lyrics. I didn't want to discuss my day with them. I didn't want to tell them how people made me feel. I didn't need to lay out the BS I dealt with on a daily basis. It was easier to game and chug Mountain Dew and destroy Doritos.

One Saturday night, they told me we had to have dinner as a family. We had to talk. Nicole was furious. One of her friends was having a sleepover and all the cool kids were there and we were ruining her life. I was annoyed because we had a raid planned and the others were playing without me but ran their mouths nonstop about me not being available after planning it all week.

My dad looked worn out, like he hadn't slept in days. It was the first time I realized I didn't look directly at him as often as I assumed I did. How long had he looked like this? The tough guy from my childhood had been replaced with a man half my size wearing a T-shirt with a cigarette ad on it and some shorts that resembled swim trunks but weren't. His foot exited and entered his hushpuppy slippers repeatedly as he tried to find his words.

"As you guys have probably heard, I've been having some minor health issues. I had some blood in my urine—"

"—Gross!" Nicole yelled.

Dad ignored her and kept going, but mom shot her the glare of death. "So, I've been seeing some doctors, per your mother's request. They've run several tests trying to figure things out."

My face burned while I muttered, "Why didn't you tell me? I would've gone with you." I wondered if he believed me any more than I did.

"I didn't want to scare anyone until I knew for sure what was going on. Your mom and I have talked about it a few times. You may have overheard some things. So, I just wanted all of us to get together so you'd hear the true stuff instead of coming up with details on your own."

"Are you going to die?" Nicole blurted out. Her face was already puffy as she teared up.

"Well, uh, I mean, we're going to fight it." Dad smiled. "It's bladder cancer. And it's a very treatable condition."

Only it wasn't a very treatable condition. Many forms of bladder cancer are, but Dad's was aggressive. Chemo didn't do anything. Experimental treatments didn't fix it. Prayer didn't work. Nothing did.

Staring into the gift shop window behind the coffee shop, I waited for my name to be called. My ears locked in on the grind, gurgle and hiss as the barista mixed my drink. Her friend packaged the six granola bars I'd ordered (I made it a point to say that I needed to bring enough for everyone, but I think the fact I only had one drink tipped them off). The magazines, comics, stuffed animals, and comfort items of the gift shop made me wish I could ignore where I was and just enjoy being a kid again.

I carried the food and my drink down the pale stretch of hallway; a private collection of metal doors with push button access, leading to further pain, fear, and disease. With each step, my shoes pounded against the shiny tile floor, reflecting the overhead florescent lighting. It was depressing to consider what lay behind each door, but it was also freeing. I didn't have to fake a smile or pretend everything was okay. There were no relatives trying desperately to keep the conversation light while not even attempting to cloak the pity in their eyes. There were no flowers to brighten the space; no color in this world of muted paint, undecorated walls and bright lighting. There was no false hope. No, these bland hallways spoke only the truth: Life isn't fair.

Entering the oncology ward, I was met with a combination of pine cleaner, astringent chemicals, and bodily fluids. These melted into the smell of some indeterminable hot food aroma, as it was almost lunch time. Let's just say it didn't make me hungry. He shifted as I entered the room, the bed creaking loudly, followed by his groan of pain.

It hadn't even been a year since The Talk in the dining room and we were nearing the end. He knew it and I knew it. He didn't always seem like it though. That day, he looked a little older and a little greyer, but his spirits were up, and we chatted for two full hours. I was hopeful but knew the odds of turning it around were not good.

The next few days were the opposite. He needed more pain medication. He was hardly coherent. Barely awake. Could almost never eat and when he did, he couldn't keep it down. He couldn't use the bathroom on his own and I couldn't handle the blood coming from that part of his body. I was useless.

He would awaken and beg to come home. That wasn't an option. Mom and Nicole and I weren't trained to take care of him. I slept in the visitors' room every night, waking up almost hourly, expecting the news. He came through every day that week, breaking my heart in a different way. As long as he was alive, so was his pain.

The second to last day, he seemed better. More aware of things. He asked to speak to each of us individually. Mom and I have never discussed what was said. Nicole and I only shared minor details. I still won't share them with you now. That's something I have that only belongs to me. But I will tell you one small part of it.

He held my hand. It hurt, but he adjusted himself in the bed to look directly at me. "I need you to promise me that you'll look after Nicole and your mom." He cut me off before I could speak. "No. You're the man of the house now. You can grieve for a while, but you need to be strong for them." Those words, and my consistent inability to live up to that demand, haunted me for longer than I care to admit.

Dr. Munson listened to the whole story without interrupting; aside from handing me more tissues. When I finished, she sat silently, letting the words roll through her mind for a minute. She pulled herself forward in her chair, straightening the skirt on her suit. "Thank you for sharing that with me. I know it wasn't easy. I'm going to say something to you and I want you to understand that I am not discounting anything your father said to you. Okay? But you need to be freed from the promise you think you made."

My eyes shot to the floor as my eye lids drooped over them. "What do you mean?"

"Phillip, you're a mess." My laughter bubbled past my tears. She smiled, placing a hand on my knee. "I mean that in the nicest way possible."

"Okay!" I said, the sarcasm dripping out of my mouth.

"Phillip, have you ever been on a plane?"

"Sure. But what does that—"

"Do you remember the speech the flight attendant gives? About the oxygen masks?"

"Yeah."

Dr. Munson wiped her blonde hair out of her face with her left hand; her red nails a sharp contract to the light locks. "And in the case of an emergency, what do you do first?"

I shrugged. "You put on your own mask."

She nodded emphatically. "Why?"

"Because you can't save anyone else until you save yourself."

"Phillip, I don't have the power to release you from the burden you gave yourself the day your father died, but you do. You have a lot more power than you think you do."

But, what Dr. Munson didn't know, is that sometimes the only way to save yourself is to save everyone else.

CHAPTER 37

Seth and Nicole held hands (her good hand) as they climbed the three flights of stairs to the Counselors' Quarters. Emily was right behind them, carrying two bats. Nicole's voice cracked as she said, "Why do you think he's doing it, Seth?"

"The Killer? Oh, could be a multitude of reasons. He could be possessed. He may be an escaped mental patient. He could have split personalities. He might have been born during a lunar eclipse. He could have even been the target of a prank twenty years ago and now he could be seeking revenge against people who have absolutely nothing to do with it. Maybe, just maybe he's not a man at all. Maybe it's the mother of a fat kid who drowned in our lake years ago and now she's gone crazy and she's killing people. OR! What if she's already dead and now his spirit is coming back for vengeance? It could just be a game he wants to play. There's really no way to tell."

Nicole rolled her eyes. "There are times I really hate you."

Emily stared out from the second landing. "Do you think Phillip made it?"

"Of course, he did." Seth said, with conviction. "He's a lot stronger than he thinks he is."

Nicole smiled. "Yeah, he is." She pointed up with her broken wrist. "But we need to keep moving." Seth and Nicole started the next flight, but Emily stayed for a brief moment; and in doing so, she saw a large man exit the locker rooms and stand in the moonlight, pulling up his pants.

"Guys! There he is!" She screamed.

Seth flipped around, almost knocking Nicole over. "The Killer?"

"No! Phillip!"

Unaware of their location, I turned toward the Rec Center. I planned to check the one place I thought Dr. Munson might hide that The Killer wouldn't have thought to look for her; the women's bathroom. Halfway to the front door of the Rec Center, I heard Seth let loose one hell of a whistle. The two tones, one low and the other high pitched, reached my ears and I turned, glancing around for them. The whistle hit again, but he held the second note longer, drawing it out into three beats. Looking up, I was mortified. Why were they going to the Counselors' Quarters of all places? They'd literally seen people killed there.

Then I realized that was true of the whole camp. They were going to try to use the phones again. Instinctively, I reached for my phone. Even after six weeks at camp, I did that sometimes. How I wished I could text Seth and tell him I needed to look for Dr. Munson. Glancing back at the Rec Center one more time, I moved toward the wooden stairs.

The walk through the middle of the cabins was lonelier than any walk I'd ever made. At each corner, I expected Eric Schultz in his hoodie and mask to jump out and stab me. Knowing Eric, he'd probably take all the money in my wallet as well. Not that I had my wallet, but that's what I told myself as I power walked. My shins and calves tightened as I walked faster than usual. I ignored it, pushing closer to the wooden stairs, but wishing I could go back and get in shape like Seth before this happened.

Emily met me at the bottom of the stairs. "We're gonna try the phone again."

"I figured."

"Why were you going to the Rec Center?" She asked, as we climbed.

"I'm looking for Doctor Munson. She might still be alive. Her husband seems to think so."

Nicole's eyes scrunched together. "I thought Greg said she was out of town."

Emily looked confused. "Yeah. And Seth said we were the only females here." She turned to him. "Remember? You said the nurse and the cook were gone so we'd have the girl's bathrooms to ourselves."

I just shrugged. I didn't know what to make of it, either, but I didn't have time to make sense of it right then. "Guys, I have to tell you something. Sarge isn't doing well. The Killer slashed his leg. He probably isn't going to make it."

I shook off the feeling of being in the hospital, making the call to Nicole when Dad finally passed away. I'd woken her up. It was two in the morning. *"He didn't make it."* Concentrating, I stared at Seth, focusing on him. Trying to keep myself grounded in the moment.

Seth stared at me. "That just leaves Greg."

"Maybe not even. On the walkie-talkie, it sounded like… like maybe…"

"We need to get help." Nicole said, saving me. "Like now."

"So, do we go back for the phones or try to make it to Burlington?" Emily asked. Her exhaustion was thick, permeating the air. There was no way she'd make it the full five miles. I wasn't sure how any of us would. I sucked up making the choice I knew no one wanted to be the one to make.

"Let's go to the phone. If that fails, we'll start the walk." I said, trying to sound like I was confident in my answer. "I know Greg already called the police, but we might as well do it again."

Seth's head rotated back and forth. "I don't think they're coming. I overheard Greg and Sarge talking about how there's only one cop in the town and he's about as useful as a sorcery speed counterspell." Immediately looking at each girl, Seth said, "I mean… as useful as an ashtray on a motorcycle."

Climbing to the top of the stairs at a speed that announced how much we didn't want to be there, I prepared myself for the worst. I fully expected a trap. The Killer had a walkie-talkie just like the counselors did. That meant he'd probably heard Greg's impassioned speech for his wife to run. The Killer had inevitably killed Greg while he was on the radio to instill fear into the rest of us who might be listening. I felt horrible knowing Dr. Munson might have been listening. I felt even worse knowing that she may not have been listening, because she may have been dead already. I expected to find her body, her throat slit, or her chest stabbed multiple times.

I shook it off, telling myself there was a chance she was totally fine. There was a chance she'd made it out alive and ran to Burlington for help.

But as I pulled open the front door of the Counselor's Quarters, I was met with something I didn't expect to find. Dr. Munson's husband lay on the floor, covered in blood.

Greg's right hand stretched for mine. "Help. Please? Help?"

CHAPTER 38

Running over to Greg, I helped him up. "It looks a lot worse than it is." He said. "We need to stop him. My wife. She may be up there. We're the only ones who can help her." He limped to one of the couches with my assistance. He barely put any pressure on his right ankle, which was covered in blood.

"Sorry for how it looks. Most of the blood isn't mine. At least not the blood up here." His hand made a circular motion over the middle of his chest. He stared at the floor ashamed of his next sentence. "I hid under a body to stay safe. I'm not proud of it, but I'm still here. I watched him go into the showers and I came up here as quickly as I could, looking for my wife."

He wiped a tear from his eye. "I haven't seen her at all during any of this. I have no idea if she's okay or not."

"I thought she was out of town."

Greg shifted on the couch; the leather scrunching and creaking as he did so. "I only announced that in hopes that if Eric was listening, he wouldn't go looking for her. But my wife is a fighter. I'd imagine she'd be able to hold her own against Eric. Anyway, I came here, looking for her. I checked all the rooms down here. I tried contacting her on the radio, hoping I could find her. No response."

"Greg, that doesn't mean anything. Sarge and I heard your broadcast. We didn't respond. And we were fine. She might be fine as well."

His head shot in my direction. "Sarge is okay?"

"Yeah. He was attacked, but he'll pull through." I hoped.

"Where is he now?"

"I'm not positive. I think he's still in the showers where I left him, but I have no way to know. I came directly here after that."

Greg's head bopped up and down. "I'm glad he's doing well. I thought I was the only one left." He held eye contact with Seth. "I mean, other than Eric, of course."

Seth's fist pumped open and closed. "I'd like to find him and show him a thing or two."

"He could be anywhere by now." Greg said. "When I returned here after using the radio, he was waiting for me. Tackled me. Sliced my ankle. That's why I can't put any weight on it."

"And you're sure it was Eric?" Nicole asked.

"I saw his face. When he sliced my ankles, he pulled down the hood and removed his little mask. He looked me in the eye and he said, 'Suffer.'"

Emily stood at the back, by the fireplace, trying to stay warm. The small amount of heat radiating from the burning logs was not enough to warm her as the draft from the broken window hit her in spurts. She picked up a trophy, carefully examining it. Her face drained of color as Greg finished.

"He got down, in front of me. He smiled and said, 'Now, I'm gonna go find your wife. And I'm gonna bring her back here. And I'm gonna fuck her in front of you. I'm gonna make you watch. And then? Then I'm gonna kill her in front of you.' And then he slapped me. Across the face. And said, 'By the time I'm done, you'll beg me to kill you.'"

White fury raged through me. The idea that anyone could even think that way about Dr. Munson, let alone say it aloud killed me. But as I looked at my sister and Emily, I couldn't help but wonder if Eric had the same thing planned for Seth and myself.

I talked to Nicole by the fireplace. It gave us the illusion of privacy without providing any. She played with the fire poker as I spoke. The wind whipped into the room through the broken window, moving her hair. "You and Emily need to take him out of here. You need to get off this property and—"

"And what? Carry his ass five miles to Burlington? I don't know the dude. First sign of danger, I'm dropping him."

I rolled my eyes. "You're ridiculous."

"Me? You want me to carry a dude with a sliced Achilles. And for what? So, you can play hero? Haven't you ever seen a horror movie? Women always win. We're the ones who kill the killer. We're the ones who break the curse."

"By that logic, it's gotta be me and Phil because virgins have to do it." Seth laughed. Nicole glared at him until he moved to talk to Greg again.

Looking back at me, she said, "Really, I don't get it. Why don't we all just face him together? That's what we need to do. Teamwork is the only way this is going to happen."

"One of us needs to make it out of here."

"There you go again, laying it all on mom."

My hand shot up in frustration. "I'm not laying it on mom. I'm not blaming mom. I'm telling you she can't survive losing us both. One of us needs to make it out of this and I don't know that we can if we don't run."

"Then we run together."

"No. You guys shouldn't even be here. You're here because of me and Seth. If it wasn't for us, you wouldn't be in this situation."

"But we are." She said. "So, let me help you."

In my mind, I sought a million reasons to tell her that she was wrong. But I couldn't find any. Her words made a lot of sense. For the first time, I agreed the girls should stay and help us fight.

Greg cut in. "Can I say something?"

"Yeah, what's up, man?"

He stared at me like I was stupid. "I don't want to stay here. Can someone help me get out of here?"

"Like to Burlington?" Emily asked.

"No." He shook his head. "Just to the Rec Center. There's a room there that would basically work like a panic room. We could ride this out until the police come."

"There's a panic room?" Nicole exclaimed.

"Well, no. It's a tornado shelter. But nothing's getting in there. Not even Eric."

I smiled. "We can stop and get Sarge on the way."

Greg nodded. "Maybe that's where my wife is."

I nodded back hopefully, but still worried I'd find the body of the only therapist who had ever actually helped me.

Nicole stood staring, arms crossed, head tilted. "And how do you plan on getting him down three flights of stairs?"

Greg smiled. "We don't have to. We'll take the elevator."

"I thought it was broken." I questioned.

"When I came up here, I took it out of habit. It opened right up."

Emily shuddered. "That's just what we need. Get caught in there with a psycho with a machete."

Greg yelled, "Jessica? Jessica?" He looked back. "I think I just saw my wife!" He exclaimed, pointing at the stairs. He jumped up, immediately falling back on to the couch with a scream. Seth dove, saving him. We helped him back on the couch, as I pondered the fact that I'd never realized I didn't even know Dr. Munson's first name until right then.

"Babe?" He yelled again.

"I'll run up and look." Seth volunteered.

"Not alone you won't!" Nicole said.

I stood up. "Seth and I will go up and try to find her. She knows us. She doesn't know you two."

Nicole nodded. "So, you want us to stay here?"

I shook my head. "No. We're leaving. I want you two to try to take him to the elevator. Seth and I and hopefully Dr. Munson will meet you. If we don't find you sooner, go to where we left Sarge.

"I don't like that we're splitting up." Nicole said. "It's dangerous."

"It's necessary." I said, heading for the stairs. "We can't keep adding more time to this than we need to."

Nicole acquiesced. "Phillip? Do me one favor."

"Name it." I said.

"Play to win."

Play to win was one of dad's phrases. He always said people don't hit the field looking to lose. They don't pull on a uniform to go out and tie. He said it was a waste of time. He couldn't stand hockey and soccer, because no one should accept a tie. "You play to win. If you're not out there trying to win, why are you wasting the space where someone else could be?"

For the first time in as long as I could remember, two unbelievable things happened. I realized I was planning on winning.

And Nicole was right about something.

The girls got Greg to a standing position. He said, "There's a small stool with wheels two rooms down. Maybe we can use it to help get me outside?"

I stood watching, but Seth's hand wrapped around my shoulder. "They got this. Let's go."

I'd waited my whole life to kiss Emily and now that I could, I stared solely at my sister, hoping it wouldn't be the last time I ever saw her. The three of them disappeared around the corner as Seth led the way up the stairs.

CHAPTER 39

After one flight of stairs, I was breathing hard, like always. Seth looked back at me and held one finger over his lips to silence me, as if I had some way to stop wheezing. I pointed to the left, toward the offices of the counselors. As impossibly unlikely as it was, I prayed Dr. Munson would simply be in her office, waiting for us. She was not. Her door was open. I quickly peeked in, looking for any additional items we could use as weapons, but something told me her inspirational plaques would not serve as tools to save our lives. Even her three-hole punch was cheap and wouldn't do much in hand to hand combat.

"What are you doing?" Seth whispered as close to my ear as he could. His warm breath didn't make me react the way Emily's did.

"Looking for anything else we can use as weapons." I whispered back.

"Something better than your bat?" He asked, pointing to it.

"Just in addition to it."

He glanced around, shrugging his shoulders. I pointed to the next office. We entered the Dietician's office but found literally nothing besides two chairs and a table. I'd only spoken to him twice, but both times had been at the Rec Center for group. Maybe he didn't even really use the office. It was more than possible. The more I thought about it, the more I questioned if he even worked every day.

The nurse's office was the direct opposite. Not an inch of space went to waste. She had a large desk in one corner of the room; her computer on one side, her pens in a jar on the other, next to a twisted bamboo plant. In front of the desk, there was no second chair. There was a hospital scale with the sliding bar on it. I hate those things. Like I want to have to guess how many things to slide on top of the bad news the scale has at the end of our time together. On the wall hung several clipboards, each facing the wall as to not reveal any sensitive health information. A black Formica counter ran the length of the wall under multiple locked cabinets. A sink with a tall vessel faucet looked brand new but judging by the lingering odor of disinfectant and bleach, it had probably been scrubbed till it shined.

Seth and I passed the cold exam table near the door. He paused, looking over some of the charts on the wall and reading flyers for upcoming fundraisers and special events. I made my way toward the red bio-waste container, looking for any sharp objects sticking out that could be used as weapons, but knowing the only things I might find would be needles. I found nothing at all. It had been emptied as well. I stood quickly, almost hitting my head on the plastic container holding three boxes of those dusty feeling latex gloves. Usually, there would be several different sizes, but she only had mediums. She probably wasn't used to anyone else requiring gloves. I could hear the *Snap!* of the gloves being pulled off in my head.

I pushed the foot-operated garbage can lid with my left foot but found it as empty as the bio-hazard can. Checking each locked cabinet, I found nothing we could utilize as weapons. I turned toward the door and my shoe squeaked loudly. Seth held his finger up to silence me again as I contemplated telling him he could screw himself.

The door to Sarge's office was not only open, it was broken. By the looks of it, someone had kicked it open with their large combat boots. The same boots I'd listened to while thinking I was about to die not long ago. I wondered if Dr. Munson had heard that same rhythmic cadence as The Killer came near her. If so, had she survived it? Seth ran to the phone, but his elation was torn from his emotional core. The cord connecting the phone to the wall had been sliced. He sat, staring at the receiver, as though a voice would greet him even without a connection. As he sat in disbelief, I searched the office quickly. I found everything that could be useful had already been taken. Even the small knife that usually hung on the wall to Sarge's left – given to him by a military friend on his arrival home from Operation Freedom – was gone.

Leaving empty handed, we expected better luck in the employee lounge area. The small kitchenette would have something we could use as a weapon, I thought. Turning toward the table and chairs, I nearly ran into a fake house plant near the wall. The soft blue light from the coffee machine was surprisingly bright. The green numbers on the microwave were not. There was no cutlery to be found in the drawers or the sink. The cupboards appeared to have nothing to help us either. Seth leaned on one of the metal chairs, causing it to scrape the floor loudly. I smiled, holding my finger over my mouth. He showed me his middle finger, as he moved toward the refrigerator.

"There's nothing in there that will help us," I whispered louder than we'd been doing.

"Not looking for that. I just need a snack." Seth said. And he found one. Removing a cold, hard, Hershey's with Almonds from the fridge, Seth smiled. "Do you know how many calories this is?"

"I have no idea."

"210." He said, opening it. The crackle and crinkle of the wrapper echoed through the almost silent room. If Dr. Munson was hiding up there, she'd find us just based off the sound. Seth smiled, taking a bite. "And what's it gonna do? Kill me? That might happen anyway. Life is short, Phillip. Shorter than we thought, that's for sure." His voice grew progressively louder. What happened to the guy trying to force me to be quiet a few seconds earlier?

I wanted to tell him to be quiet. That The Killer could be watching us. That he might tip him off that we were up there. And what came out instead was, "Is there another candy bar?" There wasn't, but he shared his with me. "You know there's no calories when you share, right?"

Seth nodded. "That's why we never gained weight at Pizza Hut."

Finishing up, I tossed the wrapper in the otherwise empty trash can. I wonder if people who smoke pot or do other drugs feel the same level of calm that settled over me after a small hit of chocolate. I knew it wasn't a long-term solution, but that momentary distraction helped me refocus. It was time to find Dr. Munson, but I really felt there was no way she was still in the Counselor's Quarters. We just needed to sweep it and be sure.

Turning the corner to the bedroom hallway, my stomach shot into my throat as the whole world spun. At the end of the hall, a blonde in a woman's nightgown sat on the floor, slumped forward. My pulse tripled. Maybe three feet closer to me, I saw The Killer; legs spread, one gloved hand holding a knife.

Neither of us moved as we stared the other down.

CHAPTER 40

I'd always been that guy who thought snakes were terrifying but when I saw them at the zoo, I'd sit close, watching them slither up the glass, flicking their tongues. Mice terrified me if I met one in my kitchen, but in a cage, it was okay. For a long time, I thought something was wrong with me that I could handle one and not the other. As I got older, I realized it was the surprise that creeped me out.

The snake was *supposed to be* in the cage at the zoo. Mice were *supposed to be* in little aquariums to run in their wheels and entertain me by filling their cheeks with vegetarian pellets, chewing them while looking around at the world. Neither was supposed to be in my house, in my kitchen, under my blanket, or in my toilet. It was the surprise that made them terrify me.

The same was true with the idea of the man standing before me, gripping the knife. When I'd expected him in the small gym next to the locker rooms, he didn't seem as horrific. Dangerous, maybe even deadly, but the terror level was toned down because the expectation led to the reality.

The monster standing in front of me was a different story. One hundred percent. His large body was postured, both arms out a little, legs spread wide. The way he overtook the entire hall was intimidating. The only light came from a small lamp on the ground behind him, illuminating Jessica Munson's nightgown, but leaving the killer in a silhouette. I'd expected the machete, but in his hand, I saw a switchblade instead. I stared at it, almost transfixed by the small diamond sparkles of light reflecting on the blade. The juxtaposition of the twinkling light against his black glove only made it more intriguing to me. But I snapped out of the spell and refocused. We stared at one another; the only sound in the room seemed to be my own breathing.

Behind The Killer, on the floor, the blonde hadn't moved. The voice inside my mind repeatedly screamed, *She's dead. Look at the angle of her head. She's been positioned there.* But I fought it. Whether I'd find she was dead or not, I couldn't do anything for Dr. Munson until I made it past the hooded menace standing between us. I took a step toward him when Seth's hand clapped down on my shoulder.

"Something feels off about this. Why is he just standing there?" Seth's grip tightened on my shoulder.

"Let me go, Seth. He killed Sarge. He killed Obi. Timothy. The others." Tears welled up so quickly the whole hall looked like it was under water.

I gripped my baseball bat and took a step forward, but Seth pulled me back, "Listen to me."

"What?"

"He hasn't moved. Why? Have you even once seen him just stand somewhere and wait? No. He always moves quickly, attacking before people even know he's there. That's how it was in the Rec Center and that's how it had to have been for Georgie." He realized this line of thought would only drive me and tried to change gears. "Think about it, Phillip. Why would you leave a light on the floor like that?"

"So that we can see what he did to Dr. Munson. To increase the fear."

I took another step, but Seth pulled on my shirt again. "Phillip. Listen to me."

But my eyes were locked on the blonde hair, covered in blood. The slumped figure that hadn't once hitched or shimmied in any direction, even minutely. The pool of blood under the white nightgown told me everything I needed to know to kill him. My fingers tightened on the bat, my knuckles drained of any blood. Angry breaths forced air through my clenched teeth as I tried to speak.

Courage ripped through my veins. Or possibly fear. I still don't know. Cocking my arm back like a catapult, I swiveled slightly to my right and brought the bat forward at full strength. I watched it spiral through the air before connecting dead center in the chest of the hoodie with the chopped sleeves. The sound of ribs cracking was followed immediately by the repeated clang of the bat hitting the floor.

But he didn't move. He still stood there, holding the knife. His head hung backward, as though he were in pain, but remained silent as he lifted it again. I ran toward him, my fist pulled back, ready to connect; but just as I reached him, Seth stopped me again. "Phillip! No!" Seth's arm reached over my shoulder, pointing at the man in front of me. "Look!"

The hood was off, lost when he'd bent backward. Eric Schultz, the former camp counselor, stood before us, tears running down his face; his mouth plastered in duct tape.

As we inched closer, I suddenly saw it. Eric wasn't standing there of his own free will at all. Each outstretched arm was held in place by thick rope. His ankles were also bound. Two more steps and I could see he wasn't holding the switchblade at all. It was attached to his glove; made to look like as though he was holding it.

My fear amplified; not because of the caged animal Eric Schultz turned out to be, but the knowledge that the real snake was somewhere else. Still, I couldn't take chances. I took the glove holding the switchblade off his hand. Even in the dim light, I could see his fingertips weren't normal. Four of his tips were the purplish hue normally reserved for having fingerprints taken with ink. The ring finger was a dark red, bordering on maroon. Each appeared slightly swollen.

Holding the switchblade to protect myself, I reached out with the other hand and ripped the duct tape off Eric's mouth. He simultaneously screamed and attempted to hold it in. "Broke my ribs," he spat out.

"Yeah, sorry about that. I was worried about her." I said, pointing to the body behind him. But as I did so, I realized it wasn't a woman at all. It was Tony, one of the overnight counselors. Someone had thrown a nightgown over his dead body. Dr. Munson was never there. As I looked back at Seth, I realized, Emily, Nicole, and Greg were in trouble. "Run downstairs. Find the girls and Greg. Tell them The Killer is still out there and it's not Eric."

Eric's eyes squinted in the darkness. "Greg. It's Greg."

The room spun as I turned back toward him, "What?"

"Greg. He's the one who did this to me." Eric swallowed with difficulty. "Can you cut me down?"

I ran the steel of the switchblade across the rope holding Eric's left hand. As the rope broke free, I found that the same rope was tied to his ankle but run through the door to the bedrooms on either side of him, making it impossible to gain any slack from either side without hurting his other limbs. Seth stood behind me, gripping his baseball bat, ready to swing if Eric tried anything; but I didn't feel the distrust he did. As soon as Eric was free, I turned to go down the hall.

"Where are you going?" Eric cried. "Take me with you."

I ignored him, turning to Seth. "Greg's got the girls. We have to get back to him."

"Wait!" Eric's voice was strained, but he managed to gain volume. "I can help you. I have a gun."

Seth pulled the bat back. "He's got a gun!"

Eric's arms instinctively covered his head as he said, "Not on me! But I can tell you where it is!" It was in his bedroom. The opposite end of the building, down another dark hallway full of doors.

Seth and I hugged goodbye, looking each other in the eye. "It's going to be okay. I'll see you in a bit." I lied. I could tell looking at Seth that he didn't want to go. He was worried The Killer would be there. But I knew better. I knew The Killer was with the girls and we only had two chances to stop him; me and Seth.

Walking away from the best friend I'd ever had, I couldn't help but wonder why I'd wanted to leave him. As I passed the hall, Eric shouted to me for help again but I couldn't waste any more time. Heading for the stairs, I took a deep breath and reminded myself that at least if I failed, Seth would give it his best try.

CHAPTER 41

I came down the stairs slowly, purposefully. With no idea where he would be, I knew only that an extremely dangerous man was waiting somewhere for me. The front door stood wide open; the top landing illuminated by floodlights. I wasn't falling for it. There's no way I was going out there. The girls were supposed to take Greg down the elevator, so I knew I needed to go down the hallway to the right of the fireplace. But I stayed on the stairs instead. I had a limited time to save them, but, at the same time, I was in no rush to find their mutilated bodies. I heard Dr. Munson in my head, as loud as if she were there with me.

When confronted with sudden danger, most people's instinctive response is not to fight or to run away. The very first response is stop moving and stay absolutely still.

To Freeze.

But, was I? I quickly analyzed my body. I could move if I wanted to, right? My foot didn't move, but maybe I didn't want it to. That's all it was.

They say it can feel pleasant. Instead of panic, one might experience comfort. Warm fuzzies. Possible even the sensation of floating.

Not even a little bit.

My rasping breaths and trembling chin and lips mixed with the pressure in my chest making me wonder if this was the heart attack I'd been expecting. Just my luck to drop dead of a heart attack when there's a mass-murderer on the loose. One more thing I did wrong in my life. My jaw clenched so tightly I thought I might grind my teeth into powder. I blinked, harder than usual; black spots racing in front of my eyes. I had to pull it together. I needed to find the girls.

I took two steps forward; I wasn't frozen. *You're in charge now, McCracken.* Sarge said in my mind.

I wasn't going out the door, so that eliminated flight; leaving only one option. *Play to win.*

"Bring it on, asshole!" The bass in my voice caught me off guard. It was quickly followed by the rhythmic slap of The Killer's boots on the hardwood floor. He was below me. I hadn't considered that. Half-expecting a machete through the wooden steps, I moved two more stairs as he came into view.

He walked past me, continuing directly to the fireplace. He didn't even bother looking at me. "Philly! Philly! Philly! You don't really think you can win, do you?"

A few minutes beforehand I wasn't sure. But now that I knew it was just Greg behind the mask, I felt a lot more confident. I still feared for my life, but with the mystery removed, things seemed more manageable.

Greg removed the hood on the hoodie. As he removed the mask, his sunken eyes announced he'd gone without sleep for days. Turning back to the fireplace, Greg poked at the logs with the fire poker. There was no indication of his previous limp and my sister and Emily were nowhere to be seen. It was only now that I noticed the machete had been resting on the mantle of the fireplace the entire time. Choking back my tears, I wrapped my hand across the handle of the switchblade, stored in the right pocket of my pants.

Without turning around, he said, "I hope you weren't too hard on Eric up there. He's had such a rough couple of days."

"I killed him. Just like I'm going to—"

His laugh echoed. "Oh my god. Really? Just stop. You want me to think you put that poor man out of his misery? Of course, you didn't. Because you don't have the balls to kill someone. You spend your life afraid that you already did."

His smile spread as he saw the confusion on my face. "I learned so much about you little creeps. My wife would come back after work and just unload everything she'd heard. Try to make sense of it all. Try to figure out how to help you. She told me all about your father. She told me how you think you killed him."

Asshole. But I wasn't going to bite. I knew he'd just throw worse at me. And I'd dealt with that part of my past. I sat with Dr. Munson and told her how I turned off the oxygen on dad's tank. And how I turned it back on less than a minute later because I couldn't handle the guilt. But he still died that night. So, it was my fault. And maybe, if she hadn't helped me deal with it, *maybe* that would've been enough for Greg to stun me and stop me. But not anymore.

Shifting my weight, I still hadn't left the final step of the staircase; feeling as though it somehow kept me separated from this insanity. That it would become real the second my foot hit the floor.

Play to win. Nicole said, in my head. *Play to win*.

Greg moved back to the fire, poking the logs further. "There's really no point in looking for her. I killed your little girlfriend."

"You're lying!" I screamed, unable to keep my emotions in check.

Greg smiled, finally coaxing a reaction out of me. "Am I? I don't think so. I slit her stomach. I watched her crawl away, begging me not to kill her. I held her by her hair and I cut her cheating head off."

"There would be blood everywhere," I reasoned, unable to see if the hallway beyond was coated in Emily's—I couldn't even finish the thought.

"There was. Oh, my god, there was. It was all over the ground. On the rocks. I covered it the best I could, of course."

"You're lying. You didn't have time to take Nicole and Emily down there."

Greg grimaced, staring at me. He touched the base of his neck as his head tilted. "I'm talking about Jessica."

The words knocked the wind out of me the same way a direct punch to the chest would have. *Jessica.* I'd only learned her first name a short while before. Dr. Jessica Munson. *Dead? Murdered?* The room spun as my anger swelled. The only thing keeping me from charging at him at that moment was the fire poker and the machete on the table nearby.

"You? You *killed* her?"

His face contorted into a smile matching a child who held the best secret ever. "Guess what, Fat Boy. She didn't love you any more than she loved me."

"I don't understand."

"I mean you're just a fat teenage boy. You thought you stood a chance with a piece of ass like her? Hell, I'm not even sure how I got her."

"I never thought—"

"—Don't give me that. I saw how you looked at her. How all of you looked at *my wife*. There's toilets that probably clogged with you horndogs jerkin' your gherkins wishing you were riding my wife. Well, you can't have her. No one can, now."

I stared at the open front door. I had no delusions that I was fast enough to make it past Greg and down the stairs. I didn't think I could beat him even if someone really cut his Achilles. But I wondered if there was a way to use the door as a distraction. I took the final step off the stairs. His hand gripped the machete before I knew what to do. Four steps later, he was within striking distance, the point of the machete pressed into the center of my shirt. "Where the fuck do you think you're going? We're having a discussion."

CHAPTER 42

Seth watched me walk to the top of the stairs and disappear. Gripping his baseball bat tightly, Seth turned back to the darkened halls leading to the bedrooms. His brain tried to write a new narrative; reminding him these were normal hotel style rooms, used as a Bed and Breakfast much of the year. But Seth knew the horror that could be waiting in any of them. He'd seen it firsthand. His mind replayed it. His imagination enhanced it.

The hallway was like so many others Seth had walked down in hotels; doors on either side of a long hallway. That feeling of dread the empty halls produce. Unlike the hotels he'd stayed in, no sound came from the doors around him. Even in the strongest daylight, so many hotels gave an impression of death; as though the halls hadn't been walked in years. This was worse. There was no sunlight and the impression of death carried very real connotations.

The silence tried to warn him as he slowly turned down the completely dark hallway. He chose to ignore it, drowning it out with the light sound of his shuffling feet as his sneakers massaged the carpet with each small step. He knew Eric was probably tied up in the other hallway, but it was impossible to discount the feeling something was near. Closing in. Ready to grab him. Drag him. Slap him in a bed. Impale him. Even in his mind's eye, Seth lived through it, screaming through the pain. Seth tried to distract himself, counting the doorways he passed on his quest for a gun. *Focus on the gun.* That thought was clear. Defined. It was enough to propel Seth forward, both hands out, the baseball bat pointing the way.

His eyes grew more accustomed to the lack of light and Seth was able to see further than before. As he looked over his shoulder he found the only thing he could find; that he was completely alone.

Reaching the third door from the end, Seth stood in front of it. His hand trembled as he remembered the CPR dummy – and worse, the counselor slaughtered in his own bed. Seth ran his hand over the dark brown wood of the oak door. His fingers gripped the shiny brass doorknob and turned it.

The warped door opened with a jerk, providing entrance to a room dirtier than any teen's room Seth had ever been in. He was supposed to find the gun in here? His heart beat faster. Harder. Louder. Without walking all the way in at first, he glanced through the room. Old cigarette smoke wafted toward his nose as he stared at the clothing on hangers in the open closet which seemed to create a waterfall of fabric into the laundry hamper overflowing with dirty clothes. Seth feared barely moving the clutter would cause an avalanche that might bury him. Orphaned socks created a trail from the closet to a pile of old musty shoes half lined up and half jumbled together. The shelf on the wall was cramped with odd electronics, a stack of comic books, and a shoebox full of photos. A duffel bag sat open on the floor, balled up socks and two empty packs of cigarettes hanging out of it.

He saw the nightstand Eric was talking about and started to make his way there, treating each step like a landmine, unsure of what was under the mess. He feared a rabid raccoon just as much as a weapon. Eventually, curiosity got the best of Seth. He used the toe of his shoe to push things aside on the floor to see what was there. He found two nudey magazines; a legend he'd heard but never seen in person, having grown up with the internet. He says he didn't look, but I don't believe him.

Seth knelt by the nightstand and pulled open the drawer. He saw it immediately. A little over six inches long the polymer skin on the M&P Shield 9mm picked up some of the light in the room. Seth grabbed the box of cartridges and quickly read, "Hornady Critical Defense. 20 Cartridges. Loaded with Patented FTX bullet." He didn't really understand any of that, but quickly saw he didn't need to, because the magazine lay next to the gun. Seth slid it in slowly, his hand shaking. He made sure to keep his finger away from the trigger as he did so. The magazine popped back out, not catching. He tried again. It came back out. Seth pushed harder this time, but the magazine slid back out again. Finally removing it all the way, Seth looked it over as though he had any idea what he was doing. This time he lined the mag up with the back of the gun and, in one quick motion, set the magazine in place.

Standing up, he held the gun with his finger extended to the side of it, careful not to touch the trigger. Looking at the floor in front of him, Seth realized he shouldn't have loaded the gun until he made it out of the room in case he fell and shot himself.

By the time he reached the hallway, Seth already felt better. He pictured being the one to shoot The Killer. In his mind, the gun fired shots as he held it horizontally like in his favorite music videos. As much as that made him smile, Seth understood that the reality would probably be very, very different.

Turning down the extremely darkened hall, fear clenched like a tight fist around his chest. The back of his neck tingled. He hadn't been able to erase the feeling Eric was in on it and coming for him. His pulse pounded in his throat as he tried to see if his fears were justified.

Seth couldn't see all the way down the hall, but he could see enough. He saw the body on the floor. Bloodied. Mutilated. The overnight counselor's body that someone had wrapped with one of Jessica Munson's nightgowns. But the body was alone.

Eric Schultz was gone.

CHAPTER 43

Greg's smirk slithered across his face like slime. "Don't piss yourself, McCracken. I'm not really going to stab you right now." He backed away from me. "What fun would that be? You caused this. So, you need to suffer through it. No early exits."

"What do you mean I caused it?"

"I saw you. At the window, in the Mess Hall. I know you saw me slit your friend Mallick's throat."

I hadn't wanted to react. Reactions gave him power over me. But I felt tears rushing down my cheeks.

"So, you did kill him?"

"Cut the performance, McCracken. I know you were watching. During the storm. Outside the window."

My head moved back and forth slowly. "The storm? No. I didn't leave Seth's cabin once I was there."

"I saw your outline in the lightning, McCracken. There's only so many kids that size."

"Someone saw you. That's why you did this. Timothy saw you do something he shouldn't have seen, and you killed him. Then someone else saw that and you don't know who." I took a step closer "You're trying to kill the witness. It wasn't me."

Greg looked up, to the right, his lips pursed tighter than any I'd ever seen. His neck rotated to the left, his vertebrae cracking loudly. "Say what you like. At this point, you've seen too much either way. What's one more body?" He spun on one heel, turning away from me. His boots clacked across the cold wood floor as he moved back toward the fireplace. "But not yet."

I ran at him. I don't think I was expecting it any more than he was. He'd just set the machete down on the mantle again and before he could reach it, I hit full force. Greg crumpled to the floor. A typical bully's reaction; dish it out, dish it out, dish it out, fall after one retaliation. I reached for the machete, but Greg's closed fist dug in my upper thigh. Pain thumped through my whole leg after that one shot. I did what fat kids do best and fell on him. My shoulder collided with his ribs directly below his left armpit. As he desperately tried to get air, the guttural screams he released were more like a dry heave mixed with a wheeze.

Rolling away from me, he was on his feet before I was. I tried to move toward the open door, unsure where I planned to go after that, but Greg's gloves caught my shirt. "You wanna go outside? Here you go." I found myself propelled not far from the ground, but not touching it. My enlarged mass hit the wooden railing on the top landing. My eyes closed as I waited for the three-story plummet, but it didn't happen. The sturdy construction had saved me. I opened my eyes, excited to be alive still, only to find Greg's boot coming at my face. I somehow swerved out of the way and used that momentum to pull myself back up.

Seth jumped off the last stair running toward us. I had no way to know if he'd gotten the gun or not, but I knew I stood more of a chance of winning this with two people than with one. Then he veered off, out of the way, not coming out. It distracted me enough that Greg was on his feet, but I understood. Seth needed me to get Greg back inside and then he'd surprise him. So, I dove for the door. He ran in after me. His fist crashed into the middle of my back. His fingers ripped at the roots of my hair as his other hand pulled back to hit me again. Seth swung, hitting Greg in the back. Greg spun around, quickly putting Seth in a rear naked choke, using Seth as a shield between us so I couldn't do anything.

"Bad choice, Jenkins. You should have run when you had the chance to live. I know you're not the one who saw me. I could've let you live." Seth's face grew darker as he fought for air. "But now I can't." Greg tightened his grip, moving to his left, putting the glass coffee table and Seth between us. I looked around for something to use to save him; but all I saw was the empty Cornuts wrapper under the glass table.

Greg released his grip. Seth fell straight forward. I screamed, trying to reach my arms out in a futile attempt to catch my friend, but he hit the glass table straight on. Shards of glass flew in every direction. Blood dripped onto the floor. As I went to check on him, Greg moved for the machete, so I abandoned my best friend to save us from the weapon instead. I hit a picture-perfect tackle. The kind that could've gotten me on Varsity; if I liked that sort of thing. The two of us fell to the floor again. His head butted in my direction four times, trying to hit me. I grabbed his cheeks with both hands and bounced his face off the floor. Planting my foot on his hand, I pulled myself to a standing position. Greg screamed as his fingers crunched.

"This fucking stops!" I screamed.

"You're right." He said. "You're right."

I'm not an idiot. I knew he wasn't done. It still didn't prepare me when he ripped a small knife from his boot and slammed it through my foot.

Imagine for a second, if you will, that you're dreaming there's a house fire. And that house is full of people. And in the dream, you're the only one awake. The only one who knows about the fire. Your eyes dart around the room, trying to take in everything at once. They grow wider; the not-so-white parts of the eye begin to burn, telling you that this is not a dream at all. You sit upright, grasping the sides of your head, trying desperately to regain control. The house is really on fire. You need water. You need to call 911. Dread sets in. You might be dying. You might be crazy. Maybe none of this is real. Only the rich oaky smell of the fire permeates every room. Wisps of silver-grey smoke curl and dance their way through the thick hazy air even as you try to deny their existence. You start throwing everything out the window, onto the lawn. You find yourself screaming for help. You're trying to save keepsakes and to wake the others. You're suddenly sitting down, double checking to ensure there's really a fire before you panic all over again and restart the panic process.

This is essentially what happens when you get stabbed in the foot. You keep questioning it, even though you can feel the cold steel against your warm muscles. Your brain shouts to the rest of your body. If you accept sitting and not reacting, you might be stuck there forever. Even when you can react, you might find your body keeps bringing you back to a place where you question the validity of the situation.

I fell to the ground as he pulled the knife out of my foot. The clacking of his boots against the wood floor matched the heartbeat pounding through my head. Sparks flew as the machete raked across the rock mantle of the fireplace. The boots hit rhythmically, coming closer to me. I slid back three times. My hand found the broken glass of the table; my eyes refusing to see Seth. Greg came closer, but this time said nothing.

My fingers wrapped around a large shard from the glass coffee table as Greg lifted the machete into the air. I held eye contact with him as I drove the glass into his upper thigh.

"Motherfucker!" He screamed as the machete fell to the hardwood floor. I grabbed the weapon and swung, but he was too far away. I held it out, pointed directly at him.

His eyes stared, half impressed, and, for the first time, half-afraid. "When did you become the physical type?"

"You made me this way." The rage boiled through my voice as we each bled.

"*You* made *me* this way!" He screamed back.

We sat in silence, each watching the other to see if he moved. Tears streamed down my face. "Just tell me why. Why? Why did you kill everyone? What did we do to deserve this?" I stared at him, as he pushed down on his thigh trying to control the bleeding. "Just tell me why."

CHAPTER 44

The toilet seat was up.

That's how it started. Greg looked around the bathroom he shared with his wife in the Counselors' Quarters, as he stood pissing in the toilet. Sure, she'd had appointments with several of the campers that day, so she'd been in her office part of the day, but it wasn't like Jessica could go more than thirteen hours without using the bathroom. Someone else had been there.

Glancing around, things were different. The shower curtain was pulled shut when it was usually open. The shampoo and conditioner bottles were nicely gathered in the corner instead of haphazardly lying on the shower ledge. The clear glass jars filled with cotton balls, Q-tips and makeup pads stood closed; not a single lid off and laid randomly on the counter. The dented tube with bits of crusted toothpaste hanging from it was nowhere to be found. The smears of dried soap and toothpaste in the sink had also disappeared. Blow dryer? Wrapped up nicely and put away. No tangle of cords. Fingerprint smudges and water droplets gone from the mirror. Jessica had straightened up; but not cleaned. The counters were not sanitized or even scrubbed. But she'd taken the time to ensure the rug was perfectly centered around the toilet.

The toilet with the seat standing in the upright position.

His head turned to the trash can. The perfectly crisp and clean bag sticking out from under the lid told him the garbage had also recently been changed. But Greg lifted the lid of the can anyway. The actual condom was nowhere to be found, but the ripped, discarded wrapper was there.

Worse. It was one of his.

Flipping through her phone as she slept, Greg read their messages. Things no husband wants to read about his wife. And while he knew he should just stop – that he was only harming himself – he kept going.

He made his way through the woods that night, knowing what he would find. *Wanting* to find it. In one hand, Greg held his phone. In the other; my nemesis. A 17.5-inch stainless steel blade sharpened beyond belief, and freshly polished for the special occasion. He rotated the Jungle Master machete in his gloved hand, repeatedly squeezing the simple wood handle as though he was searching for the tang running through it.

The subtle forward-arching edge of the weapon gave it the appearance of having more in common with an ancient combat sword than a modern cutting tool, but Greg suspected it could do equal damage to foliage and foe. At the very least, he planned to find out.

He adjusted the backpack he wore, looking down at his black shirt and pants. Greg exhaled; anger exuding from his lungs with each breath. His feet hit the soft dirt of the trail in a rhythmic pattern, but that ceased as he moved into the grass.

They were wrapped in each other's arms, their naked bodies separated only by sweat and (presumably) another one of Greg's condoms. The moon glistened off the machete the same way as their skin. Jessica rolled on top, arching back, her breasts in view. Eric's left hand reached up to cup one, while his right hand clawed deeper in the flesh of her ass cheek. Seeing it with his own eyes was more painful than Greg had imagined; but he stayed for the full show.

As Jessica rolled off Eric, Greg witnessed her last kiss. Eric stood up. "I'll be right back. I gotta piss like a racehorse." A loud *Snap!* echoed as he removed the condom.

Jessica laughed. "Hurry back, or I'll have to keep going without you."

Eric scampered into the nearby trees, not twenty feet from Greg. Peering over his shoulder to his married lover, Eric smirked. "At the very least, I'm gonna wanna watch that!"

Hands on his dick as he watered the Black Walnut tree, Eric was lost in thought. The wooden handle of the machete crashed directly into the back of his head. The momentum drove his nose into the very tree he was pissing on. Eric slumped, face first, into his own puddle. Greg checked over his shoulder. Jessica sat naked, staring out at the lake, her head resting on her knees on the blanket where she'd just had sex.

Unzipping his backpack, Greg removed three small ropes. He pulled the unconscious man's elbows together and tied them behind Eric's back. Next, he tied Eric's bare feet to one another. Not quite close enough to cut off circulation, but close to it. The final length of rope connected the two, pulling his knees up, making it impossible for Eric to move from the prone position, should he awaken. Greg didn't cover Eric's mouth. He'd rather Eric screamed where no one could hear than have the man asphyxiate before Greg could make him suffer.

Quietly, Greg grabbed Eric's hoodie off the ground. He pulled it on, not wishing to cover his own clothes with blood. Jessica smiled to herself. "Are you done already? You're as bad as my—" Her eyes met his. "Where is Eric?"

"Huh. Why would my naked wife need to know where my co-worker is?"

Pulling herself up, she stared at the machete. "Where's Eric? What did you do?"

"Don't worry, babe. You'll be reunited in a couple seconds."

She tried to run, but the machete swung, catching her straight in the stomach. It was more difficult than Greg had anticipated. Jessica panicked, turning to run, causing the blade to cut deeper and slice her side. Screaming through the tears, she couldn't see. Her foot caught a rock and she fell, the impact ripping her stomach more. Her hand moved to the cut instinctively. Thick, muscular meat threatened to escape the cavity. She felt tubing; hoses filled with air, but the sides were weak, fragile. Jessica Munson held her own intestines.

The weight of her intestines pushed against her hand as blood streamed down her arm. A hopeless yelp surrendered in the back of her throat; her teeth clenched so tightly no sound could escape. His laugh echoed behind her. She turned, trying to crawl away, but with one hand locked on her stomach, she was left with three limbs. Her balance gave way and she fell to the dirt.

His boots hit the forest floor in a slow rhythmic manner as he stalked behind her. Looking over her shoulder, she witnessed the moon reflecting on the machete blade, resembling the flash of a camera through her tears. Jessica's hand moved from her stomach, extending open, reaching for grass as though she could somehow pull herself to safety. He savored the bloodletting as her body crumpled to the ground. She spasmed with each labored breath.

"I give up." A whisper; barely audible.

One gloved hand shot out, gripping the hair near her scalp. He pulled up quickly, forcing Jessica to her knees. Not letting go, he moved in front of her and knelt. Eye to eye, a smile spread across his face. Jessica wished to apologize; to explain. But no words came out as the sound of the machete ripping through neck tendons echoed through the silent forest. He stood, staring at the moon for a full thirty seconds before releasing his grip on Jessica's dyed roots. The disembodied head bounced slightly, before resting next to her body.

Greg moved Jessica's body to a section of trees that no one really walked to. Being the counselor in charge of the treks through the forest it would be easy to redirect people away from the spot anyway. He set her head in the middle of her body. "I loved you."

Taking a precision swing, Greg lopped off Jessica's left arm. He swung again, slicing the arm in half. He'd barely finished with the arm when the screams began. "Shut up, Eric. No one cares." Swinging the machete several times, Greg brought down enough branches to cover the body. He'd have to come back to finish the job.

He walked quickly to where Eric lay. His boot collided with Eric's side. He pushed against the former counselor hard enough to roll Eric onto his side, still hogtied. "Good morning, sunshine."

Eric stared at him. "Where's Jessica?"

Kneeling down, Greg said, "You two spend a lot of time worrying where the other one is. You should've been worried about where I was." He slit the tie holding Eric's feet together and pulled him into a standing position. Flipping around to face him, Greg looked down at Eric's dick. "Well, that little thing isn't why she left me." He looked up at the moon.

Eric spit directly in Greg's eye. Wiping the spittle away, Greg smiled. "I'll give you that one. The next time you do something that stupid you get 18 inches of steel through your chest." He spun the machete in his gloved hand. "If that's how you want this to end, let's just do it now." Greg slapped duct tape to Eric's mouth. "Start walking."

When they arrived at the Counselors' Quarters, Greg led Eric to the elevator. "Get in." With the elevator door closed, Greg hit Eric full force in the face. Eric fell to the floor with a thud. "Oh, good. You're sitting down." He proceeded to tie Eric's feet together again. Instead of pushing the button to the take the elevator anywhere, Greg opened the door and left; leaving a very naked Eric to wonder what would happen next.

Greg made his way to the elevator machine room and slammed the mainline disconnect switch to the off position, before placing "Out of Order" signs on the elevator on each level.

Eric didn't see him again for almost 24 hours.

CHAPTER 45

Things slowed down at that point, but Greg's paranoia did not. Still, he tried to treat the following day as if nothing was unusual. He called a quick meeting with the other counselors and explained Jessica received a call from her mother the night before and needed to drive to Des Moines, so she was gone for the rest of the week. He broke the news that the elevator wasn't working but claimed to be on top of it, having already called a technician, who would come first thing Monday morning. No one cared, as none of them planned to be in the Counselors' Quarters that day anyway. It was the six-week mark and time to test every camper's progress halfway through Fit Camp.

The sky turned a sick green color as Greg approached his wife's decapitated body; his hands in the pockets of Eric's old hoodie. The branches were cleared out of the way, but not in any organized manner. Large sections of the torso, legs, and arms had chunks of meat ripped out of them. An animal had been here, but not a large one, judging by the damage done. Gathering the body parts in oversized outdoor trash bags, Greg tried not to think about what he was really touching.

But when he reached for her head, he was overcome with anger again. He stared into her lifeless eyes, smiling; then dropped her face first into the bag like a rotting cantaloupe.

The torso proved harder to slice than he'd expected, as he hacked at it with the Jungle Master machete. He needed something better. Running through each of the buildings on campus in his mind, he decided his best option was the electric carver in the kitchen. But he couldn't bring the torso in there and he didn't have electricity out in the woods. Rigor mortis had set in. Greg repeatedly dry heaved and gagged on the way to the locker room, but the shower there was the safest spot he could think of to dispose of the body.

Entering the locker room, Greg pulled the door closed behind him and locked it. Only counselors could get in now, and he knew Jeff and Sarge were busy with the dinner crews. Placing the torso in the shower, Greg pushed it to the corner. Then Jonathon Young made the mistake of calling out to him and Greg added to his body count.

Refusing to take more chances of running into people, Greg waited until the storm was fully raging and all the campers were in their cabins. He made his way through the kitchen, refusing to turn on the light so no one would inspect to see who was there. The constant flashes of lightning outside lit the majority of the Mess Hall Kitchen, making it easy to move effortlessly and find what he came for; the Piranha Electric carver/filet knife. His finger flipped the switch and he watched the blade slide, enjoying the whirring sound emitted. Unplugging it, he couldn't wait to feed the machine and make it live up to its name. But Timothy Mallick had just arrived, looking for a little snack.

As he drove the machete into Timothy's chest, lightning hit, and Greg saw the silhouette of a very large overweight teenager, highlighted against the window; perfectly illuminated by the blinding flash of light. When lightning struck again, there was no one at the window. Someone had seen him, and Greg had to find them. First, he had to pull Timothy's body through the mud in the downpour, all the way to the locker room. The weight of the body left a rut in the trail. After toweling up the blood in the Mess Hall, Greg made quick work of all three bodies in the locker room.

At half-past two in the morning, Greg dropped the bags of body parts into the lake, just past where campers at Wašíču weren't allowed to go. "The next day, I went back to the showers to see if I'd forgotten anything. You were just finishing up. I could've cut you right then. Instead, I just waited in the gym area until you left. Walking through, everything looked good, but I couldn't get rid of the smell of death." On his way out, he watched Roger Tonkyn take a shower. He could've easily cut Roger's throat but decided against it.

He interviewed all of us, asking if anyone had been out of their cabins the night before and kept a detailed list. That list repeatedly pointed back at me. I was one of the only people who didn't go back to my cabin and my roommate, Georgie, made sure Greg was aware of that fact.

The other three people who were out of their cabins all lived together. They'd told Greg they'd gone to watch for tornadoes and to play in the rain. The three of them were assigned to Jeff, so Greg couldn't interrogate them further. He did the next best thing and slaughtered them at the lake when the opportunity arose. Killing counselor Jeff was simply a bonus. But, Georgie escaped, running through the trees toward the camp. Greg couldn't come out of the trees with him, so he rounded the back of the Rec Center, ditching Eric's bloodstained hoodie and the machete before running through the building to come out and see us holding Georgie.

He worked hard to find out what we knew. When he found out all Georgie said was, "Sleeves," it must have entertained Greg, momentarily, but that was quickly lost when he saw Emily's phone in her hands. Attempting to coax her to the lake, he was surprised when she handed her phone over willingly. But at least she couldn't make any calls. He disappeared into the trees to make the call by the lake, but instead doubled back on the trail that ran directly to the Counselor's Quarters.

"I'd removed the other cell phones. I'd cut power to the Rec Center phones. But I hadn't cut the phones in the Counselors Quarters. By the time I arrived, Jenkins and the girl were already inside. I called Gordon's phone. If Jenkins was talking to me, he couldn't call anyone else. I told him I'd already reached medical services. Then I told him about the bodies at the lake, just to terrify him. I left out that I was the one who killed them."

Greg was also able to tell exactly where they were, saving him the time to search for them. He was the only person who knew how to turn the elevator on and off and the only one who knew it was working again. He used it to come up to the second floor unannounced.

"I couldn't risk them getting help from the overnight counselors, so I opened Tony's room, stood over his bed, and drove the machete into his chest before he even woke up. I hid down the hall in the room I'd shared with Jess, until I heard Todd talking in the hallway. Stepping out, I found myself directly behind him. Perfect positioning to take him out as well."

Greg again made use of the elevator. As they reached the bottom step of the landing, "The Killer" came out of a back room. When Nicole tackled Seth through the window, Greg attempted to follow. "That little bitch chucked a rock and nailed me in the head. I thought I was done. My hood came off. My mask came off. I thought for sure they knew who I was." But they didn't. No one mentioned it to Greg at all when he showed up in the Rec Center with the others.

Greg swung out the back door of the Rec Center and put on the costume and picked up the Jungle Master machete. The plan was to take out Sarge. Greg thought if he could take out Sarge, he'd have clear sailing, with no other counselors to stop him. At that point, he would harm himself and frame Eric. No one would believe Eric's story and Greg would get away with the impossible. But it wasn't that easy. Four kids in a gymnasium stood between him and a sleeping Sarge.

The rest, you pretty much know. He fought his way out of the Rec Center. He ended lives in the melee outside. He sliced my friend Obi's head in half. He fought me in the gym and left Sarge for dead. Making his way to the elevator, he forced Eric into the hallway and tied him up, attaching the knife to his hand, in hopes that he would get the ultimate satisfaction of making me kill an innocent man.

"Even though I knew you wouldn't do it." He said, attempting to stand up. "But, you wanna know the real kicker in all of this?"

"Sure." I said, attempting to buy time as I slowly continued to move toward Seth's body.

"Every day, Eric Schultz was a dick to me. He made fun of my ideas in staff meetings. He maintained that the campers didn't like me. He called me names. Every single day, Eric Schultz made me feel like a piece of shit. He bullied me." It was a direct reminder that the Hierarchy of Bullies never went away.

"But here's the thing, Phillip. My wife preached something else you never got to hear. She would tell me all the time. She told her regular clients throughout the rest of the year this one thing; and it's the advice I followed. She said we need to stand up to our bullies. I stood up to them. I stood up to the woman who cheated on me. I stood up to the dickhead she cheated on me with; the asshole who treated me like garbage every day at work. The guy who would walk by her office and wave like they were in high school…. Like I couldn't see them. I stood up to them. And they all fell before me."

Limping to the fireplace, he picked up the fire poker. He pushed the logs that were still burning, heating the edge of the fire poker. I used the opportunity to pull myself to my feet. Still gripping the machete, I stared at him. "It's time for this to end."

Greg turned, holding the fire poker toward me, the end glowing with embers, but not hot on its own. "I agree. Only one of us is limping out of here, McCracken. Let's light this candle."

CHAPTER 46

Seth awoke, unsure where he was. He heard a voice; Greg's voice, he decided. He was bragging about stalking Georgie Perkins through the forest. Seth remembered everything and chose not to move, out of fear of what would happen if he did. The pain around his eyes told him he'd been cut. He opened his eyes slowly to ensure they still worked. The glass shards on the floor around him came into view just after the lettering on the Cornuts wrapper cleared enough for him to read it.

Seth became aware of another pain. A bulging metal object on his side dug into his leg. Panic set in as he remembered the gun. Seth said a quick prayer of thanks that it had not discharged when he (somehow?) ended up on the floor. Thinking back, he remembered admiring the gun in the hallway right outside of the door of the bedroom and then waking up. Everything in between was a blur. Seth did not remember coming downstairs or anything that followed. But he remembered why he had the gun.

Now he just needed to find the right moment to use it.

The biggest mistake Greg Munson made (aside from slaughtering innocent people) was giving me something no one else ever had; courage. When I was forced to stand in that hallway and stare down the man I thought had killed my friends, I was scared shitless. But now, pacing back and forth, staring Greg Munson in the eye, I knew I could handle it, because I'd handled it before.

The two of us stood posing; him with the fire poker, myself with the machete. We may have posed longer than we actually fought, but I feel like that's just a male trait in general. He held the fire poker at his side but quickly raised it like an Arms Bearer in the Color Guard. I stood across from him, our eyes interlocked, my left hand out and open, my right slightly pulled back, gripping the machete. Without saying a word, we repeatedly tried to get the other offsides to start the war. A full twenty seconds later, no one had moved. I swiped sideways, knowing I was too far back to hit him, but interested in his reaction.

The fire poker came down at a forty-five angle and pulled up on the exact same trek. He took a step forward with each of the two motions.

I swiped twice horizontally again, taking two additional steps back as I did so. He moved forward, even as he arched his back outward to ensure my swings did not connect. My blade swung straight across as his weapon took two swings, connecting a giant X in the air. I lost more ground, backing out of the way, but managed to swing at a similar 45-degree angle. As I brought the machete back down, Greg stabbed directly at my chest three times in quick succession. The third time, I swung the machete, catching his right glove. He screamed in pain as blood began to pool. He dropped the fire poker, and took five steps back, giving up all the ground he had gained.

Moving toward the fire poker, I continually stabbed the machete forward, to keep Greg back. I didn't lower my eyes until I was almost to the poker. I looked away just long enough to lift it off the floor. As I looked up, Greg's combat boot connected with the side of my head. I dropped to the floor, losing both weapons.

Greg's boot swung back and forth again, this time kicking the fire poker across the room. He used the machete as a pointer as he said, "I told you that you couldn't win. You've been practicing for this your whole life; to get an opportunity and still fail. You failed at everything leading up to this moment. And you'll fail now. The only thing you've been successful at is losing." He moved closer. "Look at the upside, I'm saving you the heart attack or the diabetes."

I closed my eyes, trying to focus.

Behind me, Seth said a prayer that he could do it correctly. He stared at the M&P Shield in his hand, watching it shake lightly. He would only get one shot at this.

Seth quietly pulled himself up to his knees, ready to make a move.

"Did you really think you could win this, McCracken?" Greg ranted. "You're not in my class. You're not on my level. You're so far below me you can't see the light from this star."

Dr. Munson replied in my mind. *That thing you're describing? The feeling of being on the bottom of the totem pole? That's the Hierarchy of Bullies. It's not just you…. This is true for every level of social hierarchy, whether it's the jocks, the science kids, the gamers, the stoners, the cheerleaders, or the math club.* She leaned forward, smiling. *"It's time to change the pecking order, Phillip."*

Pain throbbed in my foot as my adrenaline dropped. His limp was more pronounced. Each step Greg took, his entire body leaned right and then shot back to the left. I watched him step, lean right, shoot back left. *Step. Lean right. Shoot back left.*

I dug into my pocket and found it. My fingers gripped the metal handle. I removed it from my pants. *Step. Lean right. Shoot back left.* Pulling myself upright, I watched the blade of the machete, at his side, as he rolled it in his palm. *Click.* The switchblade opened. I blocked Seth's view of Greg. He couldn't take the shot. The machete ripped into my left shoulder.

Greg and I stood face to face, eye to eye. I could feel his breath as he tried to scream. The switchblade came into focus, buried in the left side of Greg's neck. Blood ran down, brighter than I'd expected it to be. His neck hemorrhaged as I removed the blade. I expected the machete to slice me again, but it never came. Greg slid down to the floor, heaving blood. The sound was flat but forced. He stopped moving.

I turned around just as the gun went off three times. Chunks of the hardwood floor flew around Greg's head, but the shots didn't find their intended target. Shaking like a dog shitting tacks, Seth walked over and held the gun out. He pushed it against Greg's head. "No. Seth! No!" I yelled. But he didn't seem to hear me. His breath rasping. His eyes unable to blink. His chin and lips trembled as he clenched his eyes and pulled the trigger twice more.

"Double tap." He whimpered, lightly, just as I blacked out.

CHAPTER 47

When I awoke, Sarge was standing over me. For a second, I thought it was all a dream and he'd tell me it was time to get my rotund behind out on the track and re-run the mile I'd already dreamed I'd failed in astonishing style. But as my eyes adjusted to the room, I saw the concern on his face. Then the room came into focus and I found myself on the couch five feet from Greg's dead body.

Sarge turned, looking over his shoulder. "He's waking up. We're good." He looked back, smiling. "I might be strong, but I can't carry your ass to the elevator."

Sarge hadn't known Greg lied about the elevator. Dragging one leg behind him the entire way to the Counselor's Quarters, he'd reached the stairs and known he could go no further. Looking around, he decided he was too out in the open and moved toward the elevator on the other side. He pushed the button more out of desperation than anything. To his surprise, the shiny silver doors slid open. The bright fluorescent light beaming out from the plastic covers stood in sharp contrast to the body on the floor. He only noticed the body after his nose was assaulted by smells that belonged in a port-o-potty.

Leaning against the door with one hand as he dragged his leg in, Sarge went to push the button on the operator's panel, only to find the other person in the elevator was alive. "Are you okay?"

Eric Schultz raised his head to answer but was met with Sarge's boot to his face. The hydraulics kicked in and the doors slid shut, metal rubbing against metal, reminding Eric he couldn't go anywhere even if he could stand. The car shuddered and jerked as it began to move. Eric screamed. "Sarge. It's not me. It's Greg."

Sarge pulled his foot back, just before it connected again. He had the high ground and would be able to stop Eric if he tried anything, so he waited. "Explain. And do it fast." Sarge's hand hit the stop elevator button. The entire car hitched as the brakes ground on the cables.

"Jess and I went out by the lake to be alone. Greg found us. Knocked me unconscious. Next thing I knew, Jessica was gone. He bragged that he'd killed her. Told me it was my fault. Led me back here and left me tied up in the elevator. Then he tied me up in the bedroom hallways. Dressed me up. Tried to get the campers to kill me."

Sarge stared at him. "What the hell are you even talking about?"

"It doesn't matter, Sarge. He's got the kids. The two boys that saved me. Phillip and Seth."

Sarge hit the button. The elevator jolted alive again.

Eric couldn't stand. The pain of his shattered ribs proved too much. Sarge thought he was a whiner and said so. Coming out on first floor, Sarge was immediately met with the sound of gunshots. Three shots.

Sliding against the wall, he made his way as quickly as his body could carry him. He turned into the main lobby just as Seth pulled the trigger twice more.

"Double tap." Seth whimpered.

Sarge was on him. "Give me the gun, Jenkins." He stared at Greg's lifeless body. The hole in the man's head made it feel almost impossible to see the body as human.

Seth handed the gun over. Sarge immediately pulled the magazine. "We need to call the authorities."

Seth pointed at me. "We need to make sure he's okay."

Sarge stopped. "What the hell happened to my window?"

They found the girls tied up in the women's bathroom. It's a good thing they made noise, or it could've been weeks before anyone went in there.

A few hours later, we gathered in the Rec Center Mess Hall. Well, those of us who had survived, that is. Roger Tonkyn was on the phone with his mother, telling her how he hid as soon as he heard about Georgie's death; returning to the locker room and hiding inside of his locker until he heard police sirens. I didn't think Roger knew how close he'd come to having his throat sliced open, but I was never going to tell him. He seemed genuinely glad to be alive and that was good enough for me.

Seth, Nicole, and Emily sat eating pizza at our normal table. The one where Greg had seen someone watching him. Everything was tainted now. We'd be living with it for a very long time. But at least we were living. Seth wiped pizza sauce from his chin. "There's the hero of the hour!"

I laughed as I took a seat. "Hero? Me? I don't think so, buddy."

Emily's hand slid up my thigh as her head rested on my shoulder. "You're my hero."

Nicole stared at us in disgust, but a smile soon overtook her face. "Mine too. But don't let it go to your head."

I shrugged. "I'm just saying, I think maybe the 82 slugs Seth put into him at the end of the night... maybe that's what saved our lives."

"Funny. Whatever. We needed to be sure. I'm telling you…"
He leaned in. "Sometimes, they come back."

As if on cue, the Camp Wašíču Fit Camp sign – the one with the
kid holding his fat pants – slammed against the window, having
come undone from its metal tent stake again. From my point of
view, the sign was completely backlit and resembled someone
looking in the window. "Holy shit." I said to myself quietly.

Seth jumped, but managed not to scream. "We really need to fix
that sign."

They hauled a good majority of the survivors out via
ambulance. The ones with minor wounds went to Burlington, but
the ones more in need were taken to larger cities nearby. Sarge was
first transferred to Burlington and then almost immediately to a
specialist in Des Moines. He made almost a full recovery, showing
only a slight limp for his troubles. We text or email at least once a
week. He couldn't wait to get back to Camp Wašíču to get it ready
for the new season.

I was taken directly to Davenport. Nicole, Emily, and Seth
followed in the Ford Escape. Turns out the tires were never slashed.
It was something Greg said to instill fear, and no one had gone to
double check. The paramedics tried to get Seth to go to the closer
hospital, but he refused to leave me. The cuts in his face mostly
healed, but not all of them.

I have rehabbed my arm for the last year, but I'll never get full
functioning back again. It's a constant reminder of that night; but
it's also proof that I stood up and did what I had to do to save a few
people. If I could've done it sooner, maybe more of my friends
would still be alive.

CHAPTER 48

It's been a year since I left Camp Wašíču. A lot has changed but not everything. I've lost over a hundred pounds. But at the end of the day, I'm not sure it was ever about the weight loss. It was a need to change my view of myself. And I've managed to do that. If the changes inside of me are starting to show on the outside, that's just a bonus. I'm no longer diabetic. No longer on cholesterol medications. And I'm no longer afraid of exercise or the little bit of pain that goes along with it.

I suppose it's a lot better than the alternative.

The Perkins family almost sold Camp Wašíču two months after the events. At first, they couldn't deal with what had happened to Georgie; but with Halloween around the corner, they received a ton of calls asking about possible paranormal investigations or haunted cabin tours. Once they realized how much money could be made, the family was able to see past their pain.

Still, I get it. Each of us carries our own scars from the incident. Some are physical; some psychological. Like I said, my left arm will never function at a hundred percent. Sarge will always have a limp. In the right light, we'll forever be able to see the cuts in Seth's face from the glass coffee table exploding. He tells me he plans to grow a mustache to hide the worst one, but let's face it, the guy is eighteen and he's never had to shave yet, so that might not be the most realistic plan. Nicole will always blame herself for letting Greg capture them. Emily drinks a lot and thinks that no one knows.

I can't speak for everyone, but the four of us are each in therapy to deal with it. Dr. Rezac is an excellent therapist and he's helped me a lot. But man, I miss Dr. Munson. I feel she truly understood how to reach me. I think about her often. I sometimes ask myself what she would tell me if I presented a situation to her. Sometimes it helps. Sometimes it just leads to more questions. Would she know a better way to deal with everything I've seen? Would she apologize that this occurred because of her? There are so many things I wish I could ask her. And so many things I'd like to show her just to say that despite everything, we mostly turned out okay.

Like most high school relationships Emily and I were over almost as quickly and unbelievably as we'd gotten together. We went on a few dates, but that spark we'd felt at Camp Wašíču died pretty quickly. We had even less in common than you'd probably guess. There's only so many times you can go out with someone just because he saved your life; and only so many times you can go out with a girl just because she used to be what you wanted. We're still friends though. It has a lot to do with surviving the encounter. I think you hold on to one another because you're the only other people who will ever understand what you experienced. Emily says she likes that she's able to shift between levels on the hierarchy and exist where she wants. Being seen with her and the legend of how I stopped a serial killer have allowed me to transcend my own placement on the hierarchy and to question whether it's real at all.

Seth and Nicole are going strong. There was a time before all of this when I had a hard time accepting them making out all over my house, but when I think about how much they influence one another and keep the other moving forward, I suppose a little grossness is well worth it. Sometimes, they make out in the backseat of my car. And sometimes, I like to tap my brakes randomly to see if they'll bite each other's tongues off. But at the end of the day, I can't think of a better brother-in-law to hopefully have one day. Nicole started college, but stayed here in town, so we still see her all the time. Plus, she throws the best parties. Fine, she throws the only parties I'm usually invited to. That's where I met Rachel. I'll never forget the first thing she said to me. "Nikki and Seth have told me a lot about you. I heard what you did last summer."

I couldn't take my eyes off her; even if she was too eager to discuss what had happened at Camp Wašíču. Within a couple hours, we were making out like old friends and I realized how much I was going to love college.

The next time I saw Rachel was a double date at Nicole's house a week later. I listened to the popcorn popping in the microwave as I looked out the passthrough into the living room. Nicole, and Seth sat ignoring the horror movie they were watching. Rachel tried to look past them to see the movie as they started making out, but it was impossible. Quietly entering the room, I held a single finger to my lips to warn her and I moved toward Seth. Leaning down, right by his ear, I loudly said, "Popcorn's ready."

Seth screamed.

"Don't tell anyone I scream like that, okay?"

Rachel laughed. "I don't have to. I have the whole thing on video."

CHAPTER 49

The car stopped at the side of the small path between gravestones. If it wasn't for the rosebushes on either side, I would have had a hard time remembering where her grave was. I exited the passenger seat, quickly glancing at Nicole as she changed radio stations in the Escape. Making my way down the long, curved pathway past the other marble, granite, and concrete headstones, I read the names on different family burial plots. I admired the bright bursts of color from the silk flowers left by visitors, as the wind whistling through the trees and grass was drowned out by the low thrum of a distant lawnmower. In my right hand, I carried a single Calle Lily – her favorite – to leave next to the religious stone carvings and meaningful trinkets others left before me.

I had not visited the grave since her funeral. The headstone was larger than I'd expected. Dr. Jessica Munson. Thirty-four years old. The words carved into the stone ripped at my soul as though she spoke directly to me:

To Live in Hearts We Leave Behind
Is Not to Die
- Thomas Campbell

I stared at those words as I set the Calle Lily in front of the stone. Bowing my head, I said a quick prayer. When I opened my eyes, I stared at her name. Even seeing it written in stone didn't make it quite real. I turned, walking back to the blue Ford Escape. I crossed the small one lane road and got in the passenger seat.

Nicole smiled at me but didn't say anything until we were out of the cemetery.

"So how are things going at home?" Nicole finally said, turning the stereo down. "It's weird not being there. I miss all the crazy drama."

One side of my mouth smiled. "Oh, we got rid of that. All the drama went with you. We don't have any."

Rolling her eyes, Nicole replied, "As if I believe that. You and mom are incapable of getting along for more than an hour at a time." She made eye contact. "And that's if you're on your best behavior and she's distracted for forty-five minutes."

"No, really. We're doing well. Mom and I had a heart to heart. We talked about a lot of the crap I've held onto since Dad died. Half of it wasn't even her fault. Like how I thought she just got over Dad and didn't care. Now I've seen the nights she cries herself to sleep. Or the fact I always thought she hated how overweight I was, but she was just trying to look out for me. It's all context, really."

"Wow. Turning over a new leaf, huh?"

I nodded. "Yeah. Honestly, after what happened last year, I think she's realized she doesn't want to lose me. And it helps that you moved out, so she had to see I'm the last one."

"You know she's never going to let you leave to go to college, right?" Nicole joked.

We made small talk the rest of the way down Highway 67. At the turn onto the Walter Payton Highway, she finally gave in. "So, are you giving a speech?"

The one-year memorial had been Eric Schultz's idea. Sarge backed it immediately and made his case to the Perkins family, who eventually got behind it as well. They said it would help the healing process, but there was a large part of me that feared it would just open old wounds again. But I couldn't tell Sarge no.

Then he asked me to prepare a small speech and I told him no. I fought it for two weeks, but I eventually gave in.

I figure we all faced things at Camp Wašíču much worse than public speaking.

I looked at Nicole, "Yeah, I'm giving a small speech."

"Seth said you're like the guest of honor. He called you the Frank Doyle." She raised an eyebrow. "What the hell is a Frank Doyle?"

As we crossed the Great River Bridge into Burlington, I was overcome with the terror of being back. Every rotation of the tires meant that we grew that much closer to facing Wašíču again. While I knew it wouldn't be like last time, I'd worked hard with Dr. Rezac to overcome the trauma of that weekend; but it was all still there. Therapists can't erase it completely. They can only give us the tools to live with it.

I looked over Nicole and out the driver's side window. The Burlington Rail Bridge stood in the distance; the rust-colored vertical lift was lowered, a train running across it. Whenever we came to town, Dad would tell me the story of how that bridge helped build a train company, allowing passage from Chicago to Burlington and down to Quincy. The company grew into Burlington Northern Railroad and eventually into BNSF as it sits today. It's an easier name, but I miss the green locomotives. The yellowish-orange ones are so boring in comparison.

And yes, I was just distracting myself from the inevitability of what was coming.

But it became impossible to ignore as we drove past the hospital on the West end of the city; the hospital where many of the other survivors ended up that night. Nicole felt it as well. Her smile faded. Her eyes stared at the road ahead of her. The small talk cut down to nothing. Even the music on the radio changed.

By the time we were on the gravel road leading to Camp Wašíču, we had each teared up, but the sight of Seth sitting on his car hood waiting for us in the parking lot instantly cheered us both. Dress shirt tucked in, sunglasses on, Seth looked like a whole new man. Only somehow hilarious. We parked several car lengths down from him, as the parking lot was almost full.

Nicole barely had the car in park before she was in his arms. "You made it!"

"Where else would I be? I told you I'd make better time than you."

Nicole looked back at me. "We needed to make a stop. It was important."

Seth bowed forward a little, sweeping his hand out toward the Rec Center, "Shall we?"

CHAPTER 50

Walking through Camp Wašíču was surreal. So many things
had changed, but so much of it remained the same. An entire
section of the Rec Center had been renovated. The Mess Hall had all
new chairs and tables. The cabins looked the same on the outside,
but I didn't go in. Sarge waved to me from the top of the three
flights of stairs leading to the Counselors' Quarters. That asshole
would make me go directly there and deal with whatever it was I
was feeling.

But instead, he met me on the second landing and gave me a
hug. "Holy hell, I almost didn't recognize you, McCracken." He
shook Seth's hand. "Jenkins. Always a pleasure." Sarge's hands
went to his waist and I instantly pictured Superman. "So how the
hell are you two?"

Haunted by the past.

Terrified of the dark.

Consistently paranoid.

"We're doing great, Sarge. How are you?"

His hand tapped my stomach. "I just can't even get used to this.
You look fantastic." He stared at me, not speaking. Just smiling. It
was the opposite of the Sarge I'd known a little over a year
beforehand. "Well, I suppose we should get down there. The
speeches are about to start."

Before he could move, I hit Sarge with a question that had been
bothering me the whole ride over. "Sarge."

"Yes, McCracken?"

"You got any counselor positions open?"

He stared at me, analyzing my words. "For you? Absolutely."

"Really?"

"McCracken, if Frank Doyle was real, you'd be him. Hell yeah, I want you on this team."

Seth smiled. "Can I get some of that action? I'd love to give back to the new class." His smile faded. "Wait a minute. Did you just say Frank Doyle isn't real?"

The first day at Camp Wašíču a year beforehand, we'd all taken turns on the stage, announcing our names, our weight, and our push. This time around, we gathered to pay respects to the friends, family, and loved ones we'd lost in the incident. I listened intently to every single person who stepped up there. Fred Hoffman's father spoke about Fred's dreams. Jonathon Young's mother, Karen, related stories of a funnier side of her son than we'd ever seen. Other parents, brothers, and sisters shared family memories.

Seth went shortly before me. He talked about the darker side of our time there and how we only made it through by sticking together. Nicole placed her head on my shoulder. "Thank you for saving me that night, Phil."

"Thank you for saving me every other day, Nikki."

Sarge held the microphone as he limped across the stage. "There was a time that it annoyed the heck out of me that these kids spent all of their time talking about superheroes. I didn't like superheroes because they were unrealistic. They could fly. They could shoot webs out of their hands. One of them could talk to fish, although I'll never understand why anyone would want to do so. There was nothing realistic about superheroes, in my book."

Sarge looked down at the floor of the stage, trying not to tear up. "But a year ago this weekend, I learned that superheroes do exist." He looked right at me. "And I learned the price they pay to protect the rest of us." He limped across the stage. "We have one more speech tonight. I can't say enough things about this man. He came here to lose weight, but instead, he gained things. He gained self-confidence, self-respect, and my respect."

As I climbed the stairs to the stage, I heard Dr. Munson in my head. *We're not gone, Phillip. To live in the hearts of those we leave behind is not to die.* Looking out at the audience I understood that although we lost so many family members, each of them lived on through us. I promised myself then and there to do everything I could to make them proud.

Sarge pointed toward me and I suddenly understood the joy Frank Doyle would've felt if he was real. "Ladies and Gentlemen, our final speaker of the afternoon is a true hero, and a man I'm very blessed to call my friend." A smile spread across my face as I jogged onto the stage. The enthusiasm in Sarge's voice echoed through the speakers.

"Phiiiiillll McCracken!"

AFTER THOUGHTS

The moment that began my obsession with writing horror lives very clearly in my mind. When I was ten years old, I spent weekends at my cousin Kevin's house. We were always up later than we should have been, watching movies we had no right to be watching. One Saturday night, we happened across *The Texas Chainsaw Massacre*.

I'd heard of the movie. I knew it was a horror movie. I knew it would be scary. But I did not know what to expect. I had even less of an idea how much my entire life was about to shift because I watched this film.

From the opening when the hitchhiker cuts himself and tries to attack the others, I was sold. By the time Kirk took a hammer to the face like a cow in a slaughterhouse, I'd lost it. I was intensely frightened... but I couldn't stop watching. I didn't turn away when they impaled Pam. I couldn't close my eyes as the chainsaw ripped through Kirk's body. The level of gore far exceeded my miniscule expectations. Just when I thought it couldn't possibly get worse, the Grandfather drank Sally's blood.

I barely slept that night; a combination of terror and fascination danced circles in my head like two prize fighters. When the sun rose in the morning, I was beat, but it had been worth it. I made the five-block walk back to my parents' house; my shoes slapping the concrete a little faster than usual as I looked over my shoulder occasionally.

Easily distracted at that age, I forgot all about the film I'd watched the night before and slid into my bubble-filled bathtub, playing with whatever toys I'd brought with me. It was a lazy Sunday morning with nothing going on and soon I lay completely relaxed without a care in the world.

Until...

Brum... Brum... Brum... Brrrrrrrrrrrrrrrrrrrrrrrrrrrrrrr!

The neighbor's chainsaw roared to life, the whrrring growing louder as the chain sliced through the branches in his backyard. I took the opportunity to do what anyone would do. I cried and cried and cried. Just *bawling*.

My parents both ran into the bathroom, terrified that I'd somehow been injured. They both asked what was wrong several times, but I was so scared I'd get in trouble for watching horror movies that I wouldn't tell them.

I never told them.

That festering secret.

That fear that I couldn't tell anyone else about.

That knowledge that I was completely alone.

That's the moment I became obsessed with horror.

Over the next thirty years, there have been many other monsters who influenced my writing, whether they were in books, film, my own imagination, or occurrences in my life that I'll never be able to explain. The monsters in my head have led to many published short stories, a few novels, and selling the film rights for short films that went on to win Best Screenplay, Best Picture, and (my personal favorite) Audience Choice awards. At some point, you'd think I'd get used to the uneasy feeling I get when I'm alone.

And yet, late at night, I worry about seeing dead little girls in my mirror, old men creeping out of my closet or clammy hands gripping my exposed feet if my blanket is not properly positioned. I still pause and listen while running bathwater; awaiting a chainsaw-wielding neighbor who has long since passed.

James Sabata
May 13, 2018
Phoenix, AZ

2

PLEASE LEAVE A REVIEW

Even a few short sentences help authors immeasurably. Reviews lead to more exposure which leads to more sales.

So please, remember to leave a review of this book and any others you read... but definitely this one.

BE A STALKER!
Follow Me on Social Media:

JamesSabata.Com

Facebook.com/JamesSabataAuthor

Twitter.com/JamesSabata

https://www.imdb.com/name/nm8516263/

ALSO BY JAMES SABATA:
ZER0: Lancaster's Greatest Supervillain

Plagued by supervillains for over a decade, the city of Lancaster idolized their local superhero, Zero; oblivious to the fact that the city's great protector is also the mastermind behind the villains terrorizing the city. Exploiting his total control over the local media, the man under the mask lives out his superhero fantasies; scripting and directing events as he gains more control each day.

Looking for a new story to tell, Zero promises to make Chris Thompson his new sidekick and eventual successor. But Zero grows paranoid and flips the script on his protégé; spinning the media to make Chris the most hated villain Lancaster has ever seen.

With the line between good and evil blurred, Chris finds himself on the wrong side of the law; battling his former mentor to save not only himself, but the city that has been taught to hate him.

Available in Paperback and E-Book

James Sabata

James Sabata

HEADLESS JESS

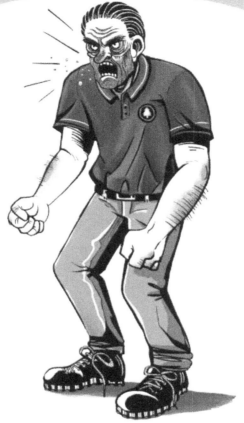

SARGE IN CHARGE

James Sabata

MINI VINNIE

James Sabata

**OVERNIGHT
COUNSELOR 2**

Made in the USA
Las Vegas, NV
30 August 2021